FATHER
OF THE
FATHERLESS

FATHER
OF THE
FATHERLESS

MARGARET E.
KELCHNER

F
KEL

Beacon Hill Press of Kansas City
Kansas City, Missouri

1

≡

"Watch your step, son," the conductor cautioned, taking note of the slender figure with bulging pockets. A tattered valise was held tightly in one hand, a paper bag in the other.

The boy climbed the high steps into the coach where he paused briefly as a hush fell over the car and all eyes turned on him. The seats were filled except two in the rear. He made his way through the aisle toward them amid curious stares and whispered comments. A young, golden-haired woman with a baby on her lap smiled at him as he passed. Choosing the seat on the station side, he was scarcely seated when the mournful sound of the whistle floated back and the train shuddered into motion, giving off great belches of black smoke.

He leaned forward in his seat, with his face pressed against the cold glass of the window, hoping to catch a last glimpse of his uncle. He closed his eyes and swallowed hard to fight the sob that threatened to escape—after all, he was almost 15 years old. An early darkness was closing in, hiding the last effects of fading sunlight when he settled back in his seat and placed the lunch sack beside him.

He stared at the back of the seat ahead with disinterest as he let his mind go back over the events of the past few weeks. So much had happened since that night his mother lay dying.

He recalled the cold touch of her hand as she reached out to him. Her voice sounded strange as she struggled to speak.

"Cam . . . ," she said weakly.

"I'm here," Cam answered, leaning closer to hear.

"Cam, you must go to live with your Uncle George."

Her hesitant voice grew weaker as Cam waited for her to go on. Her hand slipped from his, and after a moment, someone came forward from the shadows to take him by the arm. He was led from the room and told to wait downstairs. Several people were standing in the hall, talking in subdued voices. The door closed behind him. As he walked toward the stairs, he heard someone whisper, "Poor dear, I wonder what will become of him."

A shock went through Cam as he understood what was happening. His mother was dying, and he would be left alone. He fled down the stairs and out of the house with his mother's words ringing in his ears, "You must go to live with your Uncle George." Standing there in the silence of the night he welcomed the cold, crisp air against his burning cheeks. Tears flooded his eyes.

Midmorning, two days later, the black buggy passed through the small, arched gate of the cemetery. It was over. Camden Cheney looked up at the man who sat beside him. His mother had talked very little about family, so he did not know much about his Uncle George. Cam studied the grave face that was clean shaven except for a rather full mustache. He decided his uncle bore no resemblance to his mother.

The man, sensing the boy's eyes upon him, turned his head. "I hope you will like living with us, Cam," Uncle George said. "Aunt Lizzie is not . . . uh . . . well. To make things easier for us all, I'll fix a room for you in the back of my store. You can help me during the day and take your meals with us in the evening." Cam nodded his head. He settled back in the seat, watching the countryside go by. Soon the steady rhythm of the horse's hooves lulled him to sleep.

A firm hand upon his shoulder awakened Cam. "We're here, boy. Climb down now. I'll get your things." Cam climbed down from the buggy and stretched. He was standing in front of a building with a sign over the door: *GEORGE C. FOX, Merchandise.*

Uncle George retrieved his things from the rear of the buggy and motioned for him to follow. Cam made his way up the steps and walked through the door where Uncle George had disappeared. He paused to get accustomed to the darkening room, as his uncle's footsteps echoed ahead.

"The hall is straight ahead of you, Cam," his uncle called to him. Cam walked in the direction of his voice, aware of pleasant, earthy odors of soap, spice, and dried fruit. At the rear of the store he entered a short hall that led to a room with an open door. There was also a door directly across the hall with the door closed. Cam hesitated, looking questioningly at the closed door.

"Storeroom," his uncle said briefly. "Come."

The room was small with one window through which Cam could see the faint outline of some trees. There was a crude bed built in the corner, a chair, and a table with a small lamp on it. Uncle George placed the valise on the bed and lit the lamp.

"While you're up at the house tonight I'll give you a water pitcher and a basin you can put on the chest over there," he said. "Now, come with me. We'll go up to the house and have some supper. Aunt Lizzie will give you some bedding, and you can get settled later. I'll give you a key, and you can come in the back door down the hall. Take care that you always keep the door locked."

It was a short trip to the house. Uncle George stopped the buggy and told Cam to wait for him on the porch. He then proceeded to the barn to unhitch the horse and tend to its needs.

The lamplight from within the house gave a warm glow to the porch surrounding the front and side of the house. Cam climbed the steps and sat down on the swing. There were several rockers and some ferns on the porch. The house sat upon a knoll, and he could look out across the town of Norwalk, which was to be his home. He heard his uncle's footsteps and hurriedly jumped to his feet to stand obediently at the top of the steps.

George Fox mounted the steps and stood before the door a moment with his hand on the knob. He took a deep breath, opened the door, and stepped inside, motioning for Cam to follow.

"Lizzie!" he called.

A voice answered from the room to the right. "I'm in here."

Uncle George turned in the direction of the voice. Entering the room, he walked over to give his wife a dutiful peck on the cheek. Cam stopped just inside the door. Taking in the dark-paneled room at a glance, his eyes came to rest on Aunt Lizzie, who obviously had not seen him yet. She was a woman of slight build with sharp features accented by dark hair pulled tightly back in a bun.

"It's about time you got back," she scolded. "It was getting late, and I was beginning to worry. Supper is in the warmer. I'll go . . . Who is this?" she asked as her eyes fell upon Cam.

"Oh, yes, Lizzie, this is Camden, my sister's boy. I—" His voice faltered in response to her icy glare. He took a deep breath and then continued in a firm tone of voice. "I told her he could stay with us. He had no one else. Now, before you say anything, I plan for him to stay at the store. He can help me there. It will be good to have a hand with the chores." She looked as though she would speak, but Uncle George held up his hand to silence her. "We will discuss the matter later," he said.

Cam stood in silent uncertainty as Aunt Lizzie looked him over with a disapproving air, staring at his bushy head of curly brown hair, to rumpled clothing and ending with his scuffed high-topped shoes. He felt a sense of shock as her eyes, lacking in warmth, returned to his. Much to Cam's relief, she arose and left the room without a word. He soon heard the rattling of dishes and lids, signaling that she was getting supper.

"Come on, Cam," Uncle George sighed. "We'll get washed up."

Cam followed him to a sink in the corner of the kitchen
where there was a pump. He watched as Uncle George pumped
up some water in a basin and washed his hands. Cam followed
suit.

"Turn out the water, Cam. Aunt Lizzie doesn't like dirty
water left in the basin."

With that done, he followed Uncle George to the table.
Aunt Lizzie was nowhere to be seen, a relief that was short-
lived. She appeared with an armful of bedding, which she
deposited on a chair near the door, and seated herself at the
table.

"You can sit here, Cam . . . here, have some meat." Cam
took the platter offered him. "And there are some potatoes,"
his uncle went on, "help yourself."

Cam took a healthy helping of each, feeling Aunt Lizzie's
close scrutiny. He ate in silence, listening to the talk about the
funeral and the trip back. Cam felt uncomfortable as he listened.
Finishing his meal, he excused himself. He picked up the
bedding Aunt Lizzie had indicated and then left, glad to escape
those penetrating eyes.

In the twilight the stars twinkled through a clear sky. Soon
he arrived at the store and turned the key in the lock. Cam was
relieved when the door opened to admit him to the dark hall.
The lamp had gone out. Feeling his way along, he found his
room and deposited his bundle on the bed. Now to light the
lamp, he thought. Groping in the dark, he located the matches
left on the table. Carefully he removed the lampshade, struck a
match and held it to the wick. Feebly at first, and then brighter,
the light filled the room with a comforting glow. He replaced
the lampshade, adjusted the wick to prevent smoking, and
looked around the room. It was plain, but he liked it.

He picked up the valise and began putting what meager
clothing he had into the drawer of the chest when his hand
came into contact with a hard object. He turned to the light
and saw that it was his mother's Bible. He stared at it for a long
time. Then he opened it to find an inscription written in his

mother's neat hand. "This Bible is to be given to Camden, my son, to keep always. It is his richest inheritance. My love, always, Mother."

Suddenly Cam felt very lonely. He threw himself down on the straw mattress and cried with deep, stifling sobs. When the storm in his soul subsided, he sat up on the side of the bed, the Bible still in his hand. He opened it once again to read his mother's words and, with a strong feeling of conviction, vowed to read from it every day.

Placing it on the table, he turned to the task of putting away the rest of his things and making his bed. With a look of satisfaction around the room, he picked up the Bible and read a chapter. Then he blew out the lamp and climbed into bed.

Lying in the dark, his mind wandered back over the events of the day. He decided he liked Uncle George. Aunt Lizzie he was not sure about. Perhaps it would be best to keep out of her way. He turned his thoughts to the town. Working in the store would help him get acquainted quickly. He fell asleep with the faint, mingled smells of the store drifting into the room.

* * *

A sudden lurch of the train brought Cam back to the present. The loud wail of a baby broke the stillness, and he could hear the mother's soft voice quieting her child's distress. Cam remembered that the mother and child had boarded the train just ahead of him, choosing to sit near the door. Her face had betrayed such sadness, yet she had given him a friendly smile and nodded a greeting.

He realized he still wore his hat. He removed it and laid it on the seat next to him. Stretching out his legs, he surveyed the toes of his shoes and returned to his thoughts. Life in Norwalk had been uneventful. Uncle George was always busy in the store, waiting on customers, ordering stock, and working in his tiny office on the books. There was little time for conversation other than instructions for the day as to what chores Cam should do.

He had liked working there. It was easy to see that Uncle George was well-respected in the community. On Saturdays the farmers would gather out in front of the store to visit and discuss various topics of interest. When he could, Cam especially liked to listen to talk of the events going on in the country, now in its post-Civil War development. The West was opening up. People were making their way across the wide prairies and deserts in search of land to farm and ranch. There was talk of Indian massacres that would wipe out whole wagon trains. Then came the day that in spite of Indian uprising, the first United States transcontinental railroad was completed. It was a good time for the country after such a devastating war. Railroads were pushing deep into the South, and land was being offered for homesteading, bringing in many freedmen and immigrants from the North.

The weeks passed swiftly. Each day Cam awoke when he heard his uncle unlock the door. Hastily he would dress, wash his face and comb his hair, then make his way into the store where he would eat the breakfast Uncle George brought to him.

Munching on a biscuit, he would watch his uncle methodically arrange the cash drawer, then take up his stock list to check his order. After he finished his breakfast, Cam would sweep the store, remove the dust covers from the merchandise, bring up the potatoes, and check the barrels to make sure all were filled. Then he would sweep off the front walk with a broom.

In the evenings, after he had finished his chores, Cam walked the short distance up the hill to the house where Aunt Lizzie had supper ready. His world felt secure until one evening after supper he went to the porch as usual to sit in the swing before going back to his room at the store. Cam liked this part of the day best. The setting sun cast long shadows across the hills. He could see a trail of dust from a buggy going up the road to Potter's Lake.

A movement in the grass along the fence caught his eye. As he watched, he saw a rabbit scurry out to run alongside the porch and around the back. Jumping the porch rail, he followed to see it disappear under the house. Cam stooped down to take a look when he became aware of Aunt Lizzie's angry voice coming through the window just over his head.

Then he heard Uncle George's voice strained with emotion, "But you don't understand, Liz. I promised his mother he could live with us! Besides, he's not living here; he is staying at the store!"

"But it's still another mouth to cook for and clean up after," argued Aunt Lizzie. "Why can't he look after himself? After all, he's 14."

"I can't turn him out, Liz. Be reasonable!" Uncle George had shouted.

Cam felt the rush of blood to his face. He jumped to his feet and ran all the way to his room.

Even now Cam shuddered at the humiliation of that moment. He crossed his legs and turned to stare out of the train window. It was quite dark now.

The days following the incident had been full of tension. Cam did his work, noticing that Uncle George seemed drawn and preoccupied. It was with dread that he made his way to the house each evening for supper. He would eat hurriedly, excusing himself to return to his room.

One morning Uncle George had come to the store earlier than usual. Cam heard his footsteps as he came through the store. There was a pause, then a light rap on the door. "Cam, are you awake?" he called.

"Yes, Uncle George," Cam replied. "Come in."

The door opened and Uncle George stepped into the room, taking in the neat arrangement with an approving glance. His eyes came to rest on the slight figure of the boy who was busy pulling on his left shoe. He crossed the room to the chair and sat down.

Cam jerked the tie of his shoe into a bow and lowered his foot to the floor. He looked at his uncle expectantly, noticing that his face seemed more grave than usual.

Uncle George cleared his throat. "Cam," he began with a strained voice, "Aunt Lizzie and I have had no children and . . . Well, never mind that. I have been a busy man and have not spent time with you. I regret that." He stopped speaking for a moment, frowning as if some unseen thing was bothering him.

Shaking his head, he began again. "Cam, I am going to ask you to do something for me that will mean your leaving here. A while back I applied for some land in Florida under the Homesteading Act. The land will have to be cleared and improved for me to be granted ownership. I want to send you down there to live on the land and clear some of it."

It was an awkward moment. Cam reached for his other shoe and began putting it on. Uncle George cleared his throat and continued. "There is nothing on the land. You will need to build a shelter for yourself. As I can, I will send you money for food and supplies. There's a train out this evening. I can get your ticket then.

"I have put together a parcel of papers along with some money you'll need to file on the ground. I'll give them to you later. You will change trains several times. Just ask the conductor and he will assist you in finding your next train."

"When you arrive in Jacksonville, I want you to go to a man by the name of Samuel McCarthy who owns a hardware store. I have heard that he is a fair and honest man who can be trusted. There is a letter written to him in the parcel. It will instruct him to arrange for the purchase of a mule and wagon for you to drive the short distance to Palatka.

"When you get to Palatka you are to inquire for a man named Zachariah Sparks. He is well-known in the area. He has a homestead he's proving down Lake Delancy way. Give him the letter of instruction I have written to him. He will help you with the paperwork at the courthouse and will help you locate the land. Well, that's about all. Do you have any questions?"

"No, sir," answered Cam, trying to avoid his uncle's eyes by smoothing a wrinkle in his trousers.

"Very well, then. You will need to pack your things before starting your chores so you will be ready." Uncle George stood to leave. "Oh, there's one other thing." He walked over to place his hand on Cam's shoulder as he continued. "I want you to take my name. You will be Camden William Fox. It will be better that way for two reasons. You will be safer if folks don't know you are an orphan. And second, there will be less complication in filing on the land if the name is the same. . . . Is that all right with you?"

Cam lifted his head to look at the man who for such a short time had been the only father he had ever known. He was only six months old when his own father had died of consumption. "Yes, sir," he said and swallowed hard. Tears were very close to the surface.

"Well, I'd better get busy," Uncle George said, and he was gone, his footsteps sounding a hollow retreat.

Cam slid from the bed and reached underneath for his valise. Hurriedly he emptied the drawers of the chest and put his mother's Bible in his coat pocket. The bell in the store announced the arrival of an early customer. He glanced around the room. Satisfied that he had gotten everything, he went in to begin his sweeping.

It was a busy day and the time went swiftly. After closing, they went to the house for an early supper. Cam ate quickly, scarcely lifting his eyes from his plate. There was a strained silence during the meal, with each one absorbed in private thoughts. Cam welcomed the walk to the station. When they arrived, the train was pulling in and several passengers waited to board. Uncle George put his hand on Cam's shoulder. "Here's your ticket . . . keep it in your pocket. Also, here is the packet of papers and letters you will need. Be very careful with them. And here's a lunch Aunt Lizzie packed for you. Goodbye, Cam, and . . ."

* * *

"Do you have your ticket, son?" a kindly voice asked.

Cam turned his head to look up at the conductor. "Huh?"

"Your ticket. Do you have a ticket?" repeated the conductor.

"Oh, yes, sir." Cam reached inside his coat pocket and handed the conductor the ticket. "How far is it to Palatka?" he asked.

"Hmm, let's see now . . . ," said the conductor thoughtfully as he checked the ticket and returned it to Cam, "better than a thousand miles, I believe." He studied the boy, observing the tightly clutched valise in his lap. "Are you running away?"

"No, sir!" exclaimed Cam as he sat up straight and proud. "My Uncle George is sending me to Florida to homestead some land he applied for."

"You're pretty young for that, aren't you, son?" commented the conductor as his eyes took in the boy's slender form.

"I'm 14!" asserted Cam, his blue eyes flashing an inner fire and spirit. "I can use an ax . . . and cut a tree . . . and . . ."

"What's your name, son?"

"Camden William . . . Fox," Cam stammered, remembering to use his uncle's name.

"Well, Camden William Fox, I think you'll do all right!" declared the conductor with a twinkle in his eyes and a broad smile. "If you want to, you can put that valise at your feet."

Cam watched him as he moved on down the aisle, stopping to check the tickets of the other travelers. Then he took the valise from his lap and placed it on the floor at his feet. As he leaned over, the packet of papers Uncle George had given him fell to the floor. I've got to be more careful with them, he thought, picking them up. He remembered his uncle's warning, and after thinking about it for a moment, he decided to put them inside his shirt for safekeeping. He felt uneasy and looked around to see if anyone had seen him do it. Most everyone seemed busy conversing in low tones. With relief Cam noted that the seat across from him was still empty. But then he glanced back over his right shoulder to encounter the dark, steady gaze of a man sitting there. He quickly turned around in his seat, but not before noticing that the man was neatly dressed and wore a wide-brimmed hat. He wondered if the man had seen him put the packet of papers in his shirt. Still, that was the safest place he could carry them, he reasoned. No matter—he wasn't afraid.

2

THE TRAIN BEGAN TO SLOW DOWN. The conductor came through to call out, "Stamford!" Cam held his face to the window, cupping his hands, to see into the night. Lights began to appear, and the train shuddered to a stop. He heard voices outside and could see the station master's dimly lit window. A group of people were walking to the front of the car where he was seated. Good-byes were called out, and as he watched, several waved to someone who boarded the train.

There was a commotion at the door of the car, and a woman's voice said in a soft Southern drawl, "Conductor, would you please seat me away from the draft of the door?"

"Yes, ma'am," the conductor responded as he made his way down the aisle carrying her valise and hatbox. He was followed by an attractive woman who seemed to be unaware of admiring glances as she passed through the coach. She wore a brown dress with a short jacket fastened up the front, the row of buttons giving evidence of a shapely figure beneath. A matching hat held secure by a hatpin completed her attire.

Cam watched as they made their way toward where he was seated, hoping they would pass on by, but the conductor stepped aside and indicated the seat just opposite him.

"Right here, ma'am?" asked the conductor.

She seemed unaware of his question as she stood looking at Cam. Her blue eyes took in his rumpled appearance and came to rest on his face.

"I think I would like to sit here, if this young man doesn't mind," she said, smiling at Cam.

"Oh! . . . no, ma'am," stammered Cam, trying to get to his feet and not managing too well. He hurriedly removed his hat and lunch from the seat.

"Very well then, I shall sit here," she said pleasantly, and proceeded to do so. Handing her the hatbox, the conductor set the valise at her feet and went his way.

The train began to move again. Cam pretended to look out the window while watching her reflection in the glass. She removed her hat, revealing dark, shining hair, put the hat in the box, and placed it at her feet. He detected the faint odor of violets and thought of his mother. She had smelled like that.

He nestled his head back against the corner of the window, thinking about the happier years. Things had not been easy. Times were hard for a woman who had to work and care for her child alone. But there had been some good times too. He remembered walking in the woods and sitting under the shade of a tree while his mother taught him to read and write his letters. Books had been very scarce since what money she made went for food and necessities. Most had been borrowed. But there had always been a small Bible. Many times he had struggled with the words in it until he was able to master them with her help.

Cam slipped his hand into his coat pocket to feel the comfort of the Bible's bulk there. His eyes grew heavy and he slept. Cam stirred and opened his eyes to find the lady in the brown dress looking at him with amusement. He sat up quickly to straighten his wrinkled appearance when he noticed that a long shawl still covered the lower half of his body. He picked it up with a puzzled expression.

"It got chilly during the night, so I covered you. I hope you don't mind," she said.

Cam folded the shawl as best he could and handed it to her. "No, ma'am, I don't mind," he replied.

"You slept a long while. You must have been very tired. Where are you going?" she asked as she took the shawl.

"I'm going to Palatka, Fla.," he answered.

"Do your folks live there?"

"No, ma'am," said Cam. Then, feeling she was waiting for more conversation on the matter, he leaned over to inspect the catch on his valise, hoping there would be no further questions.

Not giving up easily, she asked with more interest than curiosity, "Do you have relatives there?"

"I don't know," Cam said warily, trying not to let his discomfort at her persistence show. Straightening up in the seat, he continued, "My Uncle George is sending me to Florida to homestead some land for him."

"What's your name?"

Cam looked at her a moment before answering, feeling very uncomfortable under her steady gaze.

"Camden William Fox," he said hesitantly, thinking how strange it seemed not to be using his real name of Cheney.

"Hmm . . . I don't believe I know anyone by that name in Palatka." She spoke softly as if to herself. Cam eyed her with renewed interest.

"Will someone be meeting you in Jacksonville?" she asked, then added, "That's as far as the train goes, you know."

Cam recalled the words of his uncle. "No, ma'am, I'm supposed to go see a man named Samuel McCarthy. He owns a hardware store there. He's supposed to help me buy a mule and a wagon to drive down to Palatka."

"Did he tell you how far it was from Jacksonville to Palatka?" she asked with surprise.

"No, ma'am, he said it was a short distance."

"Well, it's about 55 to 60 miles over dirt roads that at times can be impassable. Apparently your uncle is not too well informed about the conditions down there, or he would realize that the best way to Palatka is by riverboat."

Cam turned his face toward the window to hide his dismay. This was something he would have to think about. The train began to slow down again. They were entering a town of considerable size, for there were many houses built close together. Some were several stories high. Cam could see an array of articles decorating the back porches. Wash hung on lines to dry. The conductor came through and announced in a sonorous tone, "New York!"

The lady retrieved her hat from the box and placed it on her head, tucking in the hair, then fastening it with the hatpin. She turned to Cam, "You will be changing trains here. Do you know which train you are to take from here?"

"Uncle George told me to check with the conductor," he said.

"Very well then." She rose to her feet and reached for her luggage as the train came to a stop.

Cam leaned forward to get his things. It would be good to get off the train for a while.

"Here, madam, let me help you with that," said a man with a well-modulated voice.

Cam looked up to see the tall, neatly dressed man wearing a wide-brimmed hat smiling at the lady in brown as he reached to take the luggage from her grasp. It was the same man he had noticed earlier. At the sound of the voice she stiffened noticeably. Then, regaining her composure, she responded firmly, "Thank you, sir, but I can manage on my own . . . and I also have my young friend to help me," she continued, turning her head to give Cam an entreating look.

Cam saw her agitation and realized something was wrong. Who was this man, and why did his presence affect her as it had? Looking from one to the other, he suddenly realized they were both looking at him waiting for a response. "Oh," he cried as he jumped to his feet to gather up her things as well as his.

"If you will allow us to pass, sir," she said stiffly, "we have a train to catch."

"Of course, madam," he said with a hint of sarcasm in his voice. He stepped back to gesture with a wide sweep of his arm.

She walked quickly down the aisle to the door and descended out of sight. Cam followed behind her with luggage in tow.

"Come on, Camden, we must hurry," she said, stepping from the train with the conductor's assistance. As Cam started down the step, the conductor took one of the bags and set it on the platform. "Watch your step, son."

Cam picked up the valise after leaving the coach and walked to where the woman stood waiting. "I'll go ask the ticket agent where we are to catch our next train," she said in a low voice, and turned into the station door. He walked behind her, choosing to stop a short distance away while she made her way to the ticket window. From where he stood, Cam could see that the stranger had left the train and stopped to light a cigar. He turned his attention back to the ticket window.

"Let me see your ticket, madam," the agent said in a tired voice. "Your train will be ready to leave in about an hour."

"How soon may we board?" she asked.

"In about 40 minutes," he said, glancing at the clock to his right.

She walked over to where Cam stood waiting. "We'll have time to freshen up and stretch our legs. If you will stay with the baggage, I'll go first." She disappeared into the ladies' room.

Cam took their things over to a bench nearby and sat down. He was relieved to be rid of his burden for a while. The young woman with the baby sat across the room. She had removed her hat, and her golden hair tumbled around her shoulders. She seemed to be watching for someone. The stranger from the train had come into the station now and was leaning against a post. His narrow eyes took in all that moved, and Cam felt very ill at ease as the man's gaze came to rest upon him. Who was he? One thing was sure. The woman did not want anything to do with him.

A grimace came to Cam's lips, and he frowned as he took stock of his predicament. Here he was with a woman he did not know, headed for a place he had never been, to do something he had never done. One thing that seemed to be in his favor, though, was the fact that the woman apparently was familiar with the area where he was going. If she was, Cam decided, it would be good to talk to her some more on the matter.

At this point she emerged from the ladies' room and walked over to him exclaiming, "My goodness! It sure felt good to wash my face and comb my hair. Now I will wait while you go. Don't be long now." Cam sensed an urgency in her voice.

When Cam came out, he saw that she had taken their things and moved to a position near the door where several conductors stood talking. He hurriedly walked over to her and assisted with the baggage. Together they made their way to the train where the step for boarding was already in place. They paused, waiting for the conductor to arrive. Cam looked up and down the platform. No one was in sight except a man loading boxes into a car. Then a conductor headed in their direction. Cam then noticed the man from the train standing in the doorway watching them.

"Yes, ma'am," greeted the conductor. "Let me have that valise. You can go ahead and board. Watch your step! You, too, young man!"

They made their way deep into the coach where she selected the last seat on the right so no one would be seated behind them. "Here, Camden, you sit by the window," she offered.

Cam complied, glad to be near the window. He placed his things at his feet and leaned back with a sigh of relief. His companion seated herself and accepted the hatbox from the waiting conductor, thanking him warmly as he sat the valise at her feet. "There!" she said as she tucked in a wisp of her dark brown hair and smoothed her dress.

Cam waited expectantly while questions whirled in his head. Who was she? Why had that man upset her?

As if reading his thoughts, she turned to him. "Camden, I want to thank you for going along with my little charade. Allow me to introduce myself. My name is Harriet Dunn. I own a boardinghouse in Palatka. Many of the men in town take their meals at my place. The homesteaders often stay at Dunn House when they are in town. I am in a unique position to hear all the news by listening to their conversation."

Cam turned in his seat to face her, his interest growing. "The man who accosted me on the train a while ago is Clay Beardsley. From what I hear, he is engaged in some very questionable land deals in the area. There have been several cases where homesteaders have simply disappeared. The word was spread that they just gave up and went on to something else. No one has ever been able to prove any involvement Mr. Beardsley may have had in the incidents, but there are a lot of unanswered questions. For instance, those who take over the deserted homesteads are usually pretty friendly with him."

She paused to look forward in the coach to make sure they were still alone. She lowered her voice and went on, "He has taken his meals at Dunn House a few times, and the men are pretty quiet when he is there. They don't trust him. If I am any judge of character, he is a dangerous man. You will want to avoid him. I find his attention very irritating."

Cam nodded his agreement. So that's it, he thought, his hand going to his shirt to touch the packet hidden there—a movement that did not go unnoticed by Harriet Dunn.

"One more thing, it's best that you do not let him know about what you are being sent to do. Although he may have overheard our conversation," she continued, frowning at the prospect. "We'll have to be more careful in our talk."

The conversation ended and Cam turned around in his seat. Remembering his talk with the conductor last night, he was more than a little upset with himself for venturing so much information. As he straightened his coat, his hand came in contact with his Bible. He had forgotten to read from it last night! People boarding the train claimed Harriet Dunn's attention. Cam turned a little more to his right and slipped the book from his pocket and read for a while. The story of the creation was fascinating to him, and he was soon lost in its contents.

"Are you hungry, Cam?" she repeated when he did not answer her first question.

Cam had been so absorbed in his reading that he did not realize she was speaking. He closed his Bible and slipped it back into his pocket, turning toward her.

"I picked up some fruit at the station. I will be glad to share it with you." She smiled as she held out an apple.

"Oh," he said as he remembered. "Aunt Lizzie packed me a lunch. I put it in here." He reached for his valise and took out a brown sack. Inside were a couple of jelly sandwiches, cookies, and two apples. He laid the apples on the seat between them and pulled a sandwich from the bag and offered it to Miss Dunn.

"Thank you, Camden, I accept. We'll have a picnic!" She flashed him a bright smile as she took the sandwich.

"Camden," Harriet Dunn spoke thoughtfully as she munched on the sandwich, "I think I shall go with you to see your Mr. McCarthy when we arrive in Jacksonville. I have some thoughts on your plans there."

Cam took a bite of sandwich and remained silent, thinking of this possibility. He studied her face. It would be hard to guess her age, he thought. She had a pleasant face framed by dark shining hair, which she wore pinned up in a soft bun. Her full lips turned up at the corners, adding to her charm. But most of all, it was her eyes that made her pretty.

She was looking up the aisle when Cam saw her stiffen and turn her face to stare out the window. He looked to see the reason for the sudden change in her countenance. The man she had called Clay Beardsley was coming along the aisle toward them. His dark eyes glittered as they met Cam's for a moment, then moved to Miss Dunn who was still looking out the window. A dark smile spread across his handsome face as he took the seat across the aisle. He pulled a paper from under his arm, unfolded it, and began to read.

Cam finished his sandwich and decided to save his apple for later, choosing a cookie instead. When he offered one to Miss Dunn, he could tell from the expression on her face that she was not pleased to have this man's presence so near.

At the conductor's call to board, the few passengers lingering on the platform came on to take their seats, and the train began to move, slowly at first, then picking up speed.

Cam watched as they left the city and crossed the Hudson River. The sun had disappeared behind some approaching clouds, and his thoughts turned inward. There was a long train ride ahead . . . certainly it didn't look like it would be a lonely one. At first he had been cautious of Miss Dunn's intrusion into his life, but now he welcomed her presence. As he sized up his situation, he realized he needed to figure out some things and she could help him. It appeared to him now that Uncle George's knowledge of Palatka was gleaned from hearsay. So it was important that he learn all he could from her if he was going to be able to plan for himself.

Cam felt a pressure on his shoulder and turned his head to see that Miss Dunn had fallen asleep. How tired she must be, he reflected thoughtfully.

He put away what was left of the lunch, trying not to awaken the sleeping woman.

3

$\mathcal{T}$HE TRAIN TRIP THUS FAR had been long and tiring, with many delays. Cam felt that when this ordeal was over he would not wish to ever take another train ride. However, he had to admit that he had found the changing countryside interesting and was glad that Harriet Dunn always insisted that he sit next to the window.

She had been a pleasant traveling companion, pointing out things of interest, taking charge when changes had to be made, always picking up extra food for Cam during stops. On occasion, she had shared with him some readings from a book of poetry she brought along. While he enjoyed hearing her voice as she read, he was not sure he liked poetry. He found it hard to understand.

The ever-present Clay Beardsley seemed always watchful, aware of their every move. On several occasions, finding Cam alone, he had tried to engage him in conversation, but Cam had always managed to slip away with little comment.

Miss Dunn, on the other hand, had met his seemingly friendly overtures with a polite disdain that brought a cynical smile to his face and hid the cold anger just below the surface.

Now at last the train was nearing Savannah, Ga. Cam could see marshlands where long-legged white birds stalked the shallow pools. He pointed them out to Miss Dunn.

"White herons," she said, "these are the tidelands, and many waterfowl come here for the winter. See, there are some ducks!"

"Mallards," Cam said, recognizing the ducks he had seen on the ponds back home.

"The water is controlled by the tides in the ocean. When the tide is high it floods these lowlands and makes a feeding place for many species," explained Miss Dunn.

"What is that gray stuff I've seen hanging from the trees?" Cam asked. "See, there's some now."

"That's Spanish moss. You will see plenty of that before long. Down our way, folks gather it and use it for many things."

"Cam," Miss Dunn said presently, "we will have an overnight delay here in Savannah. I have a very dear friend I am going to see. I would like for you to accompany me. He is sending a carriage to the station to get me. It will give you a chance to see some of the city if we are not too late getting in. What do you say?"

Cam looked down at his travel-worn clothing. "All right," he said with modest enthusiasm, "but I don't look very good."

"You'll be fine," she responded. "We'll freshen up when we arrive. You will find him to be a congenial host who will make you very welcome."

Cam returned his gaze to the window. The sun was low in the sky. A few houses began to appear, looking quite different to him. They were long, with porches on the front and back. An open door at each end allowed one to see right through the house. Now there were more of them, close together along the tracks. A woman was taking in her wash before the evening dampness fell. Black children paused in their play to watch the train pass by.

The conductor came through to announce the approaching station. At his call, the passengers prepared to leave the train. Harriet Dunn put on her hat and tucked her hair in place around it. Cam pulled the luggage from under the seat in front of them and sat on the edge of his seat waiting for the train to stop. It would be a relief to get off the train for a while.

Clay Beardsley sat just to the front and left of them. Cam could see the brim of his hat, and while he watched, Beardsley got up and went to wait at the door of the coach just as the great steam engine hissed to a stop.

The boy and the woman sat for a few moments waiting for the aisle to clear. Then, rising to her feet, Miss Dunn remarked, "I do hope the carriage is here, Cam. If not, I'll check with the agent to see if there is a message."

Cam reached for their bags and followed her from the train. He walked to a low bench by the door and sat down to wait for her while she went in to inquire. The crowd had dispersed, and in the dim light he could see up and down the platform. It was growing quite dark now, but still the warmth of the day lingered. Cam pushed his hat back off his forehead.

A man had pushed a cart up to the mail car and was busy stacking packages being handed to him from within. He laughed and talked good-naturedly as he worked.

As Cam sat watching him, a movement beyond captured his attention. Emerging from the darkness of a nearby building were three men. Two of them quickly slipped away into the night. The other paused, struck a match, and held it to light a cigar in his mouth. Cam caught his breath as he recognized the face caught in the flash of light. It was Clay Beardsley! What was he doing and who were those men? Cam wondered as he quickly turned around.

When Clay Beardsley turned to make his way back to the station, he saw Cam sitting by the door with his back to him. How much had the boy seen? he questioned silently. Well, it didn't matter, he wouldn't be around long anyway. The men he had hired would attend to that after they had delivered Harriet Dunn into his hands. He smiled in anticipation of possessing her. It would be rewarding to see Miss High and Mighty grovel at his feet.

As Beardsley approached, Cam steeled himself against another attempt to be engaged in conversation, but the man walked on by, leaving Cam stirred with suspicion.

Harriet Dunn came back in time to see Cam looking intently at the tall figure of Clay Beardsley retreating into the darkness. "Are you all right?" she asked, noting Cam's somber expression.

"Yes, ma'am," he answered, trying to decide whether he should tell her what he had seen. Since nothing had happened to give him reason to believe the incident involved them, there seemed to be no need to worry her with the matter.

"Our carriage is here. It's out in front of the station," she said and turned to go.

Cam picked up their things and followed her through the station to the waiting carriage. Such a carriage Cam had never seen—shining black with golden spokes in the wheels and a matching gold fringe around the top. Inside the open door he could see red velvet seats. Two spirited, sleek chestnut horses stomped impatiently to get started. The driver, wearing a frock coat with shining buttons, stood ready to assist them.

"Just set those things down, son. I'll take care of 'em," he said with a big smile lighting up his black face. "Here, ma'am, I'll take that hatbox too. Watch yo' step, now!" After helping them into the carriage, he put their baggage in the rear and climbed to his seat.

When the carriage had turned out into the street and continued at a steady pace, Miss Dunn turned to Cam. "Camden," she began, "the friend we are going to see is Colonel Alexander Stothard. He is a wealthy man with great influence, and he has done much in helping the South to rebuild. He will make you feel welcome. On several occasions he has stayed at Dunn House while fishing down on the Oklawaha River."

"Is the fishing good down there?" asked Cam.

"Oh, yes," she said. "Do you like to fish?"

"I don't know. I've never been fishing," Cam said, looking out to see that they had left the city and were winding along a narrow road lined with trees.

"Well, you will have plenty of . . . Oh! What's happening?" she cried. "Hold on, Cam!" The carriage was nearly upset by the horses as they reared and lunged backward.

"Whoa! Whoa!" the driver shouted as he fought for control, holding tight on the reins.

"Hold on there, driver!" came a voice from the dark. A man ran from the trees to grab the bridle. "Just stay put and you won't get hurt," he sneered, brandishing a gun.

"Come on, Creed. Get to it!" he called to an accomplice.

The dark shadow of a man came to the door of the carriage and jerked open the door. "All right, folks, climb out of there," he growled.

"Surely there is a mistake, sir. I . . . ," began Miss Dunn.

"No mistake, lady. Now, get out of there or I'll drag you out!" he threatened as he leaped forward. "Come on, kid, you too. Move!"

Cam jumped to his feet and hurriedly stepped down from the carriage and turned to help Harriet Dunn out. "Be careful, we must do as he says," she whispered in his ear.

"Now move away from that carriage," he ordered, pushing a gun out to where they could see it.

Harriet Dunn gasped and, putting her hands firmly on Cam's shoulders, slowly backed away.

"Pull out, driver, we've no quarrel with you!" he yelled, slapping the right horse on the rump. With a leap, the horses bolted forward and the carriage disappeared in the enveloping darkness.

"Bring the wagon out, Watts. Hurry!" he called urgently.

The man called Watts drove a horse and wagon from the trees where they had been concealed.

"Now, keep your gun on 'em whils't I tie their hands," admonished the man called Creed. "Here, kid, put your hands behind your back," he commanded.

Cam complied, realizing there was nothing else he could do, and soon he was bound securely with a strong cord. As the man repeated the action with Miss Dunn, Cam could see her face, which was pale yet calm. They were then ordered to walk to the back of the waiting wagon.

"Watts, get down here and help me tie their feet, and git 'em in the wagon. Here, take the rope!"

Jumping from the wagon, Watts caught the rope and knelt to tie Cam's feet. "Haw! Haw!" he chortled. "He said it would be easy."

"Shut up, you fool!" Creed warned.

"All right, boys!" came a terse voice from the dark. "Turn around and drop those guns."

Creed spun around to face three men advancing toward them, guns leveled. Watts dropped the rope and attempted to get to his feet, reaching for the gun he had carelessly left on the wagon seat. Cam, sensing it was an opportune moment, kicked the man at his feet and sent him off balance against the other one.

Two of the rescuers jumped on the kidnappers, disarming them, while the third came quickly to release Miss Dunn and Cam from their bonds. It was only a few moments until Creed and Watts sat bound in the wagon.

"Jim, you and Bart take those two in the wagon out to the place. We'll question them later," instructed the man standing with Cam and Miss Dunn. "I'll escort Miss Dunn and this young man to Colonel Stothard's home and catch up with you later. First, bring up the other carriage."

Turning his attention back to Miss Dunn, he continued, "Allow me to introduce myself. I am Captain Brevard, Colonel Stothard's personal bodyguard. At your service, ma'am."

"But . . . but how did you know?" stammered Harriet Dunn.

"The colonel always sends two carriages; one follows at a safe distance. We saw that yours had stopped, so we stopped and came up on foot. We had to wait for the right moment so you would not be in jeopardy. Are you all right, ma'am?"

"Yes, Captain, thank you for your concern."

"Come, we must go now. The colonel will be worried. No doubt the first driver has already reported to him about what has happened." Taking her arm, he led her to the carriage, which had been brought up close.

"Oh, I beg your pardon, Camden," she said, stopping to look back at Cam who followed them. "Captain, this is Camden William Fox. He is accompanying me on this trip."

"Hello, Camden," greeted Captain Brevard politely. "You are a very brave young man." He assisted them into the carriage and joined them, calling to the driver to get going.

Harriet Dunn felt a sense of relief when a short while later the carriage passed between the gleaming white pillars of the gate house, dim in the starlight. Captain Brevard leaned forward to signal the gatekeeper, and they continued on down a long drive to pull up under the portico of a stately mansion. The lamps had been lit, giving the weary travelers a warm welcome. Captain Brevard quickly climbed out and turned to help Miss Dunn.

As Cam was stepping down from the carriage, the large door at the entrance swung open and out strode a tall, broad-shouldered man. "Harriet!" he exclaimed, concern evident in his voice. "How relieved I am that you are finally here!" Taking her by the shoulders he drew her to him and kissed her on the forehead. "Are you all right?" he asked, holding her at arm's length so he could look into her eyes.

Harriet nodded, overcome with emotion. His greeting had such a powerful effect on her that she did not trust herself to speak.

"You're shaking," he observed. "Jenny," he called to the maid hovering in the background, "take Miss Dunn to her room and stay with her." The colonel watched as the maid led her into the house.

Cam studied Colonel Stothard's face. He was a ruggedly handsome man with piercing dark eyes, standing straight in the manner of a soldier.

"So, you're the young man the driver told me about. What's your name, son?" the colonel asked, turning to Cam.

"Camden William Fox, sir," Cam answered, looking up into the kindly face. "Most folks call me Cam."

"Well, Cam, I know you are probably weary from your long trip. But come with me—I need to talk with you. Captain Brevard, join us, please." He led them through the large entrance hall into the drawing room and closed the doors. He indicated some chairs, then seating himself, leaned toward Cam.

"Son, it's very important for you to tell us all that has happened."

Cam cleared his throat and began telling them every detail he could remember about the attempted kidnapping. When he had finished he sat waiting for the two men to speak.

Finally, Colonel Stothard muttered, as if to himself, "It's clear someone else was behind this. But why?"

"Cam, did anything unusual happen on the train or at the station?" asked Captain Brevard.

"Well, there was one thing I wondered about," he answered, remembering what he had seen while waiting for Miss Dunn.

"Yes, what is it?" urged Colonel Stothard.

Cam went on to relate to them the incident involving the three men at the depot. "I could not see them very well . . . two of them were in the shadows . . . but the one I recognized. It was the man who was on the train. Miss Dunn told me his name was Clay Beardsley." The two men exchanged glances as he continued, "I didn't tell Miss Dunn about it."

Both men rose quickly to their feet and left the room. He could hear them talking in low tones. While he waited, he looked around the room, taking in the rich leather furnishings, the beautifully paneled walls, and the gold damask draperies. In the middle of the outside wall was a large fireplace surrounded by French doors. Over the mantel hung a large picture of General Robert E. Lee, resplendent in uniform. Cam could not resist walking over to look up into his face. He was so engrossed he did not hear Colonel Stothard reenter the room.

"He was a good man and a great soldier. I was proud to serve under him," commented the colonel as he joined Cam.

"Yes, sir, Colonel, you needed somethin'?" Both turned at the servant's voice.

"Jason, show this young man to his room. He is very tired and will enjoy a nice bath. Then we'll have dinner."

Cam left with the servant, and Colonel Stothard settled in his chair with a troubled look. What did all this mean? Who was this Clay Beardsley, and what did he mean to Harriet?

Something deep within him stirred at the thought that they might be involved in some way. He shook his head as if to rid it of such thoughts. He had no right to feel as he did. After all, he had no claim on her, and she was free to do as she chose.

His mind went back to how beautiful she looked as she stood there with the light on her white face. His pulse leaped as he remembered the glad expression in her eyes at the sight of him. Perhaps he had been too bold in his greeting, but he had been so glad to have her there unharmed.

He got to his feet and paced the floor as he tried to sort out the conflicting emotions raging within him. Dare he hope that she might care for him? Was her trembling response and sudden shyness because of his brash act . . . or a letdown from her ordeal?

His thoughts turned to Cam whose blue eyes were similar to hers. She had never spoken of having a son. Yet when the boy had related the story, he had spoken with the same directness and honesty. If she is in some kind of trouble I will stand by her as a friend, he concluded with quiet determination. Glancing at the clock, he went upstairs to dress for dinner.

4

*U*PSTAIRS HARRIET DUNN LAY QUIETLY resting on the bed after a relaxing bath. The maid was busy setting out her clothes. She closed her eyes and gave vent to the thoughts that belied her calm repose. Why were they waylaid by those men? They had made no attempt to rob them. Who was the "he" that one of them had referred to? Someone else had obviously hired them to do this awful deed! But who? Could it have been Clay Beardsley? And for what purpose? Cam! Beardsley must have overheard them talking about the homestead and suspected, as she did, that Cam was carrying the papers on him.

She shuddered at the thought of what would have happened to them had they fallen into Beardsley's control. Death no doubt for Cam, and a fate worse than death for her.

How grateful she was to Colonel Stothard for his carefully laid plans to protect them and provide for their safety.

Her heart throbbed when she remembered his gentle kiss. Many times before when he had been a guest at Dunn House she had caught his approving look, but this was the first sign of any affection he had afforded her. It could have been his genuine relief that she was safe. At any rate, it sent her pulse racing at the prospect that he might care for her.

She sat up quickly in bed. What was she doing to give way to such vain imaginations?

The maid stood waiting to help her dress. She had brought only one gown, a light blue with lace around the neckline and across the bosom. She slipped it on, allowing Jenny to fasten the buttons up the back. When she surveyed herself in the mirror, she was pleased with the results.

She decided to do her hair in a softer style, allowing a few curls to escape around her ears and neckline.

Jenny smiled her approval, "You sure do look pretty, Miss Dunn."

"Thank you, Jenny," Harriet responded. "Now, would you please tell me which room the young man is in?"

Harriet Dunn knocked softly on Cam's door. When he opened it she was pleased to see that he was dressed in a clean shirt and pants. His hair was neatly combed but still damp from his bath.

"Are you ready to go down for dinner?" she asked, smiling at him.

"Yes, ma'am," he answered, suddenly shy at how pretty she was.

They had started down the hall together when Miss Dunn remembered she had forgotten her handkerchief. She slipped into her room for it.

While Cam waited for her a door at the end of the stairway opened, and Colonel Stothard stepped out looking very handsome wearing gray trousers and black coat.

"Ho! There you are, son," he said cheerfully. "How about some dinner? Come, Miss Dunn will probably be down in a moment," he continued and they started down the stairs.

Cam glanced back to see Harriet Dunn at her door. She put her finger to her lips and motioned him on.

When they reached the bottom of the stairs, Colonel Stothard led the way into the sitting room. It was a pleasant room, beautifully furnished. Cam hesitated just inside the door, uncertain as to what he should do.

"Have a seat, Camden," said the Colonel, gesturing toward the couch. "How far are you in your schooling, son?"

"I haven't had much time for schooling, sir," Cam informed him as he took a seat on the couch. "I've had to work mostly."

"You mean for Miss Dunn?" asked Colonel Stothard, deciding to pursue the matter further.

"No, sir. I worked at odd jobs for my Uncle George."

"In Florida?" pressed the Colonel.

"No, sir. Uncle George lives in Connecticut," replied Cam.

The colonel studied Cam's face for a moment, then with a slight frown looked down at the ring he wore, turning it round and round with his thumb, pondering this last bit of information. Wasn't that where Harriet had written him from?

"I see you two are getting acquainted."

Colonel Stothard looked up to see Harriet Dunn standing there, and his pulse quickened at the sight of her. He had never seen her wearing other than the dark colors she usually wore at Dunn House. The blue dress, fitted at the waist, fell into soft folds accenting her slender figure.

He suddenly remembered his manners, much to her amusement, and rising to his feet he said gallantly, "Come in, Miss Dunn. I'll let them know we are ready for dinner."

Was there a difference in his manner? she wondered as she watched him leave the room.

"Cam, you must be hungry," she said, realizing that it had been a long time since they last ate.

Jason appeared in the doorway, "The colonel say fo' you to join him in the dinin' room, ma'am."

They followed him to where Colonel Stothard stood waiting to help her with her chair.

Cam took the chair across from her indicated by Jason, and when they were all seated there was a moment of silence. Finally, Colonel Stothard cleared his throat and with a smile to Miss Dunn, "Camden was telling me about working for his Uncle George in Connecticut."

"Yes, I suppose he did," she replied, wondering why the conversation started on this note. "But . . ."

The conversation was interrupted at this point when the servants brought in steaming plates of food.

Cam was so hungry he turned all his attention to his plate, while Miss Dunn and Colonel Stothard engaged in small talk.

Midway through the meal, Jason came to the colonel and announced that Captain Brevard was in the drawing room. The colonel excused himself and left the room. A few moments later he returned. Taking his seat, he looked at Cam for a moment, then turned to Miss Dunn. "Captain Brevard has just informed me that they convinced the two kidnappers to talk. They were supposed to deliver you to a man who called himself Mr. Brindley. The captain and his men rode quickly to surround the deserted farmhouse where he was waiting, but he must have suspected something went wrong and left." Colonel Stothard had been watching her face as he talked and saw no change in her expression.

"Brindley," she murmured thoughtfully, "I don't know anyone by that name . . . unless . . . did they get a description of the man?" she asked, trying to appear casual.

"Yes," he said in a constrained voice, "he was a tall, rather good-looking fellow, dressed neatly, wearing a gray hat." He noted that her face lost some of its color as she quickly looked across to Cam, who had finished his dinner and sat patiently waiting for them to finish.

Colonel Stothard pushed his plate away, no longer interested in food. He leaned back in his chair and sat watching Miss Dunn, who picked aimlessly at her plate.

She laid down her fork. "Colonel Stothard," she said, "I need to talk with you. Cam, would you excuse us please?"

Colonel Stothard and Cam got to their feet. "Of course. We'll go into the drawing room," he said helping her with her chair.

"If it's all right, I would like to go to my room," Cam said.

"You must be very tired. Good night, Cam," she said, placing her hand on his shoulder.

Cam climbed the stairs to his room. He searched for his coat, but it was nowhere to be seen. He stood looking around the room, wondering where Jason might have put it. There was a door across the room that turned out to be a large closet. He smiled to himself at the sight of his coat, which looked so small in such a large space.

He took the Bible from the pocket, and removing his shoes, he climbed onto the big four-poster bed. As he was turning through the pages, he saw his mother's handwriting. He stopped to read the words: "O God, be a father to Cam!" He read the scripture she had indicated with a check mark that seemed to describe God. "A father of the fatherless, and a judge of the widows" (Ps. 68:5). He stared with unseeing eyes at the page, remembering the good times they had shared. Mother, I miss you so, he cried within himself, as a sense of loneliness swept over him. He had not thought of himself as an orphan until now. With Uncle George there had been family, but all that was over. He was alone. She must have known.

He read the words she had written again and tried to remember the times she had talked to him about God. His mind went to the day he had come home crying after some boys had called him a bad name because he didn't know where his father was. "Cam," she had said, soothing away the tears, "your father was a fine man, and we loved each other very much. He was very sick, and Jesus came to take him home with Him. Now you have two fathers in heaven—your earthly father and your Heavenly Father. God, your Heavenly Father, will always be with you wherever you are." She stroked his head, and her calming voice had comforted him.

Reading her prayer and the scripture again, a peace settled over him. He swung his legs off the bed and laid the Bible on the table nearby. He unbuttoned his shirt and removed the packet of papers, looked at it for a moment, and decided to lay it on the table with his Bible. After taking his clothes off, he blew out the lamp and climbed wearily into bed. Lying in the dark, he thought about the attempted kidnapping and felt responsible for what had happened. He felt bad that Miss Dunn had been subjected to such rough treatment. Sleep finally overtook his troubled thoughts.

Harriet Dunn sat in the drawing room on the divan wondering where to begin. Colonel Stothard stood near the fireplace, his face expressionless. She noticed he lacked his usual cheerfulness and warmth.

"Colonel Stothard," she began, "I want to thank you for inviting me to stop over for a visit. It was most kind of you." He smiled his acknowledgment.

Taking a deep breath, she started again, "I believe the man that Captain Brevard and his men were looking for is Clay Beardsley. He was on the train when I boarded, but I didn't know it. I chose to sit with Cam . . . I don't know why . . . except he looked so forlorn and lost. Later, when Mr. Beardsley tried to force his attention upon me, I asked Cam if he would assist me. We became traveling companions, staying close to one another for protection."

As she spoke, Colonel Stothard felt as if an iron band burst around his chest, sending the blood pounding to his temples. He came over to sit beside her, listening intently as she told him information about Clay Beardsley's questionable business deals in the area, which she had heard discussed among the men at Dunn House.

"I believe Clay Beardsley is a ruthless man who will go to any extreme to get what he wants. Now, about Cam . . . I don't know the whole story on him yet. But I do know his uncle is sending him to Florida to improve a homestead. I think he is carrying the papers on him along with considerable money, and I fear for his safety," she concluded, looking down at her hands.

Colonel Stothard sat silently for a moment, thinking of what the consequences would have been had the kidnappers gotten away with their dastardly act. He reached over and took her hand, which felt cold to his touch.

"Miss Dunn . . . Harriet," he said gently, his heart swelling inside him, "why don't you stay over for a few days? You've had a tiring trip, and with the extra strain you've been under, a rest will do you good."

"I'll give it some thought, Colonel," she said, her heart pounding at his touch. When she raised her eyes to meet his, a slow blush came to her cheeks. She quickly withdrew her hand. "I'm very tired. I really must be going . . . ," she stammered, rising to her feet. "Good night, Colonel."

"Harriet, wait!" he cried.

She fled from the room, not trusting herself another minute. Her heart was racing as she entered her room and closed the door. She walked to the bed and sat down, silently scolding herself for her girlish behavior. What must he think of her? She washed her burning face and undressed, putting on the gown and robe Jenny had laid out for her.

Sleep didn't come easily even though she was tired. Searching her heart, she tried to analyze her feelings. Colonel Stothard attracted her attention as no other man ever had. During his brief visits at Dunn House, she found herself distracted, thinking about him. When their eyes met across the room, she was left breathless and shaken.

There had been no time for men in her life since her father was killed in a boating accident. An inept businessman, he was not one to keep books, spending as he had earned, leaving her only a small amount of money and the big house on Reid Street. Leola, the young black woman who worked for her father, stayed loyally on to help Harriet make the old two-story home into a boardinghouse. Good food and clean beds, along with Harriet's genuine concern for the comfort of the guests, made Dunn House a respected stopover for many travelers.

She had worked very hard to get where she was, and she was happy with her life. She was respected among the business people of the thriving river town. Oh, there had been those who wanted a romantic involvement, but she had not taken them seriously. Now, all of a sudden she was acting like a silly schoolgirl. After all, Colonel Stothard was only repaying a kindness, she reasoned, trying to calm the upheaval she felt within.

Perhaps it was just a reaction to all the fast-moving events of the day, but deep in her heart there came a strange feeling of denial to this rationale. She took a deep breath, closed her eyes, and ceased to struggle against what seemed inevitable.

5

$\mathcal{T}$HE MORNING SUN WAS SHINING BRIGHTLY as Jason entered the room to open the windows. A cool, refreshing breeze drifted in. He turned to look at the sleeping boy.

"Good mawnin', Mista Cam," he called cheerfully. "I reckon you gonna sleep all day too?"

Cam opened his eyes to watch sleepily as Jason poured water from the pitcher into the large washbowl and laid out some clean towels. He turned to look at the boy again. "You had best be gittin' up or yo' gonna clean miss yo' breakfast." He laughed good-naturedly. "I nevuh seen any growin' boy to miss his food." The door closed behind him with a click.

Cam flipped back the covers and swung his legs down to sit on the side of the bed. He reached for his trousers and pulled them on. After he had washed his face and combed his unruly shock of hair, he slipped into his shirt and walked to the window. From where his room was located he could see the stables. A stable hand emerged, leading a beautiful mare to the water trough. As he stood admiring the horse, there was a light tap at his door.

"Cam," Miss Dunn called softly through the door.

He tucked in his shirt and hurried to open the door. Her glance took in the rumpled bed with the Bible and oil-skinned packet lying on the table. Cam stood waiting for her to speak.

"I need to talk with you," she began. "Colonel Stothard has invited us to stay over for a few days. How do you feel about it? We can catch the train the first of the week." She walked over and sat on the bed, then looked at him with questioning eyes.

"It's all right with me," he answered after hesitating for a moment. "I don't have any special time to arrive, I guess."

"Good! That settles it." She reached to pick up the packet of papers. "Have you been carrying these with you?" she asked, turning it over in her hand.

"Yes, ma'am. I thought in my shirt was the safest place."

"Did anyone see you put them there?"

"I think Mr. Beardsley did," he admitted, telling her about the incident on the train before she boarded.

"Cam, I believe Clay Beardsley was behind what took place last night. I feel we would have been in grave danger had we fallen into his hands." She paused to watch his reaction. "You don't seem to be surprised."

"No, ma'am. That's the way I reckoned it after what I saw at the depot."

She sat looking at him, trying to comprehend the meaning of his words. "Tell me about it," she urged, placing the packet back on the stand.

After he finished telling her what he had seen at the station, he added, "I didn't tell you 'cause I didn't want to worry you."

"Did you tell Colonel Stothard about this?"

"Yes, ma'am. He wanted to know first off if I had seen anything unusual at the station or on the train."

"Well, now we know," she concluded. "I don't think we will be bothered for a while, but you will have to be very careful in the future, Cam. Beardsley is not a man to give up that easily." She got up and walked to the window where she stood looking down on the scene below. Cam sat down in a chair and began to pull on his socks.

"Cam," she said finally, "tell me about your folks."

Cam put on his shoe and tied it before answering. "My dad died when I was a baby. When my mother died recently, I went to live with my Uncle George in Norwalk. You know the rest." He reached for his other shoe.

She turned from the window to look at him. "Do you trust me, Cam?"

He gave the tie of his shoe a jerk and rose to his feet. "Yes, ma'am," he said without hesitation, meeting her steady gaze.

She walked over and put her hands on his shoulders. "Was your Uncle George unkind to you?" She felt a surge of emotion at the thought.

"Oh, no, ma'am," he exclaimed in defense of his uncle. "We got along . . . I stayed at the store . . . and worked there . . . it was Aunt Lizzie mostly" . . . his stammering voice trailed off, and he lowered his eyes as painful memories crowded to the surface.

Harriet Dunn gave his shoulders a firm squeeze and turned away. Her voice was unsteady. "Cam, I am going to help you all that I can. What your uncle has asked you to do will be very hard and, well, never mind right now. We had best be going down for breakfast."

At the foot of the stairs, Jason appeared to inform them that the colonel would be joining them soon. He had gone to the stables to check on a mare that had given birth to a foal.

They were waiting in the sitting room only a few moments when he came. He strode into the room looking very handsome in his gray riding habit. "Good morning! I see you two look rested and refreshed after your ordeal yesterday. Breakfast is ready. Shall we go? It is such a beautiful morning," he went on cheerfully, leading the way. "We'll eat out on the south veranda."

Breakfast was a very amiable affair. It was Cam's first taste of grits. The colonel assured him good-naturedly that he would have to learn to eat this southern dish if he was to be a true son of the South. Miss Dunn chimed in that it looked like he had done pretty well, since he had eaten two helpings.

"By the way, Cam, how would you like to see the new foal?" asked Colonel Stothard, pushing back his chair.

Cam's eyes sparkled at the prospect. "I'd like that, sir!"

"May I come along?" asked Miss Dunn.

"Of course," Colonel Stothard answered enthusiastically, rising to help her with her chair.

They crossed the veranda to a walk leading out to the stables. Giant live oak trees mingled with magnolia bordered the path. A gentle breeze swayed the gray moss hanging in the limbs. Dew sparkled on the grass and shrubs, reflecting the sun in a myriad of diamonds. Following along, Cam felt a new sense of belonging and adventure.

Colonel Stothard stopped to talk for a moment with a stable boy who was polishing a harness. "Josie, where is Cletus?"

"He's in there with that new foal, Cuhnel," he replied, gesturing toward the wide open door of the stables.

They entered the cool shade of the building to see Cletus standing at the center stall. There was the earthy smell of hay, horse liniment, and leather. Harnesses and feed buckets hung on the walls. There was a long, low bench on one side, near the door. Farther in were several bags of feed.

"Hey there, Cletus, how's the new family?"

"Jus' fine, Cuhnel, jus' fine! Why, that little felluh is all over that stall. See fo' yo'sef, suh."

"Well, well. Hello there, little fella. Come here, Cam, here is the newest member of the family. What do you think?" Colonel Stothard asked proudly, beaming down at Cam.

Cam was delighted to see the gangly-legged baby standing near its mother, head held high, already showing the characteristics of a proud, spirited horse.

"Oh, what a beauty!" cried Miss Dunn in excitement, taking hold of the colonel's arm, unaware of the effect her nearness and unconscious action had upon him.

"His mother is my best mare," he stated with an unsteady voice. "She comes from a good blood line. He was sired by King, who has great stride and stamina. No horse can outrun my King."

"Come here, little fella," Cam coaxed. But the little foal raised his head and retreated to the side of his mother, tail switching.

"I've got to find a name for the foal. Would you two have any suggestions?"

"He sure is a dandy little fellow," Cam said admiringly.

"That's it!" cried Miss Dunn. "Why not call him Dandy?"

"Dandy it will be," said Colonel Stothard, giving the hand on his arm a squeeze. "Come, we'll go see King."

They walked to the stall where King had his golden head out looking toward them. He whinnied loudly, stretching his neck to greet the colonel, who stroked his head.

"King, meet Miss Dunn and Camden. Here, Camden, you can touch him. He'll not hurt you. There, go ahead."

Cam reached up to stroke the soft, velvety nose. King raised his head to search Cam's hand for a treat. "Hello, King," he said softly, showing no fear.

"See there, he likes you," declared the colonel. "You have a natural way with horses. That's good! If you treat a horse right, he'll stand by you."

Jason appeared, beckoning the colonel aside where they conversed in low tones for a moment. Then Jason hurried toward the house and Colonel Stothard returned to where Miss Dunn and Cam stood.

"Please excuse me for a little while. I have someone waiting to see me. Take as long as you like here, then wait for me in the sitting room," he said kindly and then strode up the path to the house.

"Cam, do you like horses?" asked Miss Dunn softly, her eyes on Colonel Stothard's retreating figure.

"Yes, ma'am, but I've never been around them very much."

"You will be needing some good horses or mules to do the work on a homestead. We'll see to that."

Cletus came to lead King to water. Miss Dunn and Cam walked slowly along the path to the house, engrossed in their own thoughts until Miss Dunn asked, "Cam, did your uncle give you instructions to see anyone after you arrived in Palatka?"

"He told me to see Zachariah Sparks and that he would help me in filing the papers at the courthouse. Uncle George wrote a letter to Mr. Sparks. It's in the packet."

"Does your uncle know Mr. Sparks?"

"I don't know. I don't think so. He said he had heard that Mr. Sparks was an honest man." Cam looked up at her, squinting in the sunlight.

"Well, that he is, but he sure is a colorful person," she said with amusement. "He has been married to six wives and has about 13 children. They live out on a homestead and have done quite well, I think." She paused, then continued, "He'll be a good help. I'll have a talk with him, though he only comes into town about once a month. When Henry—he works for Mr. Sparks—comes to see Leola, I'll send a message back with him." She stopped at the bottom of the stairs to the veranda. "Cam, you can stay at Dunn House until we get things in order." When Cam did not respond, but stood there looking at some object past her, she asked, "Is there something wrong with that?"

"No, ma'am, it's just that I don't want anything for free," he said slowly, shifting his gaze to the ground at his feet.

"Well, then," she suggested, noting his discomfort, "there are some repairs that need to be·done. I've put them off until I get back from this trip. You can do those, and it will work out fine for both of us. Agreed?"

"Agreed," he answered as they continued on into the house.

Just as they arrived at the door leading into the sitting room, the opposite door opened and Captain Brevard stepped out followed by Colonel Stothard.

"Good morning, Captain Brevard," Miss Dunn said graciously, a note of gladness in her voice. A slight blush flooded her cheeks, adding to her beauty and noted by those watching her.

"Good morning, ma'am," he responded with a slight bow, smiling down at her. "You are looking quite . . . uh . . . well. I trust you are all right?"

"Yes, I'm fine," she said demurely, offering him her hand. "I want to thank you for your kindness to Cam and me last night."

He took the hand offered him. "You're quite welcome, Miss Dunn," he said gallantly. "I was glad to be at your service." He stepped back and turned to pick up his hat. "I'll take care of the matter, Colonel."

Colonel Stothard nodded his head in acknowledgment, his eyes still on Harriet Dunn as she watched Captain Brevard's tall figure walk to the door.

"Harriet," he blurted out, not noticing he had used her first name, "how would you and Cam like to take a ride into Savannah. I have a little business there that will only take a moment, then I'll be free for the rest of the day."

"We would be delighted, Colonel," she drawled graciously.

"Good! I'll have Jason order the buggy around. We'll leave in about half an hour."

"I'll get my things." She started for the stairs where she paused. "Cam, may I see you for a moment?"

"Yes, ma'am," he said, obediently following her.

When they reached the top of the stairs, she turned to him. "Cam, if you would rather do something else, it's all right. But you will enjoy seeing Savannah; it's a lovely old town."

"I'll go."

"I'm glad," she responded, then disappeared into her room.

Cam went to get his hat. The day was warm, so he decided against wearing his jacket. He was about to leave the room when his eyes fell upon the packet of papers on the table. He picked them up and looked around the room for a hiding place. A thought occurred to him—perhaps this would be a good time to take a look at the contents. Dropping his hat on the bed, he sat down and opened the packet. There were some legal-looking papers and a couple of sealed letters. One was addressed to Mr. Samuel McCarthy, the other to Zachariah Sparks. But there was no money!

He searched his pockets for what meager change he had earned delivering groceries. Most of the women had paid him with cookies, a piece of pie, or cake. He felt a rush of gratitude for Mrs. Wills, who had always given him a few coins.

He put the change back into his pocket and gathered up the papers and letters to replace them in the packet.

"Cam, are you ready?"

He looked up to see Miss Dunn watching him from the doorway. How long had she been there, he wondered. "Almost," he answered. "I don't know where to put these." He indicated the papers he held in his hand.

"Why not in my room," she suggested, "no one would think of looking for them there."

He handed her the packet, relieved to have someone share the responsibility for their safety.

"There's no money in there," he said matter-of-factly.

"No money!" she exclaimed, remembering how little he had eaten while on the train. "Do you have some money?"

"I've got what I earned delivering groceries, but it's not much."

"If you need more, I'll lend you some. You can work and repay me," she added, knowing how proud he was. "I'll only be a moment with these papers. Meet me in the hall."

While Cam waited for her, he could not help thinking about the money. Uncle George had said there was money in the packet. Had he forgotten to put it in? Well, whatever the reason, Cam decided, he would earn his own way and not accept charity from anyone. Certainly not from Uncle George and Aunt Lizzie.

In her room, Miss Dunn carefully hid the papers in her hatbox. She was very upset. What kind of a man would send a boy off alone to clear swampland inhabited with snakes, alligators, panthers, and other predators, she fumed. It was a dangerous and lonely job even for the most experienced. He needed a friend, and she intended to be that friend.

6

THE RIDE INTO TOWN SEEMED SHORT. When the carriage came to a stop before a rather pretentious brownstone building, Cam could see a sign over the doorway that read *JEREMIAH C. TEMPLETON, Attorney-at-Law.*

Colonel Stothard spoke briskly as he stepped down. "I'll only be a moment. You can come in if you like or wait here." He paused briefly for a reply.

"We will wait, thank you," responded Miss Dunn with a smile. She took a small fan from her bag.

"Cam, do you like Colonel Stothard?" she asked thoughtfully, fanning herself.

"Yes, ma'am, I do. He's been good to me when he had no call to be." Then looking at her, he continued, "You like him a lot too."

She hid her surprise at his directness, but studying his face she decided he was just speaking with an innocent frankness, unaware of the tumult that his question had aroused within her. Lowering her eyes, she murmured, "Yes, Cam, I'm afraid that I do." A slow blush made its way to her cheeks. "Please keep my secret. The colonel must not know."

"He knows," Cam said, "and I think he likes you a lot too. I've seen him looking at you."

"Shush!" she admonished him, putting a finger to her lips. The colonel had just left the building.

"There, that's done. We'll ride down through the market-place. If you see something you like, we'll stop," he said cheerfully.

When they arrived the market was teeming with activity. Wagons and carts laden with green vegetables and chicken crates lined the square. Here and there, tables had been set up to display homemade bread and pastries.

"Oh! How pretty!" Miss Dunn exclaimed, as she spotted some quilts hanging over the side of one of the wagons. "Let's get out and walk!"

The colonel signaled the driver to stop, and they got out to make their way through the crowd. Cam followed the colonel and Miss Dunn to where the brightly colored quilts were displayed. While he was waiting, he stood watching the crowd.

A buxom woman wearing a black dress with a stiffly starched collar was standing before some chicken crates. The farmer was holding up two chickens, one in each hand for her to see. She felt the breast of one and selected it. Near her stood a girl with a parasol in her hand, watching with disinterest. Cam found himself staring at her. She was so pretty in her blue gingham dress and bonnet. Long, golden tresses escaped from under the confines of the ribbon that held her hat in place. He thought her to be about his age.

The girl turned as if feeling his eyes upon her, and he found himself looking into questioning blue eyes. He smiled timidly. She looked him over with quiet disdain and lifting her chin she turned away. Cam felt the blood rush to his face. Quickly he turned his attention back to Miss Dunn, who was paying for her purchase.

Colonel Stothard motioned to his driver that they were ready, and while the carriage moved slowly through the crowd toward them, Cam looked at the buildings surrounding the square. Most of them were two story with a porch on both floors. Each porch had windows and doors opening to the square below. Turning to look at the buildings behind him, his gaze met that of Clay Beardsley, who was peering down at him from a window on the second floor. The curtain dropped quickly but did not conceal the slight shadow of movement in the room beyond. Cam stood frozen to the spot.

"Cam, are you coming?" he heard Harriet Dunn call. But still he made no effort to move, his eyes on the window above.

Colonel Stothard turned to see what was keeping the boy, taking note of his tense posture and fixed stare. He glanced up to see what had attracted Cam's attention but saw nothing unusual. "Come on, son," he urged gently.

Cam walked obediently to the waiting carriage and climbed aboard. He kept his face averted as if watching the milling crowd outside. The colonel gave one last, quick look at the buildings on that side of the square before taking his seat. Once out of the square the driver held the horses at a lively pace. Miss Dunn chatted softly. Colonel Stothard listened in an attentive but preoccupied manner, glancing often at Cam, who continued to stare out at the changing countryside. He perceived the change in Cam's demeanor and instinctively knew the boy had seen something that upset him. He was relieved when they passed through the gate and rolled up the winding drive to stop where Jason stood at the door. He stepped quickly from the carriage and turned to assist Miss Dunn, who was still in a happy mood, sensing nothing wrong. She was radiant as she expressed her appreciation for the lovely morning, excusing herself to take the package to her room. He watched until she had disappeared from sight, then turned to Cam and placed a hand on his shoulder.

"What is it, Cam?" he asked quietly.

"He's still here in town," Cam answered, lifting his eyes to meet those of the man who had befriended him.

"Clay Beardsley?"

"Yes, sir, I saw him at the window of one of those buildings in the square. He was watching us and when I happened to look up, he dropped the curtain. I think he knows I saw him."

The colonel gave Cam a pat on the shoulder and turned to instruct the driver. "Tell Cletus to saddle King for me, and get Captain Brevard and his men here immediately."

"Yes, suh!" responded the driver, and he drove rapidly toward the stables.

The colonel hurried into the house where he climbed the stairs two at a time. Cam followed but decided to wait in the hall, seating himself in a chair near the open door. In a matter of moments, Colonel Stothard came down dressed in riding clothes. He went into the drawing room and returned, buckling on his gun belt, checking his revolver to make sure it was loaded. He went out the back way to the stables where Captain Brevard and his men had just ridden up. King was prancing with excitement as Cletus kept a tight hold on the bridle. The colonel stepped lithely into the saddle and they were off, King's great stride outdistancing the others.

In her room, Harriet Dunn heard the clatter of hooves as the horses raced away. She looked out the window in time to see the men riding out. She ran into the hall where she found Cam climbing the stairs.

"What has happened?" she asked.

"The colonel and his men are going into town after Clay Beardsley."

"Beardsley? I thought . . . Cam, are you sure?"

"Yes, ma'am. I saw him when we were in the square." He related the incident to her. When he had finished she sat down on a step and didn't speak for a while.

"So, he didn't leave after all," she mused. "Beardsley is smart. No doubt he will be gone when the colonel and his men get there. Well, there's no need for us to be frightened. We will just have to be very watchful as we continue our trip. While we are on the train we will be safe."

"I'm not afraid," Cam declared.

"I don't believe you are," she said, studying his face. "The sheriff at Jacksonville is a friend of mine. I think I'll send a telegraph asking him to meet us at the station." She rose to her feet and walked back up the stairs with him.

* * *

The men slowed their horses to a walk as they approached the square. They halted briefly for Captain Brevard to disperse his men to surround the building and guard the streets leading from the area. Then the captain and Colonel Stothard dismounted to lead their horses through the crowded marketplace. Few paid heed to the men, but the spirited King drew many an admiring remark and glance. When they reached the rooming house they casually tethered the horses. Captain Brevard gave one last look around at the position of his men, and with a nod to the colonel they entered the door. The room was dark and had the odor of stale tobacco smoke. A small counter was to their left. Overhead was a light with a green shade giving off a feeble yellow glow. A stairway led to the upper floor. There was the sound of scuffling footsteps and a man wearing a green visor on his bald head appeared through a doorway behind the counter. He pushed his glasses up on his nose and squinted his eyes to look keenly at both men. There was a slight impression of a smile on his face. Tobacco stains were in the creases of his mouth.

"What can I do for you, gentlemen?" he asked in a nasal voice.

"Do you have a Mr. Beardsley staying here?" Colonel Stothard inquired tersely.

"Well, let me see," the man answered, turning to spit tobacco juice in a spittoon. "I don't seem to recognize that name."

"The man we want to see is in the room directly overhead on the left," stated the Colonel.

"Oh, that would be Mr. Blake. He . . ."

"Give us the key to his room!" Captain Brevard interrupted impatiently.

"I can't do that, sir, I . . ."

A strong arm shot out to grasp his tobacco-stained shirt, cutting off further words. "Then you get the key and open the door for us," commanded the captain. "Understand?"

With eyes bulging, the desk clerk nodded, relieved when he was freed. He reached back to get the key from the slot, then hurried before them up the narrow stairs. He stopped in front of the door to knock timidly, "Mr. Blake?" he called through the door. When no sound came from the room, he turned the key in the lock and stood aside. His eyes widened as he saw that both men stood with their guns drawn.

Captain Brevard stepped cautiously into the room. It was empty. Drawers had been left out, and smoke was still rising from an unfinished cigar lying in a tray. Beardsley had anticipated their arrival.

"He's gone, Colonel, we're too late."

* * *

Cam grew restless. He decided to go down on the veranda to wait for the colonel to return. He sat where he could see the work going on out at the stables. Cletus was busy shoeing a horse. He could hear the ring of the anvil as the blacksmith's hammer struck it. He glanced up at the sun and guessed it to be about the noon hour. The smell of apples and spice drifted through the open windows of the kitchen. He suddenly realized that he was hungry.

The sound of horses coming up the drive announced the return of the colonel and his men. Cam stood up to watch them riding two abreast to the stables. Colonel Stothard stepped down and handed the reins to Cletus, who came forward to lead King away. He stood talking to Captain Brevard for a few minutes, then turned with a wave of his hand to walk to where Cam stood waiting to hear what had happened.

"Beardsley was gone, Cam. He figured we would be coming after him. I wish we could have gotten him. We didn't miss him by much!" he said with exasperation. "Well, let's forget what is in the past," he continued in a calmer voice. "Come, we'll see if dinner's about ready."

Harriet Dunn stood watching them from her window. Her heart swelled at the sight of the two of them together. A boy she had come to love and the man who was generous and kind to this orphaned boy—"When he had no call to be," as Cam had stated. A man whose presence stirred her pulses as no other man had ever done. A man she had fallen hopelessly in love with. . . . Her heart felt as if it would burst! Oh! . . . why did I come here? What was I thinking? At the first of the week they would be leaving. She would be back to the reality of running the boardinghouse. Her busy days would leave no time for thoughts of romance. She turned from the window with a sigh. She must stop this foolish dreaming!

7

A HEAVY EARLY MORNING DEW hung in the air. The marshlands had given way to dense pine trees standing like ghostly sentinels in the gray dawn. When they had boarded the train this morning everything was wet and dripping as if it had rained during the night. The sand clung to their shoes.

The coach was nearly full of passengers. A few were talking to one another in subdued voices, but most sat quietly staring out the window, engrossed in their own thoughts. It was as if the outside gloom had invaded the atmosphere within, casting a somberness over them all.

Cam sat in a seat to himself. Colonel Stothard and Miss Dunn were sitting just across the aisle. The colonel had made a sudden decision to accompany them to Palatka, "to do some fishing up on the Oklawaha." Cam smiled to himself. He had his own ideas about that being the sole purpose of the colonel's presence here.

Cam glanced over at them just in time to see Colonel Stothard take her hand in his. When Harriet Dunn raised her eyes to meet Cam's steady gaze, a red tide spread into her face. She quickly turned her head to look out the window.

Cam settled down in his seat, pleased to have the extra space to himself. He reflected back over the events of the past week. It seemed so long ago since he had said good-bye to Uncle George in Norwalk. Remembering that evening, he closed his eyes to fight off the recurring hurt that accompanied a feeling of rejection. With a sigh, he brushed his hand across his forehead as if to erase a painful memory. He opened his eyes to find that Miss Dunn had leaned forward in her seat and was looking at him.

"Are you all right, Cam?" she asked softly, searching his face.

"Yes, ma'am, I was just thinking."

"Everything is going to work out fine. Don't worry," she encouraged.

"Yes, son, you're among friends," assured Colonel Stothard.

The car grew silent as all eyes turned toward the door where Captain Brevard had appeared. He stood there for a minute, glancing around the coach as if to locate someone, then he turned to leave. But not before Cam had detected a slight nod to a man in the front seat. It was the same man that he had seen moving restlessly back through the aisle earlier. His steady gaze and cool demeanor had caused Cam to wonder about him. He felt sure that he was one of the colonel's men.

From where he sat Cam could see the back of the man's head. A tan, broad-brimmed hat pulled low on his brow covered sandy-colored hair. He got to his feet and casually started back through the aisle again, swaying with the motion of the train. His blue eyes studied each passenger intently, lingering on Cam a little longer. Cam returned the steady gaze and was startled to receive a good-natured wink as he passed on by. If Colonel Stothard paid any heed to the man, it was not evident. He appeared to be engrossed in a book Miss Dunn had given him.

Cam folded his arms and shifted his position to look out the window. The fog was breaking up into misty clouds, allowing the sun to shine through. The thick, virgin forest could be seen more clearly now. He wondered if the trees were this dense on the land he was to homestead. If so, he certainly would have his work cut out for him! Quite a few trees would have to be cut to clear space for a cabin.

His greatest concern was the business of getting the claim papers filed and recorded as soon as possible. There would be a charge for this, and he had no money other than the few cents in his pocket. His thoughts went back to the missing money.

That morning when Uncle George had first talked about the homestead he had said, "I have put together a packet of papers along with some money you'll need to file on the ground." Since he had carefully put the packet inside his shirt for safekeeping without opening it, there was no way the money could have been removed without his knowledge. The money had to be left out or taken from the packet before it was given to him. He discounted the fact that the money may have been left out, for Uncle George had specifically said he had put it in there. He could only assume that the money had been removed without Uncle George knowing about it.

The only person who could have had access to the packet of papers was Aunt Lizzie! She would have had opportunity to remove the money. Cam remembered her angry voice heard through the window. "Uh huh!" he grunted to himself, satisfied he had figured it right. But why would she do such a thing? Was it to discredit him in the eyes of Uncle George? She probably thought he would write asking for money. Well, he certainly had no intention of doing that!

He searched his feelings and found only pity for her. Poor Aunt Lizzie, so filled with bitterness and anger that she had shut everyone out of her life. Even Uncle George spent long hours at the store, talking little when he was at home.

"I'll get those papers safely and pay for the filing from what I earn working for Miss Dunn," he vowed, dismissing the matter.

He looked over at Harriet Dunn. The soft light coming through the window enhanced the whiteness of her skin to her beauty. She lifted her eyes from the book she was reading to catch him looking at her and gave him an assuring smile. Cam smiled back at her in shy response. He was very fortunate to have such a friend. He stretched his legs and turned toward the window again. Reaching into his pocket for his Bible, he decided to read for a while. He just wished that some of it wasn't so hard to understand.

The conductor's voice calling out the station startled Cam into wakefulness. How long had he been asleep? he wondered. He picked up the Bible, which had fallen to the seat beside him, and tucked it in his pocket.

"We're just a little way out of Jacksonville, Cam. We'll soon be there," Miss Dunn informed him. "We'll get something to eat here and inquire about the next boat to Palatka."

"Now you just leave the arrangements to me," offered Colonel Stothard, getting to his feet. "I'll only be a moment." As he strode from the coach, Cam noticed the man in the tan hat get up to follow him out.

The train had slowed considerably before the colonel returned to take his seat. "Captain Brevard will see that a carriage is available to take us to the hotel to freshen up and get something to eat. He'll take care of our passage on the boat to Palatka. We'll all feel better after we've had a good meal," he said cheerfully.

A few scattered houses began to appear among the pines. The land gave way to water. They were crossing a wide river. Fishing boats dotted the shoreline. A few people sat on the pilings of the trestle, a pole in their hand and a can of bait at their side. Soon there were more houses lined along sandy streets. When the train finally came to a shuddering halt amid billows of steam, the colonel suggested they wait until the other passengers were out. They got up to leave just as Captain Brevard stepped in the door followed by the man who had ridden in their coach. He tipped his hat to Miss Dunn, then informed the colonel that a carriage was waiting to take them to the hotel.

"Thank you, Captain, good job!" the colonel responded enthusiastically. "Come, Miss Dunn . . . Cam, the men will see to the luggage. By the way, you've met the captain, and this gentleman is Mr. Scott, the captain's right-hand man."

"The name is Wes Scott, ma'am. Glad to be at your service," he said, removing his hat to reveal a boyish face.

"Why, thank you, Mr. Wes Scott," she drawled with amusement. "And this is Camden W. Fox." She put her hand to Cam's back, urging him forward.

"Hello, Cam," he said with a friendly smile that lit up his eyes. "Heard you're a great fellow! Glad to meet you."

"Cam, I do believe I'll need my hatbox. Would you bring it with you, please?" asked Harriet Dunn, pressing him on the back with her hand.

Cam gave a questioning look at the hat on her head, but at her insistence, he picked up the box and followed them from the train.

The ride to the hotel was a short distance through the dusty streets. The place was not much to look at, but it was clean and the food was good. Cam downed generous portions, taking good-natured teasing from the others. They didn't linger, but hurried on to the docks where the riverboat, a stern-wheeler, was already being loaded. Boarding was a simple procedure, and they were soon standing at the rail watching the activity on the river.

"Jacksonville is fast becoming a river port. Larger ships are beginning to put in here," explained Colonel Stothard, indicating the cargo boats moored out in the water.

At last the cargo was loaded and the gangplank raised. Deck hands stood ready to secure the ropes cast from the workers on the dock. Great belches of black smoke ascended from the stacks. Slowly the boat began to move out into the wide expanse of the great St. Johns.

"This is one of the few rivers in the world that flows north, Cam," said Miss Dunn. "It begins at Lake Okeechobee to the south and flows northward to empty into the Atlantic Ocean here at Jacksonville."

He nodded his head in acceptance of this bit of information as he watched the ever-widening gulf between the dock and their boat. He looked at Miss Dunn with a grin.

"Is this the first time you've been on a boat?" she asked.

"We . . . my mother and I were on a small excursion boat in a lake once, but this is the largest," he answered.

This was the first time she had heard him give any reference to his mother. She noticed the slight shadow of sadness that flickered over his face and then was gone. There was no doubt that his mother had been a good woman who had taught him well.

Off to the north they could hear the low rumble of a summer storm, which posed no threat in their direction. A slight breeze brought relief from the bright afternoon sun. Colonel Stothard and Miss Dunn sought refuge from the heat in some chairs farther back on the deck.

The boat had moved far out into the river now with increasing speed, leaving a wide path of foam in its wake. Cam walked to the back where he could watch the large paddle wheel swishing through the water, thrusting the ship forward. The city seemed far away now.

He returned to the rail at the side to watch the shoreline slide by. The tall trees were so dense that the sun's rays could not penetrate the dark shadows beneath them. Along the bank grew masses of green hyacinths that surrounded fallen logs as if holding them captive. Here and there in the river Cam could see floating islands of these hyacinths that had broken loose from the entanglement along the shore. Snow white cranes and blue egrets were in the shallows searching for food.

"Well, Cam, you'll soon be in your new home," Miss Dunn called to him.

He decided to join them, taking the empty seat next to Miss Dunn.

"Yes, ma'am," he replied thoughtfully, thinking about the word *home*. That's what it would be, for he knew in his heart he would never return to the north.

"Wake up Cam," Miss Dunn called softly, shaking his shoulder. "We're home."

The hour was late when the steamboat maneuvered its way to the dock in the little town of Palatka by lantern light.

Cam sat up abruptly, rubbing his eyes. He got to his feet to follow her down the dimly lit deck. Lanterns had been hung on poles alongside the gangplank to aid the disembarking passengers. Colonel Stothard was talking to the driver of a carriage.

"Yes, suh! Yes, suh!" Cam could hear the driver saying good-naturedly as he came forward to pick up the luggage.

He looked around for Captain Brevard and Mr. Scott, but they were nowhere in sight. In a matter of minutes they were loaded and on their way to Dunn House.

8

*I*T WAS LATE IN THE MORNING when Cam finally awakened. He stretched lazily and looked with satisfaction around the room Miss Dunn had given him. It was neatly furnished with a bed, a small chest with three drawers, and a washstand equipped with soap, washbowl, and a pitcher of water. Clean towels had been folded and placed on the racks alongside. A straight, ladder-back chair stood near the door with his coat and valise on the seat. There was a small closet in the corner. A cool breeze pushed through the curtains at the window, which opened out onto a side porch. He could hear someone moving around in the room overhead. There was the scrape of a chair being shoved back and the sound of a door closing. Heavy footsteps faded down the upstairs hall.

His first day in Palatka. What a strange name for a town. He pushed back the blanket and got up, turning to make the bed. Within minutes Cam made his way toward the sounds of activity in the kitchen where he found Miss Dunn engaged in conversation with a young black woman. She turned as Cam entered.

"Good morning, Cam! I looked in on you earlier, but you were sleeping so soundly I didn't disturb you for breakfast. Leola will fix you something to eat. Come, you can sit right here," she said, pulling out a chair at a small table near the window.

"Leola, this is Camden Fox. He will be staying here whenever he wants. The room at the end of the lower hallway is to be his alone."

"Yes'um, Miss Harriet," replied Leola, giving Cam a big smile as she broke eggs into the skillet.

Miss Dunn sat down at the table across from him. "When you're finished with your breakfast, I'll give you a list of repairs that need to be done." She leaned her arms on the table. "You can go over the list and see if there are any items you will need from the hardware store. If so, write it down, and I will send a note with you to have them charged to my bill. You may want to walk around a little while you are down there, to get acquainted with the town."

"Palatka is a strange name," Cam stated, nodding his head in agreement with her suggestion.

"It's a Spanish word," she said, laughing at his directness. "My father said that the town was established in 1816 as a trading post called Palatka Vaca, meaning 'crossing of the cow.' Later, Vaca was dropped and it became Palatka." She waited as Leola came to set a plate of food in front of Cam before she spoke again.

"I'm going to send a message to Mr. Sparks as soon as I can." She looked up at Leola. "When is Henry coming in again?"

"I don't know, Miss Harriet. He might come tonight if he finishes his work in time," answered Leola, setting a glass of milk in front of Cam.

"Well, let me know if he does. I'll send a note to Mr. Sparks back with him." Miss Dunn got up and walked to the door where she paused. "Cam, I'll be back shortly to go over the list with you and show you where the tools are."

It didn't take him long to finish off the hearty breakfast of scrambled eggs and biscuits with blackberry jam. He set his plate aside and watched Leola punch down a pan of dough. She dumped it out on a floured board and began to squeeze off chunks to knead and shape into loaves, placing them into pans to raise.

"Where'd y'all come from, Mista Cam?" she asked, without glancing away from her work.

"Connecticut," answered Cam, staring at the glass of milk in his hand.

She placed the last loaf in the pan and covered it with a clean flour sack before turning to look at him. "You sho' has come a long ways," she said, putting a flour-covered hand on each hip. "What ya' doin' down here?"

"My uncle asked me to come and homestead some land for him," responded Cam, slowly.

"Well, I declare!" she exclaimed, shaking her head in disbelief. "He's done sent you to do a man's job."

He drank the rest of his milk and set the glass down without replying. Leola stood waiting for a moment, but when no further response came, she went back to her work. "There's a story behind all this," she mused to herself, giving a quick look in Cam's direction.

* * *

Cam dropped the hammer into the toolbox with an air of finality. He opened the gate and let it swing to close so that he could check the latch. Wiping his brow on his sleeve, he stepped back to survey his work. This was the last item on the list of repairs. Nearly a week had passed, and there had been no word from Mr. Sparks.

He picked up the toolbox and started toward the back of the house. Miss Dunn stood waiting at the top of the steps as he approached. "Cam, Henry was in to see Leola last night and said that Mr. Sparks would be coming tomorrow." Without waiting for a reply she went on. "How are the repairs coming?"

"I've just finished all that was on the list," said Cam with a grin.

"Wonderful! Let's get out of this hot sun and have a glass of lemonade."

The next day Cam was up early and got the wood chopped and stacked on the back porch before noon. Miss Dunn had been busy all morning, but she came out to where Cam, wet with perspiration, was sitting on the porch.

"Cam, here are the wages you have earned this week," she said, taking the money from her pocket. "The going rate for a handyman is 50¢ a day."

Cam stared at the money she placed in his hand. Three dollars and fifty cents! "You don't owe me all that. I was earning my keep."

"Shush!" she said, raising her hand to interrupt him. "You have earned every bit of it and more." She took a step toward the door and stopped. "Mr. Sparks usually eats here when he is in town, so he should be coming any time now. We'll get together with him after the others are gone. I'll bring the papers then."

"That's fine with me . . . and Miss Dunn . . . thank you for the money," said Cam earnestly.

"You earned it," she insisted.

They looked at each other in silence for a long moment before either spoke. She had grown fond of this boy and would miss him. She wanted to convince him to stay here with her and not go off to that dreadful homestead, to face who knows what, but she restrained herself. Instead she asked hesitantly, "Tell me about your mother, Cam."

His eyes grew moist and he lowered his head. "She's gone . . . ," he said finally. "She passed away early last spring. Uncle George was there . . . he promised he . . ." His voice broke and stopped.

"That's all right, Cam," intervened Miss Dunn, her voice weighted with compassion. "You needn't talk about it if you don't want to."

"You're a lot like her," said Cam. "That first night on the train, you reminded me of her. It was your perfume . . . the violets. She worked hard too. Sometimes when she didn't have to work so hard we did things together."

"Thank you for telling me about her," responded Miss Dunn. "She must have been a wonderful woman." She left him then to go help Leola finish up lunch.

Cam got up shortly and went to his room. He laid the money on the bed and stood looking at it. It was the most he had ever had at one time. He bathed and put on the shirt Leola had washed and mended for him. He picked up the money, stuck it in his pocket, smoothed his hair, and walked out.

When he entered the dining room, most of the boarders, all men, were already seated around the big table waiting for dinner to be served. Cam chose one of three empty chairs and sat down. The men, who had grown accustomed to his eating there, paid little heed to his presence other than an indifferent glance, and went on talking among themselves.

Some of them Cam had come to know by name. Sam Mc-Cullough, who had lost a leg in a lumber mill accident, always sat near the wall so that he could lean his crutches there. He spoke with an accent. Down at the end of the table was Jed Philips, a jolly fellow who always had a funny story to tell. He wore his glasses pushed high on his forehead and looked at you through half-closed eyelids.

Presently, a man came in to claim the seat directly across from Cam. It was Frank Waters, who worked for the local newspaper. He greeted the others and took a paper from his pocket to read. After scanning the front page a moment, he folded it and put it back into his pocket. Cam guessed him to be about 40 years of age. The round glasses he wore made his eyes appear larger than they were in his narrow face, and his hair was combed flat to his head. He sat impatiently, drumming his fingers on the table.

"'Tis a good day to you, Mr. Waters. How are things down at the news office?" Sam McCullough asked, rolling his r's.

"Very well" was the terse reply.

"Did they ever find out any more about that homesteader they found floatin' in the river south of here?" asked Jed Philips.

"No, the sheriff is still working on it and being pretty closemouthed about it, I must say," answered Waters, taking his watch from his vest pocket to check the time.

Heavy footsteps sounded in the hall. All heads turned expectantly in that direction. A tall, broad-shouldered, thickly set man in his late 50s strode into the room with a commanding presence. He removed his dusty hat and hung it on the rack, revealing a shock of graying red hair. A full beard covered his face. He greeted those who sat staring at him as he took the last seat at the table, stepping over the seat to straddle it. His piercing black eyes surveyed the group and came to rest on Cam.

"Hey there, son!" he hailed in a cheerful voice. A smile relieved his stern appearance. "Who might you be?"

"Cam" was the reply.

"Cam, is it? That's all? Just Cam?"

Cam's eyes met the intense gaze of the older man. "No, sir," he managed to get out calmly, "Camden W. Fox."

Frank Waters suddenly remembered the watch he still held in his hand and placed it back in the pocket of his vest. Clearing his throat, he inquired, "What's happening out your way, Mr. Sparks?"

"Oh, nothing much in the way of news, Frank," Sparks replied. "Killed a big gator the other day. He kept gittin' my chickens. He got one of my dogs too."

"That so?" was the uninterested response.

"Yeah, one of my best huntin' dogs."

All conversation ceased as Leola appeared from the kitchen carrying steaming bowls of food. Everyone got down to the serious business of eating.

Harriet Dunn came in with a container of coffee to fill the cups. "How is everything, gentlemen?" she asked cordially.

Amid satisfied grunts from the others, Frank Waters responded politely, "Just fine, thank you. Very good!" His eyes lingered on her face, but she avoided looking at him as she poured his coffee. He had proposed marriage to her, but she had turned him down. He would wait.

Harriet Dunn finished pouring the coffee and set the pot down. Looking over the table she asked, "Does anyone need anything else?" When there was no reply, she went into her small office adjoining the dining room. A stack of mail awaited her attention. With a sigh she picked up the letter opener Colonel Stothard had given as a gift on his last visit to Dunn House. She sat staring at the engraving on the handle, which read "With deep affection and appreciation." A feeling of unrest stirred deep within her. What of the future?

The day he had left, he had sought her out to tell her goodbye. "I'll be back soon," he had said, holding her hand longer than necessary, a questioning look in his eyes. She had found it hard to return his gaze without revealing how she felt in her heart. But for Leola's watchful presence, she might have weakened. Instead she had murmured something that sounded unintelligible, the blood pounding in her ears, and withdrew her hand. After he had left, she had fled to her room like a silly schoolgirl to watch him ride away with Captain Brevard and Mr. Scott.

She opened the drawer and dropped the letter opener into it as if to erase the memory.

She did not know how many of the colonel's men had gone with him. There was a man in room 8 on the second floor, front, facing the street, who had checked in the same night of their arrival. Most travelers didn't stay more than a night or two. But he was still there, seldom leaving his room, requesting his meals be brought to him there. Several times he had come down in the late evening to sit in a dark corner of the porch. In the early morning hours, she had heard footsteps going up the stairs to enter his room.

On two occasions she had noticed him looking down from his window as she returned from town. Once she had observed him watching Cam as he went about his chores. He had a kind face and there didn't seem to be anything sinister in his actions. Perhaps the colonel had Clay Beardsley in mind and had left someone behind for their protection. She decided not to speculate on the matter any further.

She heard Leola bringing a tray of freshly baked pie and got up to refill the coffee cups.

The men had resumed their conversation while waiting for the dessert. With appetites appeased, they all seemed in an amiable mood.

"Clay Beardsley's back in town. I saw him get off the boat last night," Frank Waters said, watching Miss Dunn as she poured coffee. He detected a slight tremor in her hand as she raised her head to look at Cam.

"Said he'd been up in the northeast on business," he continued. "Didn't you just return from a trip up that way, Miss Dunn?" It was an attempt to see her reaction. Clay Beardsley was a handsome man who turned many a woman's head.

The room grew silent. Zachariah Sparks raised his head to glare at Waters. Harriet Dunn calmly finished filling the empty cups and set the coffeepot down.

"I find what I do is no business of yours, Mr. Waters," she responded in a controlled voice. "Now, if there is nothing else, gentlemen, I'll leave you to finish your dinner."

Cam got up to follow her to the kitchen for another glass of milk. "The nerve of that man!" she was fuming to Leola. "Was he trying to imply in front of the others that I had been off with Clay Beardsley? Oh! How dare he!"

"Don't pay him any attention, ma'am, he's just fishing," Cam said, pouring himself a glass of milk. "I saw him looking at you. He likes you and can't figure out why you don't like him."

"He's right, Miss Harriet," Leola chortled.

She wheeled around to face Cam, an incredulous expression on her face. "How absurd!" she cried, shaking with laughter. Then suddenly remembering, she added, "Frank Waters didn't meet the boat the night we arrived with Colonel Stothard!"

"No, ma'am, he wasn't there. I looked around. I would have noticed him," Cam confirmed.

"So, he doesn't know about Colonel Stothard coming in with us. Good!" She grew more serious as she turned to Leola. "Clear the table as quickly as you can, then see that we are not disturbed. Cam and I will be talking to Mr. Sparks."

Cam picked up his milk and headed to the dining room where the men had sullenly finished their meal and trooped out. Only Mr. Sparks remained. Leola came in with a large tray and began removing the plates. Cam ate his pie and sat waiting for Miss Dunn to join them.

In her room, Harriet Dunn bathed her face and smoothed her hair. Inwardly she was furious with Frank Waters for embarrassing her in front of the other guests. She stared into the mirror with angry eyes. "You've just fixed yourself with me forever, Mr. Waters," she vowed audibly. She lingered a few moments to regain her composure and retrieved the papers from the hatbox before going out.

"Mr. Sparks, Cam and I need your help," she began. "Cam's uncle has sent him down here to settle a homestead for him." She laid the papers on the table and related all that had happened.

"I believe Clay Beardsley meant to harm us. Had it not been for Colonel Stothard's protective care, I don't know what would have happened," she concluded grimly.

She handed the packet to him. "I know nothing of these matters. Please take a look at these papers and advise us on what steps to take. There is a letter there addressed to you from Mr. Fox."

Mr. Sparks opened the packet and shuffled through the papers, stopping to study two of them intently. Then he opened and read the letter, laying it aside.

"Everything seems to be in order here. His claim papers are filled out properly. All we will need to do is go to the courthouse and get them recorded." He leaned back in his chair and gazed at Cam with a grave expression.

"How old are you, boy?" he asked kindly.

"Nearly 15, sir," Cam answered.

"Just about Nan's age," he mumbled as if to himself. "Homesteadin' is a hard lot, son, even for the experienced . . . well, never mind that now. You'll be needin' some help to get started. First, we'll go to the courthouse and get your claim recorded. Then, it might be a good idea if you ride out with me for a few days. Your homestead isn't too far from us. We'll ask Henry to go over for a look at your land and see what you have." He put the papers back in the oilskin pouch and stood up.

"Mr. Sparks, I can't thank you enough!" Miss Dunn said gratefully, her eyes moist with tears, as she offered him her hand.

"Miss Harriet, I knew your daddy for years, and I've known you since you were little," Mr. Sparks began kindly, holding her small hand in his. His voice grew sharper as he continued. "I want you to know I . . . none of us . . . took kindly to what Frank Waters said in this room today! He had no call to do what he did. The way we see it, he owes you an apology."

He dropped her hand and reached for his hat. "Come on, boy! We'll go take care of your business, then you get your things together and we'll head out. I'd like to make it home before nightfall."

Cam followed him out, hurrying to keep up with his long strides.

"I'll have Leola fix you a lunch and get your clothes packed, Cam," Miss Dunn called after them.

"He ain't gonna need any lunch, ma'am," Zachariah Sparks said over his shoulder. "He can take supper with us. Just get his things. We'll be back in a little while."

9

IT TOOK A SHORT TIME to get the claim recorded. When they had finished, Mr. Sparks suggested that while he was picking up some supplies Cam could run back to Dunn House and get his belongings out on the porch to save time.

Cam hurried back to his room, and when he returned to the porch with his valise, coat, and hat, Mr. Sparks was stopping at the gate.

"Whoa! You ornery hay-eater!" he called to the horse. It stood rearing its head and chomping at the bit.

Cam grabbed up his things and started off the porch.

"Cam!" Harriet Dunn called from the doorway. "You be careful!"

"Yes, ma'am," he promised, stopping on the steps. Then remembering the papers in his shirt, he took them out and walked back to where she was. "Would you keep these safe for me?"

"Of course," she responded, taking the papers from him. "You will let me hear from you? You can send word with Henry . . . and Cam . . . you are my dear friend and will always be."

"Yes, ma'am, I'll keep in touch," Cam answered with a lump in his throat. "Give my regards to the colonel when he returns."

"I'll do that, Cam. Take care, now," she said, walking with him as far as the gate.

"I'll be back soon," he replied, as he climbed up to the seat of the wagon.

"Good-bye, Miss Harriet," Mr. Sparks said, touching his hand to his hat.

She watched them until they rounded the corner. As she turned to enter the house she looked up and saw the man in room 8 watching from the window.

Mr. Sparks held the horse to a fast trot for several hours, following a well-used clay road before turning left into a sandy wagon trail leading off through the dense, tall pines. The pungent odor of pine needles filled the late afternoon air as they entered the quiet solitude of the forest. The only sounds were the soft thud of the horse's hooves, the creak of the wagon, and the soft hiss of the sand under the wagon wheels.

Cam noticed that the pines were thinning out some and there were stands of scrub oak more prevalent now. He caught a flash of white as a cottontail scurried from the side of the road.

"That crow has probably been in my cornfield," Mr. Sparks muttered, giving a look up at the slanting rays of sunlight. "Come on, Black, let's get going a little faster there!" he called, giving the horse a slap with the reins.

The strong horse responded instantly, pulling the wagon with ease even though the wheels sank deep in the loose sand.

Scrub oak had given way once again to pine, although all at once beautiful pine trees had blackened trunks. Clumps of stunted palmetto were scattered among them.

"Forest fire," Mr. Sparks grunted. "Lightning struck that big tree over there. You'll need to clear good around your place. Don't leave a single pine tree near your house."

The two rode on in silence, both showing signs of weariness. The older man now leaned forward with his elbows on his knees, and Cam drooped in the seat beside him. It had been a long day.

The trees were casting long, blue shadows, and a dewy dampness announced the coming nightfall. The bark of a dog echoed in the distance.

When they emerged from the trees into a clearing, Cam could see several buildings across the fields. The largest one had smoke curling from the chimney. A few cattle were grazing in a fenced area beyond the barn. A chorus of barking dogs greeted their arrival.

Mr. Sparks slapped the horse with the reins and let out a loud whoop. The door of the house flew open, and a slender form followed by several smaller children ran out into the yard.

"Ho! Nan! Open the gate!" her father shouted.

The girl called Nan hurried to comply, riding the gate as it swung open. She remained perched on top, gazing curiously at Cam as they entered the barnyard. Cam caught a glimpse of a tanned, oval face with luminous dark eyes framed with raven black hair. When the wagon stopped he looked around for her, but she had closed the gate and disappeared.

Soon the horse was unhitched and led to his stall. "Grab a bucket of that grain there, son, and pour it in the feed box over there," Mr. Sparks told Cam. The boy hastened to obey, then followed Mr. Sparks from the barn, closing the door behind him.

They both loaded their arms with packages from the wagon and walked to the house. "Wife, put on another plate!" hailed Mr. Sparks, as he stooped to enter the door with Cam at his heels. "This is Cam. He'll be homesteadin' over east of here near Lake Delancy . . . chuck those things down here, son . . . we'll get back to them later." He unloaded his arms on the floor near the door, and Cam followed suit. The wide-eyed children, two boys and a girl, gathered around the packages, elbowing one another to get a better view.

Cam stood tentatively just inside the door. Mrs. Sparks, a slender woman with brown hair done up in braids piled high on her head, was standing before the wood-burning cookstove stirring a skillet of gravy. She turned to acknowledge Cam with a tired smile, her friendly blue eyes going from him to the children who were edging ever closer to the packages.

"Don't you children be gettin' into those things, now," she admonished.

Nan, who was the oldest of the children, was bringing steaming bowls of food to the table. She flashed Cam a quick smile as she herded the children to their seats at the table.

"We can wash up for supper out here, Cam," Mr. Sparks said over his shoulder as he headed for the pump on the side porch.

Cam followed and politely waited at a safe distance while Mr. Sparks washed his face with great splashes of water, then groped for a limp towel hanging on a nail on the wall.

While Cam washed, the older man stood gazing off across the fields. What kind of a man would have sent this boy down to live alone on a homestead? he wondered. A desperate man? Perhaps. The letter hadn't revealed a reason. Well, whatever help he would give would not be for the man but for the boy. He turned and put his hand on Cam's head.

"Come on, son, let's see what these womenfolk have cooked up for us," he said with a kind voice.

Supper was a pleasant affair with Mr. Sparks sharing the news from town with his wife. The very presence of the man filled the room. Nan listened quietly with an occasional glance in Cam's direction.

After supper was over, Nan and Mrs. Sparks cleared away the dishes and food and wiped the table clean. The whole family gathered back at the table.

"Nan, get those packages and bring 'em over here," Mr. Sparks instructed, waiting for her to bring an armful to the table. "Yes, just put 'em right here." He waited for her to get the rest and deposit them in front of him. After she had taken her seat, he picked up a parcel and held it out to his wife.

"Mother, here are the things you asked for. They didn't have the pink ribbon you wanted—hope you like the color I had to substitute." He sorted the rest of the packages and pushed two more toward her. "I think that is the two pieces of yard goods you ordered, the thread is in there with it."

He untied a small square box. "Here is a bag of candy for each of you. Now, mind you, don't eat it all at once! And,

Nan," he went on, picking up the last bundle, "I guess this is for you."

Nan pounced on the parcel with a glad cry and ran from the room with it held tightly in her arms. Her mother and father exchanged a pleased glance.

"It's Nan's birthday," he explained to Cam.

"Well, Mother, if you will show this young man where he'll sleep, I think we'll turn in for the night. We've had a long day!"

Mrs. Sparks picked up a lamp, and calling to the two younger boys, she led Cam into the front part of the house across the porch from the kitchen. The room in which he was to sleep had few furnishings. There were three beds built around the walls that could be folded up and fastened in place if needed. An old wardrobe stood by the door.

"I trust you will sleep well," she said, indicating the bed by the window. She waited until the two boys had pulled off their clothes and climbed into their bunks.

"Good night," she said, giving a tired sigh, and left the room taking the light with her.

Cam undressed and stretched his weary body out on the hard bed. Sleep claimed him immediately.

He was awakened before daylight the next morning by a rooster crowing outside his window. It was still dark, but already there were sounds of activity in the kitchen.

He sat up and quietly pulled on his trousers and shoes, careful not to arouse the sleeping children. The glow of a lantern and the sound of a bawling calf came from the barn. He got up and walked to the barn where he found Mr. Sparks milking a cow. Cam stood watching for a few moments.

"What can I do to help, sir?" he asked.

"Ho! You're up early, son! I like that in a man! Did you ever milk a cow?"

"No, sir, I've never been around one."

"Here, try your hand at it," Mr. Sparks said cheerfully, getting up from the stool. "Don't be afraid of her, Bessie's gentle. You'll be needin' a cow out on your place, so it's good you learn how to milk one."

Cam positioned himself on the stool and reached for the udder and squeezed as he had seen Mr. Sparks doing it.

"Lay your head against her side. That way you can hold her at the distance you want her. There, . . . that's good. I'll leave you to this and go feed the rest of the stock. You'll catch on pretty quick," he said as he walked out of the stall.

Left to himself, Cam struggled for a while, missing the bucket, the evidence of which was on his shoe, but he soon managed to hit the mark with a sort of uneven tempo.

Mr. Sparks stopped back by the door to say, "Take the milk on in the house when you're done. I'll come back later and turn Bessie out to her calf."

When he had finished, Cam took the stool away and picked up the bucket of milk. He stepped to where Bessie was cleaning up the last of the feed in the box. "You did good by this newcomer, gal," he said, giving her a pat on the back.

"Good morning, Cam," Mrs. Sparks said cheerfully as he came in with the milk. "I see you're up early. Set that bucket on the table in the corner. We'll have some breakfast soon." She expertly broke an egg in the skillet. "You'd best get washed up."

When Cam returned to the warmth of the kitchen, Nan was setting the table. He perched himself on a stack of wood by the stove where he could watch her without being noticed. Her long, black hair was tied back with a ribbon, making her face seem more slender and accenting her magnificent dark eyes. Her full, sweet lips curved up at the corners. She was dressed with a cotton blouse tucked into overalls, which could not hide the lithe grace of her slender, blossoming figure.

She looked up to catch him staring at her, and a scarlet tide swept across her cheeks. She turned quickly to help the rest of the children to their seats, where they sat sleepily rubbing their eyes.

"Go call your pa, Nan," asked Mrs. Sparks, carrying a pan of biscuits to the table. "Never mind, I hear him coming."

Devouring one biscuit after another, Cam ate like the hungry half-grown man he was, much to Nan's amusement.

When Mr. Sparks had finished appeasing his appetite, he pushed back his plate and set his coffee nearer, pouring some in the saucer to cool. "Mother, is Henry comin' today to set those fence posts?"

"I think he said he'd be here today, Zach," she answered.

"Good. I'm kinda curious about that land this young man's gonna be workin'. I'd like to get Henry to ride over there with us today. He's got a good eye for land. If it's worth anything, we'll choose a spot for a temporary shelter." He poured the cooled coffee back into his cup and drank it. Then he got up and walked to the door where he picked up his hat.

"Cam, when you're finished, you can help me saddle the mules. They'll be best for that rough country. Henry'll have his own."

"Can I go, Pa?" Nan begged. "Please?"

"You'll have to settle that with your ma. I've only got two mules, so you'll have to ride double with Cam. Cain't take any of the ponies out in that wild area," he said, as he walked out the door.

Cam got up to follow, leaving Nan to plead with her mother. He really didn't relish riding double with her. He was going to have his hands full managing a mule, he grumbled to himself.

10

*H*ALLOO!" CAME A CALL from the edge of the woods.

A young black man, wearing a white shirt and faded overalls, was riding toward where Cam sat near the saddled mules. The man sat easy in the saddle, the reins held loosely in his hand.

Zachariah Sparks emerged from the house carrying a rifle in his hand.

"Hey there, Henry!" he greeted the rider, as he stood waiting for him to approach.

Henry brought the mule to a stop in front of the gate and dismounted with a singular easy movement that left him facing the older man and the boy. He secured the reins and removed the hat from his head, slapping the dust from it.

"Good mawnin', Mista Sparks," he said cheerfully. "Mighty fine day, ain't it?"

"Did you ride out from town?" Mr. Sparks asked, nodding in agreement.

"Yes, suh, I sho did! Didn't see nobody 'cept that Mista Beardsley riding into town. 'Pears he was out mighty late or early, one of the two. He'd been out in the woods someplace."

"How do you know that?" queried Mr. Sparks.

"His horse's legs was all covered with black muck."

81

Mr. Sparks frowned at this news, looking thoughtfully for a moment. He shook his head, as if putting something out of his mind.

"Henry, this is Cam Fox. His uncle sent him down here to prove up on a homestead over east of here, near Lake Delancy. I thought we would put off settin' those posts today and take a ride out there and see how the land lays. I want you to go along 'cause you've got a good eye for that sorta thing. We can set those posts tomorrow if you can stay over."

"That's fine with me, Mista Sparks," Henry responded, a big smile breaking across his face as he looked at Cam.

"How do, Mista Cam. So you're gonna be a homesteader! Well, well. That's a big undertakin'," he said, taking in Cam's slender form. "There's gators out here bigger'n you . . ."

"I can take care of myself," Cam broke in, his voice ringing. "I'm not afraid!"

"Beggin' yo' pardon, Mista Cam, I meant no offense! What I was meanin' is yo' is gonna be needin' some help," Henry said apologetically, laying a hand on Cam's shoulder.

"Let's mount up and get to ridin'," Mr. Sparks broke in. "That sun's gettin' high!"

The men swung easily into their saddles and turned their mules down the road. Cam took a little longer to mount, struggling to get astride the big mule. He was glad Nan was nowhere in sight.

"Pa!" Nan cried, running from the house, a weighty flour sack in her hand. "Pa, wait! Ma said I can go!"

He stopped his mule and waited. "All right, gal," he said. "Climb up in back of Cam."

Nan handed the lunch sack up to Cam. "Tie that on the pommel," she said. Jumping up, she caught hold of the saddle and pulled herself onto the broad back of the mule, where she slipped into the saddle behind Cam.

"I'm all set!" she told Cam. "Let's go!"

The men had already started ahead. Cam picked up the reins holding them as he had seen the others do. The mule didn't move.

"Come on, mule," Cam said, but there was no response from the mule.

"Giddup!" Nan yelled in exasperation, kicking the mule in the sides.

The mule moved out to meekly follow the others. Cam felt the back of his neck getting red. To hide his discomfort, he pretended to check the sack to see if the knot was secure.

After they had caught up to the others, Cam found that all he had to do was hold the reins, for their mule maintained the same gait as those ahead.

He was conscious of Nan sitting close behind him. He had never been this close to a girl before. He could feel her warm body against his back and the whisper of her breath on his ear as she watched the trail over his shoulder.

"Are you going to homestead all by yourself?" she ventured to ask.

"I sure am," Cam replied firmly, squaring his shoulders a little.

"That's going to be hard."

"I can do it. I've been thinking a lot about it."

"Where are you going to live? There's gators and snakes, panthers, and lots of wild things out there in the swamps."

"I'm not afraid," Cam answered. "I'm going to build me a cabin. Then, I'm going to get me a dog and a cow. Later I'll get me a horse."

"If you're gonna have a cow and a horse, you will have to shut them in at night or something will get them for sure. Pa has lost stock to wild animals."

Cam made no reply to her last statement.

"A good hunting dog will help you," she went on, unperturbed. "Our coon dog, Millie, is gonna have puppies. I'll get Pa to give you a puppy if you want one."

Cam brightened at the prospect. "I sure would like to have a dog of my own," he asserted.

"Pa said you were from Connecticut. Do they have snakes and gators there?"

"I don't know, I don't think so," he answered slowly. "I lived in town and worked at a grocery store."

"A city boy, huh?" Nan said archly.

Cam felt uncomfortable with the way the conversation was going and fell silent.

Nan sensed the change in his demeanor and kept her thoughts to herself. There was so much she wanted to ask him. Her inquisitive mind yearned so much to know what was going on in the world beyond the small perimeter in which she lived. She longed to live in a big house in town and wear pretty dresses like Miss Dunn. She didn't want to be stuck out in the woods on a homestead like her ma. With a deep sigh, she looked at the dense forest around her, the forest that was a prison from which she must somehow escape. The heat of the day began to press in upon them now even though they were under a canopy of trees. A gentle drift of air gave no relief from the stifling humidity. The only sound in the stillness was the far-off call of a crane and the plodding of their mules. A sweet, familiar odor filled the air, drifting up from plants crushed beneath the feet of the animals.

"Wild vanilla," Nan said, breaking the silence. "That plant with the broad green leaf is rabbit tobacco. Holly smoked it once, and it made him awful sick."

Cam made no response other than to look at the plant she pointed out, although inwardly he wondered who Holly was.

The riders ahead had halted before a small creek when Cam's mule caught up to them. Henry was saying, ". . . full of moccasins! We'd better not cross here—too dangerous. I'll ride downstream a ways and check for a better place."

"All right, Henry," Mr. Sparks replied. He turned to Nan as Cam brought their mule to a stop. "How are you two faring?"

"Fine, Pa," Nan laughed, "once we got ol' Jacob started. I had to give him a kick in the ribs. What are we stopping for?"

"Take a look at that creek there," he said, pointing to a big moccasin coiled on the bank, sunning himself.

"Moccasins!" she cried, grabbing Cam by each arm.

Cam sat stiffly in the saddle as if frozen, his eyes on the big snake. A few feet away was another and another. He felt his flesh crawl.

"They are very poisonous, you know," Nan whispered in his ear.

"Keep that mule steady, Cam," Mr. Sparks warned. "They're all around us. We rode right into a nest of 'em."

The minutes ticked by in endless suspense. Nan sat motionless, her fingers digging deep into Cam's shoulder. She watched with fascination as her father drew his rifle slowly from its scabbard. "Don't move, either of you!" he commanded in a low, stern voice. His eyes were terrible, fixed on the ground beneath him. She knew when he spoke that way there was danger.

Henry had returned and was sitting quietly in the saddle taking in the serious situation.

"Yo' can't shoot, Mista Sparks," he said quietly, "that'll get 'em all riled up. Just hold steady, everybody, and hope this party breaks up before that mule sees that bigg'n under his belly."

What seemed like an eternity passed before Nan, from the corner of her eye, could see the big snake continue on its way into the thick palmettos at the water's edge. She saw her father's face relax, and he wiped his brow on his sleeve. He slowly nudged his big black horse close to them.

"Throw those reins to me, boy," he said in a strained voice, catching them as Cam complied.

"Which way, Henry? Look sharp . . . they're crawlin' for the water."

"Cut through ova' theah, Mista Sparks," Henry instructed, pointing to a clearing where the undergrowth was far enough apart to allow safer passage.

Nan's father urged his mule forward slowly, warily picking his way toward the clearing. Cam's mule followed obediently.

"That's right, Mista Sparks, come on, yo' almost in the clear," Henry encouraged. "Hang on, Mista Cam and Miss Nan. Yo' is gonna be all right in a jiffy."

When they reached safety where Henry waited for them, Mr. Sparks expelled a deep sigh of relief and tossed the reins back to Cam. "Here you are, son. We're out of our bind now, but stay close. Better yet, you ride in behind Henry and I'll bring up the rear," he said, nudging his mule to one side.

The sun was directly overhead when they rode out into a parklike clearing in the tall trees. The ground was covered with pungent pine needles and here and there patches of white sand glistened in the sunlight.

Henry halted his mule and climbed out of the saddle. "We'll stop here a spell," he said, fastening the reins to a tree.

The rest did the same, with Nan slipping down to the ground quickly.

"Pa, I'm hungry," she announced. "This would be a good place to eat the lunch Ma fixed."

"All right, Nan," he responded, pleased with her suggestion. "Get it ready. I'm hungry too, and I reckon Cam could eat anything that isn't snake meat. Haw! Haw!"

Cam untied the flour sack from the saddle and handed it to Nan. It took only a few minutes for her to spread a small cloth on the pine needles and lay out a lunch of biscuits, ham, and oranges.

Sitting there crosslegged on the ground, Cam felt a kinship with these people. They had extended friendship and a helping hand to him without question, sharing their food and shelter. It seemed so natural to them to help one another. Suddenly, the thought came to him that these people were doing this for him, not for his uncle.

He found it hard to keep his eyes off Nan as she conversed with her father, teasing him into laughter. Her musical voice rose and fell as she kept up the lighthearted banter.

Cam decided he liked the way she tilted her head slightly forward and looked you straight in the eyes as she talked to you.

She must have sensed his eyes were upon her, for she turned and gave him a long, disquieting look. Cam felt as if he was falling over a precipice. He forced himself to look away. He got to his feet to walk over and stand by the mule. From there he watched her as she gathered up the food that was left to put back into the sack. She didn't look his way again.

Henry got to his feet, slapping the dust from his hat. "Mista Sparks, y'all be needin' to gimme some landmarks to go by."

"Well, as I remember," began Zachariah Sparks, getting to his feet, "the land is bordered by that moccasin creek back there on the west and then goes east to a huge live oak on the northeast corner." He paused to pick up a dead branch from the ground. Clearing away the pine needles, he began to draw in the sand. "Here's the creek. The live oak should be there, and straight south from there should be a marker in the southeast corner, then back to the creek. The size of the parcel of land should be determined by that big oak tree and the marker."

"If y'all are ready, we better be ridin' out to see if we can locate that tree," Henry commented.

When they had all mounted they rode out single file following Henry who had turned his mule in a more northerly direction, quickening the gait.

They had been riding for what seemed a short time when they spotted the big oak standing above the other trees. From this Henry set their course southward, and soon they found the marker.

"Now, Mista Cam, let's see if we can find a good location to build yo' shelter," he called over his shoulder to Cam as he rode on, taking a diagonal route toward the center of the homestead.

Cam's mule, with little on his part, followed Henry's. He was delighted with this gentle animal and was beginning to feel more confidence and ease in the saddle.

Nan, showing the strain from the long hours of riding, was sitting behind him in quiet lassitude. He could feel her leaning against his back. Her hair had escaped the bonds of the ribbon she wore and wisps of it blew against his ear, causing a riot of emotion within him. The blood pounded in his temples. He scarcely saw Henry's upheld hand signaling him to stop and almost ran into him before hauling back on the reins.

They had been skirting around a small pond filled with water lilies. Henry got down from his mule to peer closely at the ground.

"What's the matter, Henry?" queried Mr. Sparks, catching up to them.

"Horse tracks," he answered. "Fresh, maybe a day old." He took his hat off and mopped his face with his bandanna. "Black muck around this pond too."

"What are you thinkin'?"

"Well, like I said, Mista Sparks, that horse had black muck dried on his legs. 'Pears to me, we's not the only ones interested in this homestead," Henry answered, scratching his head.

Cam sat listening silently to the men. Nan looked at her father's somber face, trying to grasp the meaning behind Henry's remark. As they moved on, Henry kept his eyes on the ground watching for the tracks that were going the same direction. He paused when they suddenly veered off to the east and disappeared in the undergrowth. He made no comment but continued on engrossed in his own thoughts. He would come back to investigate those tracks. There was no doubt in his mind as to who had made the tracks. A heavy sense of foreboding settled in upon him. He recalled what Leola had told him: "You hep that boy. Miss Dunn thinks a heap of him, and she cain't hep him way off out there."

"Henry, look ahead there!" called Mr. Sparks, bringing him back to the present. They halted the mules to look around them. A great live oak tree stood before them, its limbs reaching almost to the ground below. It was a beautiful spot dominated by the big umbrellalike tree.

"Whatta yo' think, Mista Sparks?" said Henry, being the first to speak.

"Think? Cam, look at this! We've just found your new home!" Mr. Sparks boomed enthusiastically.

Nan uttered a delighted cry and slid from the mule to run over to one of the low-hanging limbs. She climbed up on it and sat down, swinging her legs.

Cam got out of the saddle and led the mule over to join the men who were tying their animals to a low branch. All three stood for a moment, studying the lay of the land around them.

"Very little clearin' will be needed to get started. There are almost no palmettos here," said Mr. Sparks, thinking out loud.

"Here's where yo' should put yo'sef a cabin," Henry suggested, standing in a clearing just in back of the big oak. "There's plenty of pine nearby for that, and yo' can fetch in some of those big palmetto leaves for yo' roof thatchin'."

"He'll have plenty of moss to pack his mattress," Nan called to them from her perch.

Mr. Sparks was busy pacing off a place to build pens for the animals. "I would suggest placin' your fences here where you can keep a close watch on your stock," he said.

Cam nodded in agreement, sharing in their exuberance. He took a deep breath and looked at his surroundings with great satisfaction. He liked it here. He glanced over at Nan, who was watching him, and grinned.

"I like your tree, Cam," she said saucily, using his name for the first time. Removing the ribbon from her hair, she flipped the wayward strands back over her shoulders and re-tied the bow.

"I guess we should be thinkin' about headin' back," her father announced, squinting up at the sun, "if we're gonna make it before sundown."

* * *

After supper that evening, Mr. Sparks pushed away the plates and sat with Cam, making plans. The first things that must to be done were to mark and cut a road, purchase and haul in materials, then drill a pipe for safe water. Cam worked patiently over the list of supplies.

Later he stepped unnoticed out into the cover of darkness and sat on the bench near the gate. The night reverberated with the cadence of calling insects. Here, alone, he sat gazing upward to the sky where myriads of stars gave off a dim light.

The memory of summer nights he had shared with his mother came back to him. Sitting on their front step after the work was finished, she would often say, "Learn to appreciate the darkness, Cam, and you will never be afraid. Take your direction from the stars, and you will never lose your way. Many a ship has gained the safety of the harbor because the captain knew the position of the north star."

"Mother," he cried softly, "I wish you were here with me, but since you cannot be, I want you to know I am happy. I have friends who are helping me, and there is your Bible that helps me feel near you." A great sob choked him as he once again realized his loss. He dropped his head into his hands and gave vent to the pent-up emotions he had suppressed so long. Finally he grew quiet and spent. A new peace settled over him. He remembered the prayer she had written in her Bible, "O God, be a father to Cam." She had always told him that God was everywhere. Was He here?

The murmur of voices came to him from the porch. He could hear Nan's merry laughter as she teased the other children. He returned to the house to join them, glad for the darkness that hid the telltale tears and reddened eyes.

"Tell him, Pa," Nan urged.

"Tell me what?" Cam asked, trying to see her face in the blackness.

"Cam," Mr. Sparks said hesitantly, as if unaccustomed to what he was going to say, "tomorrow is Sunday . . . and we always ride over to the church if we can. You're welcome to come along. You'll get to meet some of the other young folks from around here. There'll be dinner on the grounds."

"I'll be ready, sir," Cam replied, accepting his invitation.

The next morning, Cam helped spread blankets in the wagon and loaded the baskets of food under the springboard seat out of the sun. At Mr. Sparks' call, the children came running, dressed in their best. Nan appeared behind them, wearing a light blue dress. Her dark, shining hair was wound tightly and coiled high on her head.

Cam stared at her in admiration, becoming embarrassed as she returned his gaze. She gave him a shy smile, then climbed into the wagon with the rest.

He helped Mr. Sparks fasten the tailgate into place and waited to close the gate behind them before climbing in.

It was a glorious morning. A heavy dew had fallen, and every tree glistened in the early sunlight. As the wagon proceeded at a leisurely pace, Nan laughed and played games with the children. Soon they entered an open glen where shouts of greeting were called out to the new arrivals.

The wagon had scarcely rolled to a stop before a group of young people ran to surround them, hailing Nan in boisterous, happy voices while casting inquisitive glances at Cam. He climbed down to open the tailgate, ignoring their apparent curiosity.

Nan jumped down to help Cam lift the smaller children out before she yielded to her friends' demands that she come with them to sit on a bench under the trees.

Cam sensed he was the object of their conversation and decided to walk into the church where he chose a seat off to one side. It was cool in the building, and through the open window he could see people standing around in small groups talking. The room was crudely furnished with long, homemade benches. A pulpit stood in front with an old upright piano off to its right. In the center and off to one side was an old potbellied stove. Well-worn songbooks lay scattered about. Someone came in and began ringing the bell. When the sound of the bell had died away, he heard footsteps coming toward him.

Cam looked up to see a man in a dark suit beaming down at him. "You must be the young man who is staying with the Sparks family," he said. "I am Rev. Underwood."

"I am Cam Fox," responded Cam, getting to his feet respectfully.

"They tell me that you will be homesteading out toward Lake Delancy. That will be pretty lonely for a young man your age."

"Yes, sir, but I don't think that will bother me none," Cam replied guardedly.

The people began to drift in from outside, taking their seats. The parson excused himself and went to the front to sit down. A woman went to the piano and began playing a hymn. The group of young people along with several men and women trooped in to take their place in the choir. Sitting beside Nan was a pretty girl with unruly blond hair and bold blue eyes. Every time she caught Cam's eye she flashed a radiant smile, exposing an even row of white teeth. He squirmed as he felt a warm tide spread to his face and turned his attention to what the preacher was saying. He didn't look that way again throughout the service.

Cam stood leaning against the wagon, watching them as they approached. The long service had been a pleasant experience, but at the conclusion, he had hurried out to help Mrs. Sparks get her food carried to the long table under the trees.

"Cam, they want to meet you, but I declare, you sure make yourself scarce," Nan complained, coming near. She took the girl with the riot of blond hair by the arm and pushed her forward. "This is Henrietta, and that's Joey, her brother," she continued without giving any of them a chance to speak. Joey was a tall lad, about 17, with blue eyes like his sister. Unlike her, he had dark hair. He stood with hands jammed into his pockets.

"Hey there, Cam," Henrietta drawled, her eyes sweeping over him.

Joey nodded in greeting. "Welcome to homesteading. Heard you're working a place over near Lake Delancy."

"That's right," Cam replied, with calm dignity, searching Joey's face for any sign of animosity.

"Good luck," Joey said without rancor, "hope it goes well for you."

"I do too," chimed in Henrietta. "If you need any help, we will come and work, won't we, Joey?"

"Cam looks to me like he can take care of himself, Henrietta, but if you do need a hand, let me know," he said to Cam.

"And this is Ellie Mae," Nan broke in before Cam could reply, "and her brother, Holly—that's short for Hollister."

Cam liked Ellie Mae's pleasant, straightforward manner. "Hey there, Cam, I hope you like it here." She looked at him with frank blue eyes. A dusting of freckles across her nose gave her face an honest, open expression. Her hair was a dark carrot color. Holly favored his older sister, except that his hair was a much darker color and the freckles were less prevalent.

"I'm glad to meet all of you," Cam said, acknowledging the group. "When I get my homestead settled, you are welcome to come for a visit."

Any further remarks were stopped by a call to dinner. As they headed for the tables, Henrietta fell in step beside Cam. There was no indication that Nan even noticed; she was walking with Joey and seemed to be very interested in what he was saying.

11

CAM HAD JUST FINISHED THE MILKING and was carrying the brimming bucket to the house when he heard Henry's call from the edge of the woods. He waved and went on into the kitchen to leave the milk. Returning to the porch, he washed his hands and waited for Henry to ride in.

The sun was only a rosy glow on the horizon, yet the morning was already hot and sultry. The air was heavy with dampness.

Mr. Sparks came from the house and sat down on a chair to pull on his high-topped boots. "Good mornin', Henry," he called out cheerfully. "It's sure gonna be a scorcher if we don't get some breeze."

Henry stepped down from the saddle and walked toward them, leading his mule. "Mawnin', Mista Sparks. We'll be needin' to get those posts set early. That sun sho gonna be leanin' on us today!" He tied his mule to the gate and came to the porch to stand in the shade, fanning himself with his hat.

"Mista Sparks, as I's been a ridin' back and forth on that road, I's been a lookin' for a place for Mista Cam to cut a trail through to his place. Well, back the road a ways, I spotted a kinda low ridge that takes off over his way. Didn't 'pear to be much undergrowth along there either. Mebbe Mista Cam can ride out there today and mark hissef a road."

"Well, I dunno but what that's a good idea," Mr. Sparks said thoughtfully, stroking his beard. "Cam, when you eat breakfast, stick a few extra biscuits in your pocket. I'll go saddle the mule . . . sit down, Henry, the Missus will have somethin' ready to eat soon." He headed for the barn.

* * *

Cam rode the mule more slowly now, feeling that he was surely in the vicinity where Henry had said he would find the low ridge. The pines were more sparse here, but still there was no indication of a ridge running along either side of the road. When he got to the road that turned off to the church he knew he had gone too far. Patiently, he turned the mule back in the direction he had come, watching the winding road for any detectable rise or fall. There was none! He had ridden back for some distance when he stopped the mule to study the area. He was about to give up on finding it when he noticed a long, low clump of palmettos off to his left. They seemed to grow in a straight line. The few pines nearby appeared to be growing out of the top of them. He urged his mule forward to get a closer look.

There was a break in the ground about 50 feet away. The ridge didn't extend out far enough to affect the road, and with the palmettos camouflaging its existence, one would have to look closely to see it. Cam guided the mule off into the woods. Henry was right. The undergrowth was mostly small, scrubby plants. He rode only a short way, then returned to the road where he slid from the saddle and tied the reins to a tree.

Taking down the ax Mr. Sparks had tied to the pommel, he began marking the trees that needed to be removed. After he had gone a short distance he would return to get the mule and move him up. He kept repeating this action until the sun was high overhead.

He stopped long enough to devour the cold biscuit and egg sandwiches he had brought with him. Sitting there with his back against a tree, he felt an affinity with the quiet solitude of the forest. He liked the smell of the pine mingled with wild vanilla. It was hard to figure how far he had come. He felt that the lower end of the creek should be pretty close and that would be about half way. He was going to have to make better progress to at least get to the marker in the nearest corner. He decided to try marking the trees from the back of the mule.

The hour was getting late when Cam reached the big live oak tree that stood where he was to build his cabin. He was hot and tired, but he knew he dare not tarry. To make it back to the road before dark, he would have to see the marks on the trees to show the way. He tied the ax back to the saddle and headed the mule home. Darkness overtook him long before he reached the road. He gave the mule free rein to choose the way and was relieved when finally they turned into the wagon trail leading to the house.

Off in the night, a dim light appeared, bobbing through the trees. As it drew nearer, he was glad to see it was Henry who had come to look for him.

"Heah yo' are, Mista Cam. We was beginnin' to worry 'bout yo'! Mista Sparks tol' me to come a lookin' for yo'. He thought mebbe you'd gone and gotten yo'sef lost . . . or sumpin'." Henry swung his mule around and waited for Cam to catch up. "Did yo' find that little ridge I was talkin' 'bout? How far did yo' get?"

Cam was pleased with Henry's response on hearing he had chopped the trail all the way in.

"Mista Cam, yo' is some worka!" Henry said, shaking his head in disbelief. "Mebbe tomorra we can get out there and start clearin'."

* * *

Cam stood surveying his cabin with a feeling of pride. It had been four weeks since he had said good-bye to Miss Dunn.

Mr. Sparks and Henry had come to help nearly every day. Together they had cleared the road, cut and stripped the trees,
driven a well, and built the cabin. It was just one room built
high off the ground for protection against predators. There was
a door and two windows, one on each side. He chuckled to
himself at the thatched roof of green palmetto leaves that made
the cabin look like it was wearing a hat.

Night came early in the forest. Already the dark shadows
were creeping beneath the trees, even as the last rays from the
sun etched the tops with gold. Cam wearily climbed the steps
and sat down in the doorway. It had been a long, hard day.
While he and Henry had gathered palmettos and fixed the
roof, Mr. Sparks had built the bed and some shelves.

He sat gazing up at the large oak trees in front of the
cabin. He liked this part of the day best. Far off in the woods
he could hear the cry of a whippoorwill. The last fading light
reminded him the hour was late. He got up and went in to
light the lamp. It gave off a comforting glow. Closing the door,
he threw the latch in place.

Mr. Sparks had built the bed along the back wall. On it was
a mattress tick that Mrs. Sparks and Nan had sewn together.
Following Henry's advice, he had stuffed it firmly with dried
moss. Several boxes and his valise had been laid on the floor
near his bed. A chair and a small table were under the window.
When Mr. Sparks had gone in for supplies, Miss Dunn had sent
them back with him, along with a note. The note! He had put it
in his pocket and forgotten about it. Pulling it out he sat on the
bed to read.

> *Dear Cam,*
>
> *I miss you so. Do take care of yourself. These are some things*
> *I had stored. Please accept them as a loan until you can do*
> *better. Come to see me soon, won't you?*
>
> *Your friend,*
>
> *Harriet Dunn*

On the chair was a large paper sack. In it he found two sheets
and several towels. How thoughtful of her! These were things

he had not remembered to get. His eyes fell on the boxes on the floor. The one contained canned goods and a few staples, the other he didn't recall bringing in. He pulled it over to the light. It held a skillet, pan, two forks, a sharp knife, two plates and cups, and a bucket. They were not new, but that didn't matter to him. There was a short note from the Sparks family wishing him well. Cam's eyes filled with tears of gratitude for the kindness of these good people who had helped him. He placed it all back in the box and pushed it against the wall. Taking the bucket, he went out to the pump for water. The stars gave off a dim light, and the night was cool and fresh.

Aware that it was not wise to linger, Cam reluctantly strode back inside where he carefully closed and barred the door. He set the bucket down on the table and turned to search his food supply for something to eat. A can of beans and a cold biscuit left from lunch became the first meal in his new home. Tomorrow he would spend the first part of the day getting things organized in the cabin. When he had finished eating, he made up the bed and stretched out to read his Bible.

Henry rode away with misgivings at leaving Cam alone. The tracks he had seen over by the pond were still on his mind. While he had worked on the roof today, he'd had the uncanny feeling that someone was watching him. He rode well out of sight of the cabin before turning the mule off the road to make a big circle. He kept his eyes on the ground, searching for any unusual sign. He was not surprised when he came across the tracks of a horse. The rider was headed directly toward Cam's place.

"Uh huh, we'll just see what yo' is up to," he mumbled to himself. Henry dismounted, tied his mule to a tree, and followed the tracks on foot. They led him into a thicket of scrub oak, not more than a hundred yards from Cam's dwelling. The area showed ample proof that it had been used more than once. Someone had been spying on them and would no doubt be watching Cam's activities. From where he stood, Henry could see Cam moving around in the cabin. He retraced his steps and climbed on his mule and headed out to trail the rider in the other direction, moving cautiously through the brush.

"First off I'm gonna get Mista Cam to clear out that stand a oak," he vowed.

* * *

The daylight was fading fast when he smelled the smoke of their fire. He rode on a little farther until he could see a glimmer of light through the trees. Henry got down and tied his mule securely. "I might need yo' in a hurry and I don't want yo' to be goin' off," he whispered, giving the animal a pat. Starting out, he placed each foot carefully so as not to make a sound. He knew well it would not be healthy for him to be caught slipping around their camp. He paused to wait for the night to settle in before going further. He could see their movement as they walked in front of the blazing fire. The trees were thinning out, and most of the underbrush had been cleared away by the former homesteader. It would be too dangerous to try to get in any closer. Henry looked about for a better approach and saw none. Deciding it best to give up, he made his way back to his mule and rode off toward town.

When Henry reined in at Dunn House and climbed wearily out of the saddle, Leola spotted him from the kitchen window and ran to open the back door.

"There yo' are," she cried. "I thought yo' done lef' the country! Where yo' been, man?"

"Now, don't yo' go jumpin' my hide, woman. I been workin' hard out at Mista Cam's place. We got him a road cut, a well driven, and a cabin built. Just finished puttin' the roof on today."

"Um humph! Yo' sure been workin', all right. Sit down here and drink this coffee. It'll perk yo' up some," Leola said sympathetically, as she poured him a cup.

"But that's not what's got me so tired. I been a ridin' all night." Henry paused to take a sip of his coffee before going on. "Woman, I been followin' tracks. The ones that led back to town was that Mr. Beardsley's horse. I's sneaked into the stable to make sure. But the others led over to that homestead where that man is missin', and there's two strange men campin' over there. They's been sneakin' 'round watchin' us out there at Mista Cam's . . . and now he's out there by hissef! Woman, I don't feel right about this atall!" he moaned, rolling his eyes at her.

Leola stood staring at him, trying to comprehend the full meaning of what he was saying. "I'll go get Miss Harriet," she said and left the room.

When Harriet entered the kitchen, she wasn't sure what she would be hearing from Henry. The urgency she heard in Leola's voice, however, let her know that it somehow concerned Cam.

"What is it, Henry?" she asked, searching his face anxiously.

"I don't know, Miss Harriet, but I been a followin' those tracks out at Mista Cam's, and I's worried. It jus' don't look safe for him to be out there by hissef. That Mista Beardsley's been out there traipsin' 'round, and so has those men from over at that camp where that man's missin'. They's been watching us while we been workin' out there. I don't like it, Miss Harriet," he concluded, wagging his head back and forth.

"When were you supposed to go out that way again, Henry?" Miss Dunn asked, a worried expression on her face.

"I told Mista Cam I'd be back sometime today . . . but I been ridin' all night, and I cain't work that mule no more today, Miss Harriet."

"That's all right, Henry. When you've rested you can go . . . have you eaten?"

"No, Miss Harriet, I just been ridin'," he replied, shaking his head wearily.

"Leola, warm up some food and fix Henry a place to rest in the storehouse," she instructed, leaving to go to her room.

She paced the floor trying to think of what she could do to help Cam. Mr. Sparks would not know to go to his aid, for Henry had not gone by there to inform him of his latest findings. There was the colonel's man upstairs. Would he go? Other than a nod of greeting on a chance encounter, she had never exchanged more than a few words with him. She wasn't even sure that the name on the register was correct.

She slipped quietly up the stairs with her heart pounding. Fortunately all the doors were closed as she made her way noiselessly along the hall. She was uncertain of what to say as she approached his door. He answered her light tap on the door immediately.

"Good morning, madam," he said in a subdued voice, bowing slightly. "May I be of service to you?"

"I hope so, sir," she replied softly, looking back through the hall. "May I speak with you in my office?"

"No, madam, I'd rather not be seen talking with you."

"Then may I come in?" she asked, breaking for the first time a rule she had always upheld until now, not to enter any of the rooms that were occupied.

He stepped aside to allow her to enter, noting the strained expression on her face. He looked along the hall again and closed the door silently behind her.

She glanced at the neat appearance of the room. The rocking chair had been pulled over by the window where she knew there was full view of the street below.

"Mr. . . . uh . . . ," she stammered, turning to face him.

"Bonham, madam, Robert Bonham."

"Mr. Bonham," she began again, "I need your help. Cam is out on his homestead alone, and I have reason to believe he is in danger. Henry, Leola's friend, has just come in with some very disturbing news."

He listened attentively while she related the details, taking notice of the way the dim light in the room made her wonderful eyes seem even more luminous in her fair face. No wonder the colonel cared so much for this breathtaking woman. He realized suddenly that she had finished speaking and was standing there waiting for him to answer.

"Begging your pardon, Miss Dunn, I cannot go out there to see about Cam. He is a fine lad, and I would like to help him, but the colonel gave me strict orders to watch for your personal safety."

"Very well then . . . will you go with me?" she persisted.

"No, madam, I cannot allow you to do such a thing."

His answer drew the fire into her eyes. "I am sorry to have disturbed you," she said stiffly. She brushed past him to the door where she let herself out. Rigid with anger, she swept quietly down the hall to her room. What did he mean he would not allow her to go out to Cam? She had a right to do as she chose!

Henry was just finishing his meal when Harriet Dunn came into the kitchen dressed in a brown riding habit. She threw a hooded cape over the chair.

"Henry, I must have a horse. Will you go to the stable and get me one before you rest? Here is the money."

"What yo' 'bout to do, Miss Harriet?" Leola asked.

"I'm going to ride out to Mr. Sparks and get him to ride over to Cam's with me."

"You oughtn't be doin' that, Miss Harriet," Henry implored, pushing back his plate. "I'll catch a short rest and get on back out there."

"Tell me the way, Henry. You need the rest," she insisted.

"I'll go now, Miss Harriet," he moaned. "I'll just doze while that mule keeps on goin'. 'Sides, yo' need to be here to feed folks and not 'tract attention."

"Leola can handle that. I'll ride out with you and go on to get Mr. Sparks. You run along and get me a horse. Bring him to the back of the house. I don't want anyone to see me leave." Miss Dunn watched Henry leave through the back door, then turned to Leola. "Fill a sack with a loaf of bread, and some of that ham, oh, yes, put some jelly and fruit in there too. Henry can take it to Cam."

While she waited for Henry to return with the horse, Harriet Dunn left instructions for Leola and warned her not to tell anyone where she had gone. If she was not back by morning, Leola was to notify the man in room 8.

When Henry appeared at the back gate with a bay mare, Miss Dunn quickly donned the black cape, pulling the hood up over her shining hair and walked swiftly out to climb easily into the saddle. Wheeling the horse around, she rode out ahead of Henry. When she was a safe distance from Dunn House she reined in to wait for Henry to catch up.

"Miss Harriet, if yo' don't beat all," he said admiringly. "Yo' handle that horse like yo' always been on one."

"My father put me on a horse when I was very young. I shared his love for fine thoroughbreds, and we rode together a lot. This is a beautiful animal. She has good gait. Does she have a name?"

"The boy at the stable called her Star," he recalled.

"When we get out a little farther, I'd like for you to adjust the stirrups a little higher, Henry. I didn't want to take the time there at the house."

"I'll do that, Miss Harriet, 'n then we better be a ridin'," he responded.

When they turned off the main road into the wagon track leading through the forest, Miss Dunn gave a cry of delight. It had been a long time since she had been out in the pines. She took a deep breath of air laden with the clean scent of dried pine needles and gave her attention to the trail ahead.

They had ridden a long way into the woods when Henry pointed out the road leading off to the church.

"It's only a little further to where I turn off to go over to Mista Cam's cabin," he said.

As they reached the place where Henry was to turn off, he stopped his mule. "Miss Harriet, you just keep ridin' down this road. Ride hard now, yo' hear? Don't stop for nobody!" he warned, kicking his mule into a fast trot.

12

CAM HAD BEEN UP FOR SEVERAL HOURS, quietly working on the inside of his cabin. He put the last of the canned goods on the shelf and stood back to admire his handiwork. The empty box, he decided, would make a good stand by the bed to put the lamp on. He could use the inside for storage. He looked around the room, pleased with the arrangement. The bed was left to be made, and when he had finished this task he sat down to wait for Henry. He should be riding in soon. He picked up his Bible to read for a while.

Later, laying it aside, he sat trying to recall what the preacher had said in the last service. "The just shall live by faith . . . faith in God . . . faith in the Word of God . . . and faith in one another." Cam grinned at the last part. That would take some doing with some folks.

It was beginning to get warm in the cabin, so he got up to open the door. As he was about to lift the bar, a sound caught his attention. Was that the snort of a horse?

Cautiously he crouched down and moved out of view of the window. Someone was out there! He could hear the creak of leather as the person dismounted. It wasn't Henry—he would have called out to him.

Cam crawled on his hands and knees to the bed and slid underneath. Perhaps they would think no one was here and leave. His heart sank as he heard the sound of a boot on the step outside. Whoever it was tried to open the door. They could tell it was barred from the inside and knew he was there. There was a surprised grunt, then all was quiet.

Cam stayed where he was, scarcely breathing for fear he would be discovered. The blood pounding in his temples sounded like a loud drum. He detected a movement near the window, then suddenly there was the scrape of boots on the wall of the cabin. The intruder was trying to climb through the window. Cam could hear his labored breathing. The struggle ceased abruptly, and the man held his breath as if he were listening to something. A soft thud gave evidence that he had dropped to the ground. A minute later he rode away.

Cam stayed where he was, waiting and listening, hearing nothing. When he felt it was safe to leave his hiding place, he scooted out to risk taking a look out the window. There were tracks in the soft sand, but no one was in sight. He sighed with relief and sat down on the bed, aware that his legs no longer wanted to hold him up. He wished Henry would come.

There! That sound . . . was he coming back? Cam looked around the room, unsure of what to do. Should he try to run? He wouldn't stand a chance against a man on a horse. It would be better to hide under the bed and hope he would not be seen. He was just about to dive for the floor when he heard Henry's call. What a welcome sound! Cam unbarred the door and flung it open. He stood waiting for his friend.

"Henry, I'm sure glad you came along when you did," he exclaimed. Henry drew rein and looked around when he spotted the tracks of the horse. He realized he was a target for anyone who had a gun and lost no time in urging his mule in close to the cabin. He jumped to the ground, grabbed the sack of food, and hurried up the steps, taking quick note of the large footprints in the sand. Cam stepped back to allow him to enter, then closed the door and dropped the bar in the slot.

Henry tossed the bag onto the bed. "Miss Harriet sent yo' sumpin' to eat. Better get some vittles inside yo' . . . I got a feelin' we're gonna be in fo' trouble soon." A scowl appeared on his face as the reality of their predicament hit him full force. He stared out of the window.

Cam made himself a sandwich and sat on the side of the bed eating. He had put off fixing something to eat earlier, waiting for Henry to come, and he was hungry.

"What happened heah this mawnin'?" Henry asked, studying the ground under the window. He could see where the hoof marks led off toward the scrub oak thicket.

Cam related to Henry what had taken place as he helped himself to more ham and bread.

Henry backed away from the opening and stood deeper in the dim interior of the room. The tracks revealed there was only one of them here. Where was the partner? There was no opening in the back of the cabin, and one would have access to the rear without being observed. That worried him as he glared at the blank wall trying to figure it all out. No doubt one of them overheard him saying he would be riding over here today. If they did figure on taking the boy this morning, they wouldn't want to risk being seen. The other man could be watching the road coming from the Sparks' homestead, intending to waylay him. A growing fear swept over him as he thought about Miss Harriet riding that way. Why did he give in to her coming? Yet he knew there was nothing he could have said to keep her from doing what she set her mind to.

Henry rolled his eyes heavenward and wagged his head as he always did when he was distressed. A deep moan escaped his lips.

Cam looked up at the sound and saw the anguish in Henry's face. "What is it, Henry?" he implored with alarm.

"It's Miss Harriet. She's on her way over to Mista Sparks! When I left yo' yestuhday, I rode off in a circle and came across some tracks comin' into that oak grove out there. I found someone had been watchin' us all the time we been workin'. I foller'd them tracks, and they led to that camp where that homesteader's missin'. There was two rough-lookin' men there. I couldn't get close 'nough to see who they were. If . . . if only one was here after yo' . . . then the other'n could be hidin' on that road to waylay me, thinkin' I'd be a ridin' over from there!" Henry's words tumbled over one another. "Miss Harriet won't know, and she'll be . . ."

"Do you smell smoke?" Cam asked, breaking in on Henry.

Henry's eyes bulged as he saw the wisps of smoke coming up through the cracks of the floor under the bed. He stood petrified, wondering what they could do.

"All right, you two, move on outta there or you'll burn to a crisp!" a coarse voice shouted. "Come on, don't take all day! Open that door and move out with your hands in the air if you want to live!"

"We better do as he says, Mista Cam," Henry urged with a strickened cry.

Cam dropped his half-eaten sandwich and jumped to his feet. The smoke was filling the cabin and pouring out through the windows. Henry felt his way to the door and lifted the bar. With eyes smarting from the smoke, they groped their way out into the bright sunlight, putting their hands high over their heads.

"Now, that's more like it!" growled their captor, a big, burly looking man with a dark visage and cruel, squinted eyes that looked like slits in his head.

"Stan' over this way and don't move!" he ordered, waving the rifle in the direction he wished them to go. When Henry and Cam had complied, he backed up to kick the fire from under the cabin.

"Haw! Haw! Don't wanna burn this nice cabin you built for us!" he laughed with derision.

"Climb on that mule, black boy, and ride out ahead of us," he snarled at Henry disrespectfully. "The other is gonna walk in front of this gun. One wrong move and he's a goner. Understand? We're moving over to that scrub oak."

He poked Cam in the back hard with the barrel of the rifle. "Move out, boy."

Cam spun around and struck the rifle aside. "Don't you dare do that again!" he cried in a ringing tone, his eyes flashing fire. "I'll walk without you prodding me." He turned and walked away after Henry's mule.

"Haw! Haw! So I've got a little rooster on my hands. This oughta be some entertainment," the man chortled.

Once they reached the trees, the man ordered Cam to climb up in front of Henry, then mounted his horse, a roam with a black mane, and pointed the direction.

"Mista Cam, we's in an awful fix," Henry whispered in his ear. "If Miss Harriet don' make it through, nobody's gonna know 'ceptin' Leola, and she's not 'spose to tell 'til mawnin'. We gotta do sumpin'! He's takin' us over to that other homestead where they's been campin'.'"

Cam gave no reply except to nod his head. There wasn't much they could do against a man with a gun. They would have to outsmart him somehow.

* * *

Harriet Dunn waved a hand at Henry and rode off like the wind. What fun it was to be on a horse again! Star seemed to anticipate what her rider wanted and stretched out in full stride, increasing her speed. The trees flashed by as horse and rider became one racing down the road.

An instant later she felt the grit of sand between her teeth as stars exploded in her head from the fall. She never saw what caused her horse to stumble and throw her forward to the ground. The breath was knocked mercilessly from her lungs. She couldn't move.

She felt crude hands roll her over and heard a grating, nasal-sounding voice exclaim, "Well, I'll be . . . I've done gone and caught me a woman!" Rough hands brushed the sand from her face and caressed her hair. She felt herself being picked up and carried. She struggled weakly to get free, but he only tightened his hold on her. He tossed her, facedown, over the saddle and climbed up behind her. Consciousness left her as she faded into a black swirling vortex.

* * *

How long she had been unconscious, Harriet Dunn had no idea. When she opened her eyes, she could see the horse's feet and the ground beneath her. Her head throbbed with pain, and her mouth was sticky with sand and blood. One arm was caught under her body and her legs were numb. Where was she? When she tried to pull her arm free, a hand restrained her, pushing her back down.

The horse came to a stop, and the rider took his hand from her back. Getting down, he led the animal a little farther. She heard a coarse voice call out.

"What you got there?"

"Got me a woman!" was the reply.

"A what?"

"A woman, I said. Cain't you hear all of a sudden? A real beaut too! Wait'll you see her," her captor said, gleefully. He pulled her roughly from the horse, her feet hitting the ground hard, and stretched her out on the dirt. She could smell the sweat and tobacco odor as he leaned over to peer into her face. She kept her eyes closed, scarcely breathing.

"She took a nasty fall when I pulled that rope up. Don't think she's hurt bad, though," he said, as he pulled at her arms and legs. "Nothin' seems broken, at least yet, noways! Haw! Haw!"

Cam and Henry sat speechless as they watched the horse approach with Miss Dunn over its back. She was hanging there so limp, they thought surely she was dead. They struggled with the ropes that bound them to a tree as the man dragged her so ruthlessly off his mount. On her cheek was a red bruise that stood out in the whiteness of her face.

"Miss Harriet! Miss Harriet! Tell me yo' ain't daid," Henry wailed brokenly.

The big, burly man was in the act of building a fire when he heard Henry's cry. He stopped dead, a piece of wood in his hand, his head jerked up and he looked at Henry and then at the woman. Letting the wood fall, he stood up and walked over to where Harriet Dunn lay. He looked into her face and let out an oath as he straightened up to glare angrily at his partner.

"You've gotten us in a fine mess, now! Do you know who that woman is?"

"Whatta I care?" the younger man snarled, blinking his weaselly eyes. "I caught her and she's mine, all mine." He picked her up and carried her into the cabin, leaving the older man to stare after him thoughtfully.

Cam was relieved when he returned right away, closing the door behind him. The older man, he noticed, had also taken several steps in that direction but stopped and turned away as he saw the younger man emerge.

After the fire was built the two of them went aside for what seemed a heated argument, with much gesturing. Cam strained to hear what they were saying, but to no avail. The younger man was red in the face and at one point slammed his hat to the ground. Finally, they appeared to come to some agreement between them, and they returned to the fire to go on with the preparation of a meal. The younger of the two helped little but sat on a low bench sulking. Every now and then he would bestow a malevolent glance on the big man, who was down on his knees making biscuits.

"Why should he have her? I'm the one who got her!" he raged, unable to contain his contempt.

"Shut up!" the other ordered, leaning into a crouching position, his hand not far away from the guns by his side. "Just hope he doesn't find out what you were up to, or it will be trouble for you!"

The jaw of the weasel-faced one snapped shut, and his face blanched a little as he fell silent and watchful. His close-set eyes darted back and forth.

Cam knew instinctively there was some evil scheme beginning to take form in his depraved mind. There would be no sleep in this camp tonight.

Apparently the older man sensed this scheming in his partner, for he casually moved his position to face him as he placed the biscuits, one by one, in a deep cast-iron pot on the hot coals. He dusted the flour off his hands and wiped them on his pants. Picking up the rifles, he walked over to sit down on the well-worn stump of a tree.

13

*I*N HIS ROOM AT DUNN HOUSE, Robert Bonham was restless. He had been keeping watch from the window to see if Harriet Dunn might leave the house. So far as he knew she had not, yet as he opened the door a crack to listen for the usual sound of her voice from the floor below, he could hear nothing except the clatter of dishes from the kitchen and Leola humming to herself.

A frown furrowed his brow as he stood pondering the situation. Had he been too direct, too forceful with her? He recalled the blaze of color that had flashed into those glorious eyes as she hesitated, poised for flight. Had he misread the whole thing? Did his refusal to go to Cam's aid challenge her to do something rash? A woman with her spirit would not be above taking things into her own hands.

Bonham stepped out into the empty hall and slipped to the head of the stairs, treading softly. He stopped to listen for anyone moving around in the room below. Hearing nothing, he descended noiselessly to the lower hallway leading to the back of the house, pausing only to glance in the direction of Miss Dunn's unused office. A sense of urgency swept over Bonham as he made his way to the gate at the end of the path. The hoofprints in the damp sand, just beyond the fence, told the story.

Bonham quickly returned to the house and entered the kitchen. Leola was removing a big batch of freshly baked bread from the oven. The aroma filled the room. She looked up, startled, to see him standing there. Her eyes widened as she turned to set the hot pan down on a rack.

"Miss Dunn! Where did she go?" Bonham cried, taking her by the arm.

"I don't know," Leola stalled, trying to free her arm from his grasp.

"Tell me!" he persisted. "It is important that I know. I want to help her."

"She made me promise not to tell nobody 'ceptin' that man in room 8!" she responded fearfully. "Now, yo' let me go, mista, or I'm gonna start yellin'!"

"Tell me . . . I am the man in room 8! Hurry! She could be in danger!" he insisted, shaking her arm.

Leola told him all that had taken place in a breathless voice, her words tumbling over one another. After asking several questions as to directions, he ran from the kitchen and up the stairs, taking them two at a time.

Once in his room Bonham strapped on his gun belt, checked the guns, and stuck a knife in the sheath of his belt. Putting on a long coat to cover the fact that he was armed, he picked up his hat and left the house, going out the rear entrance.

He pulled the hat low over his eyes and strode swiftly along the side streets to come up in back of the livery stable. There was a door there that opened into a small, fenced-in area. Jumping the fence, he stopped to peer into the dim interior. No one was in sight, so he saddled a big black horse, laid some money in a feed scoop, and led the horse out into the corral and through the gate.

Bonham rode hard with no letup, pressing the big horse to his greatest stride, the thundering hoofs leaving a trail of dust behind. He was relieved when he reached the turnoff to the wagon trail. Not lessening his speed, the horse raced on through the woods. It was some time before he came to the road Leola had said would lead off to the church. With only a glimpse in that direction, he rode on, slowing his horse's gait only slightly. He could see the tracks of Henry's mule plainly now. Alongside were the smaller indentations made by Harriet Dunn's mount.

Bonham slowed his horse to a trot, watching for any deviation in the hoofprints he was following. When he came to the newly cut trail going off to Cam's homestead, he paused. He could see where they had split up, with Henry riding off toward Cam, and Miss Dunn continuing on to the Sparks' home for help.

Prodding the horse on in a fast trot, he kept his eyes glued to the trail in the soft sand. His heart sank when he came to the place where she had been thrown from the saddle. He pulled up his mount sharply and leaped to the ground. Leading the horse to one side, he tied him to a branch, then walked back to carefully study the imprints in the sand.

It was an old trick. Someone had carefully buried a rope beneath the dirt and then concealed himself by the side of the road. When the unsuspecting rider came along, he simply jerked the rope up, tripping the animal and throwing the person forward from the saddle. The rope marks had not been removed.

Bonham could see where the horse had recovered and raced on down the road. Miss Dunn had fallen in the sand, scooting it before her as her body projected forward to finally come to rest at the side of the deep rut. One of the combs from her hair was stuck in the pine needles a few feet away. He picked it up and put it in his pocket.

Footprints led from behind a bush near the edge of the trees. The man had walked with a shuffle, pushing the pine needles along with his heel. The mark left by the man's knee showed where he had stooped to pick her up. Bonham followed the footsteps, deeper now with the extra weight, to where a horse had been waiting. There had been no sign of struggle. Miss Dunn must have been knocked unconscious, or worse.

Climbing back on his horse, Bonham swung off on the trail through the woods. The kidnapper did not seem to be in a hurry. He must have had a destination in mind, or his camp was not too far away. He had been riding for some time when he came to the creek. The trail led down into the water. Bonham looked for tracks on the opposite bank but saw none coming up out of the water. Did the man ride up or down the creek? he wondered. He searched his mind to remember what Leola had told him about Lake Delancy. It lay to the south, she had said. He looked up at the late afternoon sun. He had been traveling to the southeast. This creek would be emptying into the lake. He decided to go downstream, splashing through the clear water. He could see the white sand bottom.

Bonham was watching the other edge when the black horse reared back with a snort, nearly unseating him.

"What is it, boy?" he said, reaching out to pat the animal on the neck to quiet him. There were no snakes in view. Could it have been a panther? He dismissed that idea; it was too early in the day. He backed the black horse up and turned him to the bank. He dismounted and picked up a fallen limb. Carrying it along the bank, he threw it into the water, watching in horror as it was sucked down rapidly by quicksand. A cold sweat broke out on his forehead.

Bonham walked back to the horse and stood there thoughtfully stroking his neck. He felt sick to his stomach. Surely they . . . Miss Dunn . . . He pushed the thought abruptly from his head. He went back to the bank again to study the ground. A thick blanket of brown pine needles covered the area. If they had come up out of the water here, the needles would have been disturbed. He was just about to go upstream when he noticed several strands of dark brown hair caught on a bush.

Stooping down, Bonham brushed away the layer of pine needles and found the faint outlines of a hoof mark. The cunning of the man let him know what he was up against. In case someone did try to follow, they would assume he had gone downstream, since his tracks had been bearing that way, and unknowingly be trapped and dragged under by the quicksand.

"That was a close one," he muttered.

Climbing back in the saddle he rode on in a southeasterly direction. About 50 feet away from the creek, he picked up the trail again. The green bow of a pine tree had been dropped nearby. The abductor had taken the time to rub out his tracks.

The signs were easy to read now, and Bonham made good progress through the trees. No doubt the man he was following thought he had covered his tracks pretty well, for no further attempt was made to throw him off the trail. The smell of smoke warned him to check his horse. He looked around for the best possible approach. A short distance away was a small stand of scrub oak. Bonham made his way over to them. They were not as dense as he had hoped, but it would be dark before too long and the black horse would not be seen.

Starting out on foot, he cautiously worked his way forward. The trees were beginning to thin out. Many of them had been cut for building or firewood. In some areas where there was little cover, he was forced to crawl on his stomach. Proceeding in this manner to a clump of palmettos, Bonham was finally able to get a better view of his position. He was coming up to one side of the cabin. He could see the flicker of the fire but little else. He would have to get in much closer. He decided to circle more to the right so that he could come in behind the cabin and be less visible.

He painstakingly crawled until he found himself behind the crude building. From what he could see there appeared to be only two of them. He must wait and see on that score.

He settled down to bide his time until dark. In his mind he tried to formulate a plan, but everything he came up with hinged on where they had the woman and if there were more than the two moving around the campfire. He drew one of his guns and held it ready should he be discovered. Somewhere off in the distance came a low rumble of thunder. The woods were quiet except for the occasional hoot of an owl.

* * *

Henry sat with stoic expression, watchful, never taking his eyes off their captors, who were greedily devouring their food. His fingers were getting sore and cramped as he continued to work with the ropes that bound him to the tree. What he would do once he was free, he did not know. He glanced longingly at the rifles that were never far from the big man's side.

One of the men looked over at Cam and made some low comment, which brought loud laughter from them both.

They had been careful not to refer to one another by name when they were talking, so Henry had no idea who they were. The big, rough-looking man who had taken them prisoner seemed to be in charge and held the younger man in check.

There was something about the latter that Henry disliked very much. It wasn't just the dark, darting eyes, but a deeper, more sinister quality. He had a cruel mouth that rarely parted to show tobacco-stained teeth.

As Henry watched him, the man set his plate down and got up to walk over toward the makeshift cabin to listen at the door. Giving a furtive glance back at his burly companion busy at the fire, he opened the door and slipped inside, closing it behind him.

Henry sat frozen. "Miss Harriet!" he shouted, as he heard her cry out.

The big, burly man spun around with a roar. He ran to jerk open the door, diving into the darkened room. There was a noisy scuffle, and when he finally emerged he was dragging the agitated younger man by the collar. He dropped him sputtering in the sand.

"Don't you go near her agin. You hear?"

"Aw, come on, Cl- . . ." He didn't get to finish the name. The big man gave him a swift kick and walked off to gather up the rifles and placed them near his side.

As dusk overtook the daylight, the men sat silent before the fire, staring somberly into the blaze. Neither made any attempt at conversation. The younger was nursing scratches on the side of his face, which were beginning to welt up. Every now and then he would cast a baleful glance at the big fellow across from him.

Cam was sitting quiet, staring in the direction of the cabin. Henry looked over at him with compassion, waiting to give him a smile of encouragement, but Cam did not move or turn his head. Henry went back to watching the men who had captured them while he continued the struggle to free himself.

A movement in the shadows beyond the building had caught Cam's attention. Whatever it was came crawling along the ground toward them. Suddenly, it stood up and ran without a sound to the corner of the hut. It was a man! Cam quickly looked at his captors. They showed no sign that they were aware of the presence lurking there in the dark. The bright light of the fire would have blinded them. Who could it be? Mr. Sparks would not know they were in trouble; Miss Dunn didn't make it through to warn him. Whoever it was came to help them, or he would have called out to the men by the fire. With the big, gruff man facing that way, so as to keep watch on the cabin door, Cam knew that the person hiding in the obscurity of the night could not approach the camp without being seen. Someone would have to divert their attention.

He looked over at Henry and was sure he had not seen the shadowy figure. Beginning to strain at his ropes and kick what little he could manage, Cam cried out as if tortured. The two men turned to look at him with consternation.

"What's the matter with you, boy?" the big man asked, reaching out to grasp his rifle

"Snake! . . . it bit me . . . on the arm . . . help me . . . !" Cam wailed.

"Haw! Haw! Is that all! That snake saved us some trouble!" they guffawed and got to their feet to walk over to him.

"Mista Cam, lay still . . . don't move!" Henry wailed in despair.

"Hyar now. You shet up!" hissed the young thief, giving Henry a hard kick to the face.

Both men leaned over to peer into Cam's distorted face. Neither was aware of the figure creeping stealthily up behind them. Cam continued to struggle, begging for help, while Henry stared in disbelief.

"Shut up, boy, before I put you out of your misery," growled the one with the rifle. He raised the gun butt up as if to hit Cam with it.

"I wouldn't do that if I were you," Bonham said in a stern voice. Whirling around, they found themselves looking into the barrels of the two guns aimed directly at them.

"Throw those rifles down!" Bonham ordered in a commanding voice. The two men stood dumbfounded, frozen to the spot. The rifles fell to the ground.

"Now get those hands up high over your head and move away from the boy," Bonham commanded.

Cam ceased his writhing and crying and sat quiet.

"Are you all right, son?" Bonham asked anxiously, without taking his eyes off the captives.

"Jest yo' lay quiet, Mista Cam, we'll take care of that snakebite," Henry assured, trying to comfort his friend.

"I'm all right, Henry. There was no snake. I was just trying to get their attention," Cam replied.

"Good job, Cam," Bonham acknowledged as he holstered one of his guns and reached for his knife. He cut Cam free and tossed the knife down by his side.

"Free Henry, Cam. Then you two tie up these vermin."

Cam hastened to cut Henry loose and together they bound the hands and feet of those who had treated them so cruelly.

When he was satisfied they were tied securely, Bonham handed Henry a gun to stand over them. He then ran to the cabin door, Cam close on his heels.

"Wait here, son," Bonham said gently, taking Cam by the shoulders to restrain him. "Let me check on her first."

Inside the room, Harriet Dunn had crawled into the darkness of a corner. She had fought off her attacker and was relieved that he had been dragged to the outside. With great effort she had rolled from the bed to the floor in search of something to protect herself. Feeling her way along the wall, her hand came in contact with a piece of metal. Her grasping fingers took hold of a round rod, and she dragged it along with her.

When she reached the adjoining wall, she pulled herself up to a sitting position, clutching the rod in her lap. Was that a sound outside the cabin wall? Her head was pounding so, she couldn't be sure. Through the window she heard Cam's cry. She fought off the despair that swept over her. She must not succumb to weakness but must keep her wits about her. If she could stall long enough, Leola could get the message to Mr. Bonham.

The shouting outside had ceased, and footsteps could be heard coming toward the door. There was a pause, then she could see a man entering the room silhouetted against the glow from the fire. She crouched to spring up, the metal in her hand, as the man moved on into the room.

"Miss Dunn, where are you? This is Robert Bonham. Don't be afraid."

She uttered a cry and sank to the floor, shaken and spent. He came over to where she was and lifted her to her feet, supporting her with his arm.

"Come, everything is all right now," he said gently. He put his long coat around her and carried her out into the firelight where he sat her down.

"Cam, is he . . ." Her voice broke.

"I'm here, Miss Dunn," Cam spoke up, coming to her side. "I'm fine."

"But you . . . I heard . . . ," she stammered.

"I was just getting their attention 'cause I saw this man in back of the cabin, and he needed help."

"And Henry? Is he . . ."

"I's right here, Miss Harriet, guardin' these tough guys that don't look so tough now," he said, giving her as good a smile as he could manage with his swollen face.

"Cam, bring Miss Dunn some water to drink. She will want to wash her face too," Bonham instructed. "I'll go in the shack and see if I can fix her a comfortable place to rest."

"No! Please! I don't want to go back into that place," she cried, looking pathetic with a large red bruise on her white cheek. Her rich brown hair was in disarray. She clung to him, shaking her head back and forth.

"Very well, I'll make you a bed here by the fire. Here's Cam with some water. Stay with her, son," he said, leaving her in Cam's care. While Cam held the bucket, she rinsed the sand from her mouth and face.

Bonham busied himself fixing something to eat from what stores they could find. When they had finished, he cut pine boughs and fixed a bed for Miss Dunn, spreading his long coat out for her to wrap around herself.

Later, while the others fell into an exhausted sleep, he sat tending the fire and keeping watch through the night.

Tomorrow he would send Henry over to the Sparkses for a wagon and then they would start the long ride back into town with the prisoners. He glanced over at Harriet Dunn, who lay with the firelight playing on her hair. She was the colonel's lady, and he was a very fortunate man.

14

SUMMER HAD COME ONCE AGAIN to the St. John's River country. The day had begun hot and sultry with only a slight breeze offering relief from the heat. Cam sat on a bench he had built alongside the cabin, sheltered from the hot sun. A bridle he was mending lay forgotten in his lap as he languished in the shade.

He had been living on the homestead for over two years now, and there was little left to do other than tend the live-stock and take care of his own needs. The first year passed quickly. He had been busy clearing the land and building the pens for the animals. But now the days and weeks seemed long, broken only by an occasional visit from Mr. Sparks and Henry. The books and papers Miss Dunn had been sending out helped him to endure the long, lonely hours, but lately, an inner restlessness had come upon him and would not go away.

Could it be that he was growing tired of this lonely exis-tence in the forest? Questions began to crowd his mind. He had improved the land, and Uncle George now held title to it. He had done what he set out to do. But what of the future? He would be 18 soon. Wasn't it about time for him to start out on his own? How long should he feel bound by loyalty to Uncle George?

Brindle, a female hunting hound, came pattering from the cabin to lay at his feet in the cool sand, eyes fixed fondly on her master. As Cam looked down at her, she wagged her tail expectantly. "Got too hot in there for you, huh, girl," he said affectionately, rubbing her ear with his boot.

Nan had kept her word, prevailing upon her father to give Cam a puppy. He would never forget that day. Mr. Sparks and Nan had ridden over with a wiggly, tawny-colored pup tied up in a flour sack hanging from the pommel on the saddle. He had been so glad to see them and was really delighted when Nan handed the squirming little bundle to him. When Cam had placed the puppy on the ground, they had all laughed at the antics she displayed as she ran around the yard, tumbling over her feet. Together they had chosen the name Brindle.

Nan had brought a lunch, which they shared under the big oak tree. The tiny Brindle had entertained herself by chewing on acorns and tossing them in the air, much to Nan's amusement. Tiring of this, Brindle curled up beside Cam to sleep.

Brindle had awakened while he was showing Mr. Sparks and Nan the new cattle pen and shelter, and wandered off into the woods. Cam and Nan had heard her yipping off in the distance and had run to rescue the tiny stray who had gotten into a patch of sandspurs. While he held the writhing pup, Nan had pulled the sharp spurs from its feet. Nan's face had been close to his, her warm breath fanning his cheek.

Cam felt his pulse quicken as he recalled that wonderful moment when his lips met hers. He had drawn back, shocked at what he had done. Nan had stood motionless, looking at him with wondering eyes, before turning to hurry back to the cabin.

"Nan! I'm . . . ," he had tried to apologize in a strangled voice. After that day she had not come again, except with the young people from the church who had ridden out on a Sunday afternoon, bringing a picnic dinner with them. They were a lively crowd, teasing one another in fun while downing fried chicken, ham, cold biscuits with homemade butter, and a cake that Nan had brought.

They had given Cam ample praise on his neatly arranged homestead, but Joey, most of all, had a more appreciative eye, talking at great length about the quality of the soil and what could be done in raising crops.

The day had not ended soon enough for Cam. Henrietta had been overwhelming in her attention to him, much to his discomfort. Nan had stayed close to Joey and the others and avoided looking at Cam most of the time. Only once did she give him an accusing look as Henrietta sat close to him with her arm through his.

Cam squirmed and frowned as he remembered the embarrassment and confusion he had felt under her direct gaze. He had jumped to his feet to stalk off toward the cabin. Since that day he had avoided Henrietta as much as possible.

Nan remained friendly to him, but he was baffled by her quiet, reserved manner when around him. She no longer teased him as she had done in the past. Often when in her presence, Cam would turn quickly to find those wonderful dark eyes upon him with an expression he could not fathom.

A sigh escaped his lips as he admitted to himself that he was in love with Nan. It was her face that kept haunting him during the long, lonely hours he spent in the evenings, appearing in the flames of the fire, the page of his book, and his dreams. But what could he do about it? He had no means to support a wife and provide for a home. Would she even have him? What about Joey? Was she in love with him?

Next week was her 18th birthday, and she was having a party. He dreaded to go. Henrietta would be there, but he knew he could not stay away. Just to be near Nan, listen to her merry voice and musical laughter, would have to suffice for the time being. Perhaps when he had more to offer than the drudgery of a homesteader's wife, he could let her know how he felt.

The neighing of a horse broke into his reverie, bringing him back to reality. Dandy stood with his proud head extended over the fence calling to him.

"I'm almost finished, Dandy," Cam said.

He picked up the bridle and finished tacking the torn headstall. With this done, he went out to put the saddle on

Dandy, leading him around to the front of the cabin. He glanced up at the sun and realized he would have to hurry if he was going to meet Henry out on the road in time to ride into town together.

He hastened out to check on the feed for the mother cow, then turned the calf in with her.

"There, little fella, you can have all you want for the next couple of days." He stood watching the calf nudge its mother in search of food, then closing the door he latched it securely so the wild animals could not get inside. He returned to the cabin to get his hat and the Bible, which he put in his jacket pocket. Cam looked around the cabin. Then taking up his shotgun, he went out and locked the door.

Giving Brindle final orders to take care of things, he swung up on Dandy and was off. The horse was anxious to run, so Cam gave him his head. He needed no guiding on the familiar trail. Before long Dandy settled into an easy canter and did not slow until he reached the creek. Cam allowed him to drink, then urged him on. With the horse's speed, it didn't take long to get to the fork in the road. Henry was nowhere in sight. Cam stepped down from the saddle and sat down on a stump to wait. Henry had taught him to track and read signs while hunting together. He could tell by the marks in the soft sand of the road that Henry's mule had not been there yet. Cam grinned with satisfaction. Henry should be coming along any time now. Cam valued the friendship of this man who had been a true companion, helping him on the homestead, teaching him to cook over an open fire, and patiently showing him the ways of the forest.

The heat had grown more intense, and the forest around him was still. It was as if everything was held captive in limp, silent suspense, waiting for a cooling breeze or a refreshing drop of rain. Cam removed his hat and wiped the perspiration from his brow. The low rumble of a thunderhead warned of rain.

"Hello," he muttered to himself. "You'd be welcome if I wasn't riding into town."

It wasn't long before he spied Henry riding toward him down the road. Climbing back into the saddle, Cam sat waiting for Henry to catch up. Dandy pranced in anticipation of another run.

"Howdy, Mista Cam," Henry called in greeting. "Has yo' been a waitin' long?"

"Not long, Henry, are you ready to ride? I'm not anxious to tangle with that storm I hear rumbling out there," Cam replied, as another clap of thunder came closer.

"I sho is, Mista Cam, but don' you let that Dandy horse of yo's go a racin' off leavin' me in his dust, yo' heah?" Henry answered, rolling his eyes dubiously at Dandy, who was ready to be off.

"All right, Henry, I'll hold this Dandy horse to a fast trot," Cam laughed, mimicking him.

The sun was below the horizon, and the coolness of the twilight was giving welcome relief from the heat when the two riders reined in and stepped down at the back gate of Dunn House. Leola waved at them from the window and ran to inform Miss Dunn of their arrival. "Mista Cam's here, Miss Harriet!"

Harriet came from her office to stand in the door, waiting for Cam to come up the walk. He had matured into the lithe form of an outdoorsman with broad shoulders and lean brown arms. His clean-shaven face was tan from long hours in the sun, making his blue eyes appear gray.

"Cam! I do declare, you are sure getting to be a handsome young man," she said, greeting him happily as he strode up the steps.

"And you, madam, you are a very lovely colonel's lady," he responded as he bowed playfully, taking her hand in his.

"Perhaps soon, my friend," she demurred, a slight flush stealing to her cheeks. "Have you eaten? No? You must be starved. Take care of Dandy, and I'll get Leola to fix you and Henry some supper."

Cam pushed back his plate and poured the coffee he had put out into the saucer to cool, back into the cup. Miss Dunn came into the kitchen and got herself a cup of coffee and sat down opposite him. He waited for her to add cream and sugar before he spoke.

"Miss Dunn," he began hesitantly, clearing his throat, "Nan's birthday is next week, and I want to get her something. Will you help me?"

Harriet gazed at Cam fondly. "Of course, Cam. Do you have something in mind?"

"No, I figured you'd be better at knowing about things like that."

"You lo- . . . like Nan a lot, don't you, Cam?"

"I love her. I'm planning to ask her to marry me."

"How wonderful, Cam! When?"

"I don't know yet. I guess when the time is right. I need to find a steady job first. I can't and I won't ask Nan to share the drudgery and loneliness of homesteading," he answered.

"I overheard the men talking at the table last night about Mr. Wilson needing someone as a night watchman at the lumber mill," she suggested thoughtfully.

"I'll ride out and check on it in the morning!" Cam exclaimed. "It would be good if I could get a job at the mill. I like working with wood."

"You can stay here at Dunn House and work for me during your off hours and work nights there. That would be perfect."

"Only thing, I will have to think about what to do concerning Uncle George and the homestead," Cam said soberly.

"I think you have done your duty there, Cam, and the way I see it, you have no further obligation to your uncle," Miss Dunn said sternly.

"You may be right," he responded. "He's got the deed to his land now. I've been thinking it's time for me to get on with my own life."

Miss Dunn finished drinking the last of her coffee and set the cup down. She sat silent for a moment before speaking again.

"Clay Beardsley is back in town. He was here at Dunn House for dinner one day. Leola warned me that he was here, and I didn't help with the serving. She said he kept watching the doorway, thinking I would come in. How bold of him. I wanted to remember to tell you. You will need to be more watchful."

Cam pushed back his chair and stood up. He put his hand gently on her shoulder. "And you too, ma'am; it was not only me he wanted," he cautioned, his serious blue eyes studying her face.

She had recuperated quickly from the hard fall she had taken when thrown from her horse, but the emotional scars took much longer. In those first few weeks after their traumatic experience, Cam had seen very little of her. He had no way to get into town except to hitch a ride with Mr. Sparks or ride double with Henry.

Colonel Stothard had come as quickly as he could to be near her, taking care of all the legal matters to spare her the pain. As her love for the colonel deepened, she had become more and more disenchanted with running the boardinghouse.

Her eyes filled with tears at the young man's sudden tenderness and concern. She reached to cover his hand with hers.

"You have been a good friend, Cam. After father died, I had no one to really care for until you came into my life. Now there is Colonel Stothard. He has asked me to marry him." She wiped the tears away and gave him a radiant smile. "I am so happy!"

"So, you really are going to be the colonel's lady! I like that, ma'am," he said softly. Cam picked up his hat and coat and walked to the door where he turned to look back at her. What a good, brave, and honest person she was. "Yep, I really do like that. Good night, ma'am."

"Good night, Cam. I'll go tomorrow morning and find a gift for Nan," Harriet Dunn promised as she got up to leave the kitchen.

Cam walked the few steps to his room. Leola had thoughtfully lit the lamp for him, and the light gave off a soft, comforting glow. He glanced around the familiar chamber. Everything was as he had left it. Cam stood for a moment, trying to sort out his thoughts, his brow knitted in a frown. Change was coming into his life, and he could not hold it back but rather welcomed the challenge of a new start.

Harriet Dunn would soon marry Colonel Stothard and go to live in Savannah. He felt sure the only thing holding her back was her concern for his welfare. In his mind he knew she was right about his further obligation to Uncle George. If he got on at the mill, he would write Uncle George and let him know he was leaving the homestead.

Cam grunted with satisfaction at having reached a decision in the matter. He dropped his coat and hat on the chair and sat down on the bed to pull off his boots.

Taking his Bible from the pocket of his jacket, he turned the lamp up and stretched out on the bed to read. He opened the book at Proverbs and was about to turn the pages to where he had left off reading the night before, when his eyes fell on a verse that had been underscored. To the side was a note his mother had written. "In all thy ways acknowledge him, and he shall direct thy paths," the scripture read. In the margin his mother had penciled the words, "Father, I cannot be with Cam to direct him. Take him into Thy care and lead him in the paths You would have him to go."

Cam read the scripture and his mother's prayer again. She knew then she was not going to live! Her concern was not for herself but for him. He closed his eyes and thought back to the night when she died. Her last, gasping wish was that he be cared for. She had no other choice than to ask her only brother to take him into his home.

The awkward, uncertain boy who had stumbled down the stairs into the night to cry alone, had become a man. Gone were the tears and the hurt. He had good friends and a new life in the frontier of the south. Harriet Dunn coming into his life had been a good and establishing influence.

Cam recalled what Rev. Underwood had said in his sermon the week before. "God works in the order of things." Did that mean that God had a hand in bringing Harriet Dunn into his life? If so, what about Nan? Would he be amiss in asking her to marry him? The image of her sweet face blotted out the page. The Bible lay forgotten in his hands as he dreamed of what their life could be together.

There was a light tap at his door. Cam swung his legs off the bed and got up to see who it was. Harriet Dunn stood in the hall.

"Cam," she whispered, "I thought you would like to know that Mr. Sparks and Nan will be in town tomorrow. Leola just told me. They will be eating here at Dunn House at noon."

Cam's face brightened in anticipation. "I'll be looking forward to that!"

"Sleep well," she said softly as she slipped noiselessly down the hall to her room. Cam closed the door and went to bed.

Leola was busy in the kitchen making breakfast when Cam rolled out of bed. The smell of ham frying in the skillet permeated the air, mingling with the aroma of fresh-brewed coffee. All over the house, he could hear movement, as if some silent alarm had gone off in the stomachs of the guests. He grinned at the thought as he washed and dressed with great care. Leola's cooking was enough to wake up the dead.

When he presented himself in the kitchen for his breakfast, Leola smiled her approval.

"My, my, just look at yo'—yo' sho is spiffed up this mawnin', Mista Cam. Must be somethin' special is gonna happen today!"

"I'm going to the mill to see Mr. Wilson about a job this morning. Miss Dunn told me he was looking for a night watchman," he answered, taking a seat at the table by the window.

"Oh, I see," Leola nodded knowingly, placing a plate of ham, eggs, and hot biscuits in front of him.

"I'm sure it wouldn't have nothin' to do with Miss Nan coming t' town," she went on, undaunted by this piece of information, turning to the stove to pick up the coffeepot.

"My man, Henry, says that girl is plumb crazy 'bout yo'. He says she's allus asking what yo' doin'," Leola continued in mock innocence, pouring his coffee.

Cam kept his eyes on his plate for fear of betraying the riot of feelings her words had set off in his breast. He laid the biscuit and knife down on his plate, his trembling hands no longer able to hold them.

Leola glanced at him from the corner of her eye. He sat constricted, staring at his plate.

Finally, unable to control his emotions, Cam got up and bolted from the kitchen, unseeing eyes not noticing Harriet Dunn coming toward him in the hall as he rushed to his room.

Leola stared after him round-eyed. "Umph, umph! I had no idea it was that bad! Leola, yo' don' gone to meddlin' now," she scolded herself.

Harriet Dunn came into the kitchen, her eyes taking in the uneaten plate of food.

"Leola, whatever has gotten into Cam?" she asked with consternation. "He just rushed past me in the hall as if he didn't see me."

Leola busied herself at the stove. "I don't know, Miss Harriet, we was jus' talking 'bout his goin' t' see Mr. Wilson at the mill, and Miss Nan comin' in t' town," she answered naively, keeping her back turned.

Miss Dunn watched her cook for a moment, keeping her suspicions to herself, then turned back to the hall as she heard Cam leave his room.

"Cam, are you all right?" she asked hesitantly.

"Yes, ma'am," he grinned, reassuring her. "I was just getting ready to leave for the mill. I thought I'd go to see Mr. Wilson about that job before starting my chores."

"Good luck!" she called out to him as he walked out the door.

Wilson's mill was located on the river's edge, south of town. Pilings had been driven deep in the water to support docks laden high with lumber. Cam had always liked the clean smell of wood drying in the sun. He found the office without any trouble. The door was open, so he walked right in. A clerk working at a counter looked over his glasses at him.

"May I help you with something?" he inquired of Cam.

"I'm here to see Mr. Wilson," Cam answered.

"He hasn't come in yet," the clerk informed him, going back to his work. "You can wait if you like."

Cam sat down to wait. A big clock on the wall ticked off the minutes, the long pendulum swinging back and forth. A whole hour had passed when a tall man dressed in khaki pants tucked in high-top boots stepped in the door. His gray eyes took in Cam without recognition as he hung his hat on a rack by the door. Tucking in his shirt, he strode toward his office.

"Good morning, Mr. Wilson," the clerk said stiffly, "this young man wishes to see you."

Cam stood to his feet as Mr. Wilson came over to him.

"What is it you wish to see me about?" he asked, giving Cam a keen, appraising look.

"I heard you were needing a night watchman, and I came to tell you I want the job," Cam replied, looking directly into his eyes.

"So you want the job, eh? What's your name, son?"

"Camden W. Fox, sir. Miss Dunn told me you were needing someone."

"Harriet Dunn?" Wilson asked.

"Yes, sir."

"That's good enough for me. When can you start?"

"I've been taking care of a homestead for my uncle. I will need to take care of some business on that and sell my cow," Cam explained.

"Will a week be enough time?" Mr. Wilson asked.

"I'm sure it will, sir. It may not take that long."

"Fine! I'll see you in a week, if not before. Report to me when you are ready, and I'll show you around," Mr. Wilson concluded and walked on into his office.

Cam was elated as he walked back to Dunn House. This would change things considerably. He would have a steady job. Now he could pay his way and even save some money for the future. Cam stopped walking and stood still.

"Nan," he muttered as he stared out across the wide expanse of the untamed St. John's River. Would he dare to hope that she cared for him as much as he loved her? What Leola had said this morning had spurred him on to believe that was possible, yet, it could have been Nan was just expressing interest in what he was doing.

Cam shook his head as if to rid himself of the doubt that threatened to extinguish the faint ray of hope in his heart. He determined the first chance he had alone with Nan he would declare his love for her. Now that he had a job, he could even ask her to marry him, he thought happily, continuing on toward the boardinghouse. When he came in, Harriet Dunn was in her office.

"How did it go, Cam?" she asked, looking up as he walked through the door.

"I've got the job. He gave me a week to close up the homestead. I'll need to get a letter off to Uncle George after a while. Right now, I'd better get started on the storehouse door."

"While you are at it, Cam, take a look at the roof. Leola said there was a leak in there the last rain."

Cam went to his room to change his shirt and then went out to get the tools. He found the door frame on the storehouse was rotted and splintered where the hinges were. He would have to go over to the lumber yard and get a new board to replace it. Since it was getting close to the noon hour, he decided to wait until after he had eaten to finish the job, choosing instead to fix the leak in the roof.

Nan and her father had not arrived when Cam took a seat at the table. In fact, Leola was already bringing in the food when they came in. Nan appeared in the doorway ahead of her father. She hesitated briefly when the circle of faces turned toward her with admiring glances. The dark hair framing the golden tan of her face was coiled and piled high on her head, held in place with combs. A light dew of perspiration lay across her lips. She wore a pink blouse tucked into a black skirt, which clung to her slender figure. Her eyes glowed as she took in those seated around the table. When her glance fell on Cam, he couldn't help but notice a slight start as she became aware of his presence.

Suddenly becoming shy, Nan slid into the empty chair opposite Cam, keeping her eyes lowered, hands folded in her lap.

Zachariah Sparks hung his hat on the rack and sat down at the end of the table.

"Hey there, Cam, what brings you into town?" he asked, beaming at his young friend.

"A couple of things," Cam replied quietly, hardly able to keep his eyes off Nan. "Supplies and some work for Miss Dunn."

Mr. Sparks nodded agreeably but made no further attempt at conversation as dishes of food were passed around the table.

While eating, Cam listened in on the talk at the other end of the table. Nan sat picking at her food without saying anything, and her father was engrossed in appeasing his appetite.

"Heard tell that job at the mill was taken by some young fella who just walked in and said he wanted it," commented Sam McCullough, who used to work there.

Cam held his breath, hoping he would not say more. He wanted to tell Nan himself.

"That so?" answered Jed Philips.

"Yep, some home- . . . ," McCullough halted midsentence as Leola came in with a tray of assorted pies and cakes, much to Cam's relief. Miss Dunn appeared to pour the coffee and replenish the water glasses.

One by one the guests finished their meal and filed out of the dining room leaving Cam, Nan, and her father at the table. Leola began busily removing the dishes, and Harriet Dunn sat down with a cup of coffee to chat with Zachariah Sparks.

Nan got up to walk out to the porch where she sat down in one of the many rocking chairs. Cam excused himself and followed her out. Fortunately none of the other guests came out to the porch. He took the chair next to Nan.

"Nan, I've been wanting to talk to you," he began in his direct manner. Nan turned her head to look at him. Her dark eyes were luminous and questioning.

"Nan . . . I have been thinking a lot about you . . . about us," he said, reaching to take her hand in his. She made no attempt to withdraw it. This gave him the courage to go on.

"Nan . . . what I am trying to say is . . . I care about you . . . I . . . I love you," Cam stammered. "I hope . . . you care for me or will come to love me. I want you to marry me."

Cam watched Nan's face anxiously as she lowered her eyes and pulled back her hand, sitting quiet for what seemed like an eternity, before she spoke.

"Cam . . . I am fond . . . I—I do care about you . . . I may even love you . . ." Her quavering voice trailed off into silence at hearing her father's footsteps coming through the door. She jumped to her feet and stood looking down the street, averting her face, trying to gain her composure.

Zachariah Sparks stomped out on the porch followed by Harriet Dunn, whose gaze took in Cam's troubled face and Nan's agitation. All this was lost on Nan's father, however, as he brushed past Nan to head toward the wagon.

"Come on, gal, we got a lot of runnin' around to do. I'll drop you off at the dry goods store and you can get what your ma wanted while I run by the feed store."

Nan dutifully followed him to climb in the wagon, tucking her skirt in around her. She didn't venture to look at Cam, who had followed them to the gate, until her father was busy coaxing the horse into action. When she did, what Cam saw expressed in her eyes both startled and thrilled him.

"Good-bye, Nan, I'll be out soon," he called to her, standing to watch until they were out of sight.

Harriet Dunn had discreetly gone back into the house. When Cam entered, she appeared to be busy in her office. She looked up as Cam came through the hall, but he gave her no notice, going into his room.

When he came out some time later, he had changed his shirt in preparation for work on the storehouse door. Stopping by her office Cam informed her that he was going to the hardware store and lumber yard and would be back shortly.

Harriet Dunn watched his tall, lean figure until he disappeared from sight, conscious of a nagging thought. Cam was lonely! He had reached a time in his life when family and friends could not fulfill the longing of his heart. It was the age-old instinct passed down through a long line of generations before him, the primeval urge to seek a mate, surging through his veins. The boy she had championed had become a man, virile and strong. He had fallen helplessly in love and would soon marry.

Her thoughts turned to the decisions she would have to make very soon. They could not be put off much longer. Colonel Stothard was pressing her to set a date for their wedding. She had been uncertain because of her concern for Cam, and too, what she should do with Dunn House.

Leola and Henry would soon marry, she was sure, but how would they make it without Leola's pay. Henry's odd jobs would not be enough. Decent work for a black man was scarce, and with the threat of a secret organization of men taking their warped idea of justice into their own hands, she could not desert them and leave them to their own resources.

Cam would have work at the mill, and if he and Nan were married they could room at Dunn House for a while . . . an idea began to beat its way into the foreground of her thinking. Why not turn Dunn House over to Cam and Nan after they were married!

Leola would be assured of a place to work and perhaps Cam could help Henry get on at the mill. Happy and pleased with her train of thought, she went back to work on the books.

15

CAM STRODE SWIFTLY ALONG the short distance to the hardware store. As he rounded the corner on Lemon Street, he came to an abrupt halt. Nan was in front of the dry goods shop talking with Clay Beardsley, her vivacious face turned up to his, hands gesturing. Cam could hear her familiar laughter.

Beardsley was dressed impeccably in a white suit and wore shining black boots. He held a cane in his hand. He presented a figure that would turn the head of any woman, and Nan appeared to be flattered by his attention to her.

From what Cam could tell, neither of them had noticed him standing there. He felt a rush of anger and something akin to jealousy as he watched Beardsley lean his handsome face toward Nan. Forceful strides brought him to where they stood. Taking Nan by the arm, he drew her away.

"Go into the store, Nan," Cam ordered in a quiet but firm voice, not taking his eyes off Beardsley. "You should not be talking with the likes of this man!"

"Cam, you have no right to interfere in my affairs!" Nan protested, her face growing white as she stared from one to the other.

Beardsley stood still, his face frozen into a sardonic smile, black eyes glittering with obvious satisfaction at this encounter.

Cam's blue eyes flashed with fire as they glared at Beardsley, his body stiff, his fists clenched, the blood pounding in his head. "Beardsley," he ground out in a tense voice, "you leave my girl alone! Don't you ever lay a hand on her!"

"Oh, so it's the little rooster again," Beardsley taunted, as he turned an insolent gaze on Nan.

Nan drew back farther into the doorway of the store as she saw her father's wagon round the corner toward them.

Zachariah Sparks took in the scene at a glance and drew his wagon to a hurried stop. He knew Cam would not stand a chance in a fight with Beardsley. The man was not to be trusted to fight fair. He jumped down and put himself between the two men.

"Hello, Beardsley!" he thundered. "When did you get back into town?"

From the doorway, Nan strained to hear what was being said as her father and Beardsley talked. Peering out, she noted that Beardsley backed up a step as her father advanced toward him with head thrust forward and fists threatening to strike. There was a scowl on Beardsley's face as he turned to walk stiffly up the street.

Nan picked up the things for her mother and went out to the wagon where she deposited them under the seat. She didn't look at Cam or her father.

"I'll be there in a minute, Nan," her father said, entering the store.

Cam came over to help Nan up to her seat in the wagon.

"Don't you touch me, Cam Fox!" Nan blazed at him. "You . . . you . . . oh!"

"Nan, please, I love you . . . I . . . I just didn't want my girl talking to a man like Beardsley. You don't understand!" Cam pleaded.

"Cam Fox, I am *not* your girl, and I wouldn't marry you if you were the last man on earth . . . you . . . you . . . home-steader!" she stormed at him.

Ignoring his outstretched hand, she climbed into the wagon and flounced down on the seat. She lifted her chin and stared away from him, her face resolute.

Cam was stunned at the furious onslaught. Her flashing dark eyes were full of scorn as she denounced him. He stepped back before the verbal attack, dropping his arm to his side, his face turned white.

Mr. Sparks came from the building and climbed grimly to his seat. Nan sat by his side, unyielding and indifferent. She did not look back. He gave a flip of the reins along the back of the horse and they were gone.

How long Cam stood and stared after them he did not know. Eventually, after father and daughter were long out of sight, his leadened feet carried him to the hardware store where he purchased the nails he needed and on to the lumber yard to pick up a board. The hurt inside was overwhelming. He felt as if he were in a daze. When at last he arrived back at Dunn House, Cam went directly to the storehouse and began feverishly working on the repairs. So intense were his thoughts, he did not hear Harriet Dunn approach.

"Cam," she called the third time, coming nearer.

She was shocked at the hurt she saw in his face as he swung around to confront her.

"Cam! What is it?" she exclaimed.

"I reckon nothing, ma'am," he managed to say, trying to smile. "I guess I took for granted something that wasn't there."

Harriet Dunn knew instinctively that Cam and Nan had quarreled. Perhaps worse. Nan had spurned Cam's declaration of love and proposal of marriage. Frowning at this prospect, she suddenly remembered the letter in her hand.

"Cam, this letter from your uncle came today. I thought I'd bring it to you and see how you were coming along on the door."

Cam dropped the hammer on the floor and took the letter. He opened it to find a short, brusque note, written in the manner Uncle George always did things. He had sold the homestead, he informed Cam, to a Mr. Beardsley who had come to see him, offering cash payment. He considered himself fortunate to be rid of the property since it was such poor land. Cam had 10 days from the receipt of the letter to remove his personal belongings.

Cam stared at the letter in his hand. All he had worked so hard for, Clay Beardsley now owned. He handed the note to Miss Dunn and turned away to lean against the wall of the building, trying to collect his whirling thoughts.

Uncle George had not taken the time to come down to see his property, so he would not know he had been misled into believing the land was worthless. Beardsley, no doubt, had simply walked into the store presenting himself as someone of importance in the area. Using his cunning wit, he had persuaded George Fox that his land was of little value.

His uncle could not have known who he was dealing with since Cam had not felt it necessary to inform him of his suspicions involving Beardsley. After all, they had not been able to prove anything.

Cam was convinced in his own mind that the purchase of the homestead was a direct blow to him personally and afforded the crooked land-grabber a great deal of satisfaction at having set Cam off the property—a satisfaction that would be short-lived when he found that Cam was leaving the homestead anyway.

He felt Harriet Dunn's firm grip on his shoulder as she stood quietly at his side.

"Cam, don't be bitter. Your life will take a new direction now. You are free of any obligation to your uncle, and you have a job at the mill. You have your own future ahead of you. Time heals all wounds," she said, trying to comfort him.

Cam sat down on the bench by the door, his head in his hands. Harriet Dunn sat beside him.

"You don't understand," he whispered hoarsely, giving her a troubled look. "Beardsley is after Nan." He went on to tell her about what had taken place on the street.

"Beardsley has taken the land I worked so hard to clear, and now he will try to get Nan. She will surely be in danger with him out riding around in those woods."

"Things look very dark to you right now, Cam, but Nan is square and honest. She will think over whatever she said to you and will want to make amends. You'll see. Just give her time to cool off. Women sometimes have a way of saying things they don't mean in a fit of passion," Miss Dunn asserted, going to Nan's defense.

Cam offered no reply, so she got up to walk back to the house. "I'll put this letter in your room," she said, pausing to give him one more concerned glance.

Cam got up and went back to work on the door, grateful for something to occupy his mind. He could probably start at the mill in a couple of days if he rode out to the homestead and removed his possessions tomorrow.

Harriet Dunn placed the letter on the stand in Cam's room and went to find Leola. She was in the linen room folding the wash.

"Leola, when Henry comes tell him it's urgent that I talk with him."

"Yes'm, Miss Harriet. He should be back this evenin'."

"Good. I want to talk with him privately. Can you arrange that?"

"Yes'm, yo' can meet in the storehouse. I'll keep watch."

Harriet Dunn returned to the kitchen where she stood watching Cam from the window. Long curls of shaved wood fell to the ground as he planed the door to fit smoothly against the new board. His shirt was wet with perspiration as he worked in the heat.

What Cam had told her was very disturbing. Clay Beardsley's intense hatred for Cam was becoming a personal vengeance, far beyond a land-grabbing opportunity, and could only mean harm to him. Beardsley's encounter with Nan was certainly not just a coincidence, Harriet Dunn concluded, although she had to admit, Nan's dark beauty would attract any man's attention.

It was some relief to know that Zachariah Sparks had been made aware of Beardsley's sinister plots and reputation with women. From what Cam had told her of Sparks' reaction to what had taken place today, he would certainly try to hold Nan in check, if that was possible. Nan was pretty headstrong.

However, Zachariah probably did not know that Beardsley had gained ownership of Cam's homestead and that it would not be safe for Nan to ride off alone as she often did. Miss Dunn decided to send a message of warning out to Mr. Sparks.

Cam opened and closed the door several times to make sure it wasn't binding against the molding. With a grunt of satisfaction, he picked up the tools and put them away. After he cleaned up the chips, he threw the old board on the woodpile and went into his room to wash up.

Hanging his shirt on the chair, he stretched facedown on the bed. The incident with Clay Beardsley and Nan kept running through his mind. The vision of Beardsley's smiling face leaning down to Nan's rekindled the anger deep within him.

Beardsley was a handsome, dashing figure of a man and could turn any girl's head with his smooth talk. Nan had been flattered by his attention. The fact that he was much older than she would not affect Nan's thinking. Her father was a great deal older than her mother.

Watching the two of them standing there laughing had been more than Cam could stand. It was Beardsley's obvious interest in Nan that had triggered his rude behavior, Cam reasoned in his own defense—he was only trying to protect Nan.

Even as he thought it, Cam knew in his heart it wasn't true. He had reacted like a jealous lover, thrusting Nan aside, treating her rudely, and standing there like the "rooster" Beardsley had called him.

He recalled what his mother had said many times: "Cam, when you let someone else's behavior dictate your own, you have lost control of your actions and are no better than they."

Realizing it was his own fault that Nan was angry with him, Cam felt ashamed of the childish way he had treated her. What right did he have to call her his girl? She had made no commitment to him and was free to talk to anyone she chose. He owed her an apology and when the time was right, he would make amends and face the fact that he had been wrong.

Cam remained prostrate on the bed, coming to grips with his emotions and the chaotic imagination of his mind. Finally, the storm in his soul subsided and he sat up on the side of the bed worn and spent. Night had replaced the day, and the room was dark. He fumbled for matches and lit the lamp with unsteady hands. Wearily he removed his boots.

His mother's Bible was on the table where he had left it the night before. The cover was frayed, showing long years of use. Cam stared at it thoughtfully. She had often said that the Bible held the answers to all man's difficulties and needs. He heaved a long sigh. If only there was an easy answer to his problem.

Reaching for the book, he opened to the middle, intending to continue reading where he had left off. He was about to turn the page when a notation his mother had made caught his attention. "Forgive me, God, that I may be pure in Your sight. The end is near. Please don't let me do anything wrong." It was written above the 51st psalm. Cam read the entire psalm, going back to read the 10th verse again. "Create in me a clean heart, O God; and renew a right spirit within me."

Bowing his head, he searched his soul. He had always been honest, truthful, never taking God's name in vain or using profanity. What was it he lacked? He had always treated others with respect. "But you didn't have respect for Nan's feelings today," came an accusing inner voice. Cam's spirit wilted before the incriminating charge. Restlessly he closed the book and put it aside. A strong knock at his door startled him. He opened it to find Leola standing there with a plate of food in her hand.

"Mista Cam, Miss Harriet said I should be bringin' yo' some food, since yo' didn't come fo' yo' suppa," she said, her round eyes peering at him in the dim light. "Is yo' all right, Mista Cam?"

"I'm all right, Leola," Cam responded slowly, taking the plate from her.

"Does yo' want sumpin' to drink, Mista Cam?"

Cam stood staring at her and didn't respond to her question, the plate forgotten in his grasp.

"Mista Cam, are yo' sure yo' is all right?" Leola queried, concern evident in her voice.

"Leola, what does the Bible mean when it says, 'Create in me a clean heart . . . and renew a right spirit within me'?" Cam asked, giving no indication he had even heard her.

"I don' know, Mista Cam," Leola answered, thinking for a moment. "I think it means, if yo' has done wrong, you should ask forgiveness and let the Lawd do the rest. Has yo' done wrong, Mista Cam?"

"I . . . I think so. . . ."

"Well, yo' is on the right track," she encouraged, shaking her head.

"I'll bring yo' that drink."

Cam left the door ajar and sat down on the bed to eat. Surprisingly, he found he was hungry.

"At least that part of me is normal," he mused to himself. "A man would have to be dead not to enjoy Leola's cooking."

She returned with his drink and closed the door softly after her as she left. Hesitating outside his door, Leola stood in the dimly lit hall, her brow furrowed with worry.

"Sumpin' is really botherin' Mista Cam," she reflected out loud. "It must have sumpin' to do with that letter Miss Harriet gave him today."

She hurried on to the kitchen to finish the few tasks left to do. Henry would be by pretty soon. She would find out from him.

* * *

Cam had just finished his breakfast and was sitting there staring glumly out the window when Henry appeared out of the heavy morning fog, riding up to the back gate.

"Hey there, Henry, come on to the house and sit a spell. I'll get yo' sumpin' to eat!" Leola sang out to him from the window.

"Hey there, yo'sef, woman, I'm a comin'," Henry answered in mock derision as he slid from the saddle and tossed his rein over the gatepost.

Cam pushed back his chair, took up his cup, and went out to join his friend. He sat on the floor and leaned back against the wall, sipping his coffee.

"Where you headed this early in the morning, Henry?" Cam inquired as the broad-shouldered man perched himself on the edge of the porch, removing his hat to lay it beside where he sat.

"Well, I kinda figured I'd ride back out with yo' this mawnin'. Don' have much a doin' the next coupla days. Was thinkin' maybe to get out fishin' with yo' this evenin'," Henry replied innocently, as Cam gave him a curious look.

"All that riding for a little fishing, Henry? You could do that right here in the river or out on Dunn's Creek."

"I know, Mista Cam, but I heard them fish over in that creek emptyin' into Lake Delancy is a bitin' their heads off. Iffen we gotta chance, maybe we could ride over that way and check on it," Henry insisted, scraping the sand with his boot.

"Can't do it this week," Cam chuckled. "We'll have to give it a try later. I've got to rent a wagon and move my things out of the homestead today. My uncle sold the land to Clay Beardsley."

"Beardsley!" Henry exclaimed with pretended dismay, not lost to Cam.

"Henry, you're not a very good actor. What's the real reason you came to ride out with me? Does Miss Dunn have something to do with this?"

"I gave my word not to tell," Henry responded indirectly.

"Uh huh, well, whatever the reason, I'll be glad to have you along. There might be some unlikely varmints running around out there in those woods again. No use for you to ride your mule out there. You can ride in the wagon with me, unless you're going to stay over at Sparkses." Cam felt a twinge of pain as he spoke the name.

"Naw, I was a goin' to ride out and back with yo' just in case yo' was needin' some hep," Henry offered.

Cam nodded his head. Drinking the last of his coffee, he set the cup down and slipped off the porch.

"Give that cup to Leola, Henry. I'll get Dandy and go on down to the livery to pick up the wagon while you're eating. We'll have to hurry a little going out, because it will be slow coming back with the cow and calf following along behind. I'll be back in a little bit to pick you up."

The morning fog had lifted when Cam drove up in the wagon to get Henry, who was waiting out front of Dunn House. At first, Dandy had not been happy about being hitched to a wagon. Now he pranced in anticipation, starting off at a fast trot, slowing only when he reached the turnoff into the trail leading through the woods. Cam let the reins hang loosely in his hands, giving Dandy the freedom to choose his own pace. The strong horse didn't falter even when the wheels sank in the loose sand of the trail.

Neither man made any attempt at conversation. Each sat silent and watchful, engrossed in his own thoughts as the wagon creaked and bumped along. To Cam, the forest suddenly seemed a lonely place. No longer was there any desire in him to be a homesteader. Perhaps someday, a farm near town would be nice. He liked to grow things and work with his hands. He would work and save his money. If all went well, he could probably start his job at the mill tomorrow or the next day.

"Mista Cam, when you figgerin' to start at the mill?" Henry asked, breaking the silence.

"Soon as I can sell my cow and calf and dispose of the rest of the things, I reckon."

"I know a man that's lookin' for a good milk cow . . . don't know about the calf though. He lives about three miles out on the Springside road. I'll ride out there and see him if yo' want me to," Henry offered. "Yo' want to sell the feed too?"

"I need to sell it all, except the things the Sparkses sent over. If you don't mind, you can return those for me when you're riding out that way. The rest goes back to Miss Dunn."

They were not far from the cabin when Brindle heard them and came running to greet them, jumping up at the side of the wagon, her ears flapping. Cam pulled Dandy to a halt and helped her up to the seat between them. She barked noisily at Dandy to get started. He didn't need urging, however, for he took off so abruptly it nearly unseated them all.

Cam backed the wagon up to the door of the log house and tied the reins to a limb of the live oak tree. It didn't take long for them to load up what was there. While Cam carried the sacks of grain to the wagon, Henry fixed a rope around the neck of the mother cow and led her to the rear to tie her securely to the tailgate. The calf would follow.

When all was ready for the trip back, Cam gave one last look around, calling to Brindle. "Come on, Brindle, you get to go this time," he said, lifting her up to the seat as he climbed up beside her.

They left the yard slowly, watching for the calf to get the idea that it should follow its mother. Progress was slow at first, but soon they were able to pick up the gait. Cam didn't look back—ahead lay a whole new life.

16

Nan RODE AWAY BESIDE HER FATHER in silent fury, her back ramrod straight. She did not look back at Cam standing there in the street. Her father kept the horse moving quickly along and soon the town lay far behind them. Neither spoke. It was only when her father slowed the wagon to turn the horse off the main road into the worn, sandy ruts of the trail leading through the woods that Nan ventured to glance at her father. His stern expression had not softened. She knew by the set of his jaw he was upset.

The heavy load of feed for the animals had slowed their progress along the sandy roads, making what had always been a pleasurable trip seem long and tiring. Daylight had faded into darkness when the wagon rolled to a stop in front of the barn.

Without a word, Nan jumped nimbly to the ground, gathered up the parcels for her mother, and carried them into the house. Her mother was in the kitchen, putting some sticks of wood in the fire to warm up their food. She looked up when Nan entered the door, her tired face brightening.

"You're later than usual, Nan, any trouble?"

"No, Ma, just a heavy load. Are the children already in bed?" Nan asked, changing the subject.

Mrs. Sparks drew the pot of food over the fire to heat, then turned to look at her daughter, noticing the paleness of Nan's face.

"Are you all right?"

"Yes, Ma, just tired is all," Nan answered impatiently, turning to unload her arms on a chair. She heard her father's footsteps on the porch and quickly slipped into her seat at the table.

While they sat waiting for Mrs. Sparks to bring the food to the table, Nan could feel her father's eyes upon her. She kept her face turned toward where her mother was dishing up their supper, not daring to look at him.

The meal was a strained affair, with her father saying little except to answer her mother's questions. Nan sat quietly toying with the food on her plate, making no comment. Twice she had caught her father glancing at her with that strange, thoughtful look.

Mrs. Sparks, sensing that something had happened, went back to her work, pausing to study the two of them with a troubled expression. Nan ate very little, escaping to her room up under the eaves as soon as possible. There she sat staring blindly out the window. She was still smarting over Cam's egotistical treatment of her earlier. She had not seen him coming and was totally surprised and shocked when he had taken her by the arm. His strong, tense grip had hurt as he pulled her back. The nerve of him! But what could you expect from a . . . a homesteader. He would pay for this.

Nan rested her head on her hands, giving little heed to the cool night breeze or the shining stars overhead. Brooding over the events of the day, she felt almost consumed by the turbulent emotions raging within her. When her father had left her at the store, she had taken her mother's list in to the clerk. While waiting for him to fill the order she had restlessly wandered from the stuffy store to get some air. Standing there on the street she had seen the man in white emerge from the courthouse and start up the walk toward her. Fascinated by his good looks, Nan had not realized she was staring at him, until suddenly there he was before her bowing slightly, a smile breaking across his dark, handsome face.

"I must admit I am unaccustomed to a beautiful woman staring at me. It is usually the other way around," he teased, his black eyes flashing with an inner fire.

Nan felt the heat come into her face as she remembered that moment. She had laughed up at him to hide her confusion and embarrassment at being caught, a red tide surging into her face.

It was then she had felt Cam's firm grasp drawing her back. Why he had been so angry, she couldn't understand. He had never objected to her talking to Joey and the others. Why had he confronted this man in such a defiant manner? It had all been so innocent on her part. However, Nan had to admit she was flattered by the compliment from the dashing older man. She wondered who he was. He must be wealthy . . . the clothes he wore were expensive.

Dreamily she saw herself in a beautiful pink gown riding by the side of the man in white. People along the street turned their heads to look at the comely couple in the black, shiny surrey. A long sigh came from her lips as the vision vanished and reality returned.

Turning away from the window, Nan undressed in the dark and sought her bed where she remained wide-eyed, listening to the sound of her father and mother talking in the room below.

Presently, there was the scrape of a chair and she heard her father's footsteps on the narrow stairs leading to her room.

"Nan," he called with a gruff voice, "are you awake?"

"Yes, Pa, I'm in bed, but I'm awake. Wait, I'll light the lamp."

"Cover up, I want to talk to you."

"It's all right, Pa, you can come on up," Nan said, replacing the globe on the lamp and getting back in bed to pull the sheet over her.

His bulky presence filled the small room. Stooping to keep from hitting his head on the rafters, he stood looking at her with that strange look on his face. He brushed his hand across his eyes and reached for the small chair by the window, pulling it over to sit by the side of her bed.

"Nan," he began in a strained voice, "not until today did I realize how much you had growed up. You are a woman now. I suppose soon you'll be a marryin'," he paused, "but not to the likes of Clay Beardsley if I kin help it." His voice broke with emotion.

"Nan, he's not a man of good reputation. You . . . you would not be safe in his company. Do you understand what I'm trying to say, gal?"

"I . . . I think so, Pa," Nan stammered.

"What Cam did today was for your good. You gotta understand that, gal. The boy loves you!" he said explosively.

"But he was so rude, Pa, and he humiliated me!" she cried.

"Be that as it may, gal, but I don't want to see you talking to Clay Beardsley again, you hear?" Mr. Sparks said in a stern voice. "He is a dangerous man."

He put a hand on each knee and raised himself to his feet, pushing the chair back. Walking to the head of the stairs, he turned to look back at her.

"Get some sleep, gal," he said gently, and he was gone with a heavy tread.

Nan blew out the lamp and climbed back in bed, grateful for the darkness. Her father's concern had touched her heart. She knew he was right. In times like these in the South, no decent man would have made such an overture to a young woman on the street.

"Even if that young woman was staring boldly at him?" her conscience accused her.

Nan's face burned with shame as she realized she was partly to blame for his advances. What must the people who were in the store think of her? Two men almost at blows over her there in the street!

The vision of Cam standing there in her defense, fists clenched and blue eyes blazing, generated a new and strange emotion she tried to deny.

She had always liked Cam. He was different from the young men Nan had grown up with—better educated, more mannerly. She had found his directness rather disconcerting at times, but she preferred that over deceit.

Nan recalled the day he had kissed her there in the woods. Cam had not meant to insult her, it was just something that happened. She had fled rather than let him know how much his action had affected her. She had avoided being alone with him after that because she did not want to fall in love with him and be doomed to a life of homesteading.

Yet in her heart, Nan knew it was hopeless. Whenever Cam was around, she had felt his adoring eyes upon her. She had denied her feelings for him, trying not to encourage him in any way. After all, he had nothing of his own, even the land he lived on belonged to his uncle.

Nan sat up in the bed with her arms around her knees and gazed out the window again. The stars still gave off a dim glow, although there was a low rumble of an approaching storm.

Cam's stricken face as he stood there in the street appeared before her. The pain she had seen in his eyes was as if she had fired a bullet into his heart. Nan had not cared at the time that she had hurt him deeply. She stretched out again in her bed and turned to bury her face in the pillow. What had she done? Cam had acted only out of love for her. Shaken and wretched, tears came to her rescue. In the hours of distress that followed, one growing resolution took hold, and she slept.

* * *

Three weeks had passed and Nan had not seen or heard from Cam. Her anger had long since subsided, replaced with a longing to see him, to know he was all right. He had not been back to the little church. That worried her.

Sitting there in the shade under the chinaberry tree, her lap full of peas she had picked for her mother, Nan stared out across the fields to where the road entered the woods. Who she was watching for, she didn't know.

Remembering her mother wanted the peas for supper, she slowly began the task of shelling again, finding it hard to keep her eyes from searching out the road as she looked up from her work.

Nan had just finished shelling the last of the peas and was emptying the hulls from her apron into a bucket when she heard Henry's call from the edge of the woods. Her heart leaped with gladness as she shaded her eyes to look down the road at him, then she picked up the peas and took them into the kitchen and left them on the table. Her mother was in the other part of the house. She could hear her talking to the younger ones, who were getting up from their nap.

Nan stood in the doorway of the kitchen to watch Henry ride up to the barnyard gate. Her father came striding in from the field to meet him. The two men talked for a moment, but Nan could not make out anything they said.

Henry untied a sack from the pommel of his saddle and handed it to her father, who opened it to look inside. Nodding his great shaggy head, Sparks laid it on the ground. With a look toward the house, he drew Henry around the barn out of sight.

Nan's curiosity about the bag gave way to a sense of foreboding when she saw the scowl on her father's face. Obviously he didn't want their conversation overheard. Why else did he take Henry aside.

Quietly, she slipped out to where she had left the bucket of hulls. Picking it up, she went to the barn to pour the hulls to the animals as her father had instructed her. He would not think much about it if she got caught coming from there.

Once inside, she put the pail down and crept to the other side where she heard the murmur of voices.

"Yes suh, Miss Dunn wanted me to warn yo' that it ain't safe for Miss Nan to be ridin' out alone no mo'. Since that land-grabbin' scalawag don' gone an' got Mista Cam's homestead, there's some mighty rough men out 'n these woods."

"How's Cam taking it?" Mr. Sparks asked.

"Oh, Mista Cam, he's a doin' fine. I don' see much of him 'ceptin' at night. He sleeps most all day," Henry replied, as she heard them moving away.

Nan hurried back to where she had placed the bucket of hulls. Quickly she emptied the contents into the feed box and ran out. She had barely made the safety of the porch when the two came around the corner of the building. Mr. Sparks stooped to pick up the bag and brought it to Nan.

"Here," he said, "give these to your ma, and see if there's any coffee left in the pot."

Nan carried the heavy sack inside the kitchen, setting it down with a clank, then went to see about the coffee. She knew without looking that Henry had brought back the things they had given Cam when he had started homesteading. Her heart was heavy as she warmed the coffee and took some to the men waiting on the porch. Her hand shook as she handed Henry his cup. He looked up at her curiously, taking note of her white face and troubled eyes.

"Aftuhnoon, Miss Nan," he said congenially. "Fine day, ain't it?"

Nan smiled and nodded in the affirmative, afraid to speak for fear of revealing the tears so near the surface.

"Uh huh," he mused to himself, "Miss Nan has don' gone and got hersef a heart full o' trouble."

"Yes suh, I jus' thought I'd better ride out and let y'all know about Mista Cam," Henry said aloud, unperturbed by the warning glance Mr. Sparks shot at him.

"He's doin' all right, considerin' him havin' to move offen his homestead 'n all. Sho he's been some heartbroke lately, moonin' round down at the mill, not sayin' much . . ."

Henry ceased speaking as Nan fled into the house leaving her father to stare blankly after her.

"Mista Sparks," Henry stated, "that girl's gotta heap a heart trouble . . . she loves that boy iffen she knows it or not, and I know he's a pinin' away over her!" Henry set his cup down and stepped to the ground.

"Well, I'll be ridin' on, Mista Sparks. I'm a thankin' yo' fo' the coffee. Let me know if yo' is a wantin' hep with clearin' them stumps," Henry offered, walking off to mount his mule.

"All right, Henry, give my regards to Cam and Harriet. I'll be comin' into town soon; I'm 'bout out of feed," Sparks called after him.

"Yes, suh, sho will, Mista Sparks," Henry responded with a wave of his hand.

Nan didn't stop until she reached the privacy of her room, where she flung herself facedown across the bed. Her trembling hand clutched the pillow and drew it to her. Tears of relief flooded her eyes. Henry's last remark, which she knew was for her alone, had released a flood of emotion within her.

Somehow, Clay Beardsley had taken over the homestead, forcing Cam to move. That would explain why Cam had not been back to church. He was probably staying in town at Dunn House. Poor Cam! All he had worked for, gone!

"Even *you* failed him" came an accusing voice from within her. Anguish and heartbreaking loss swept over her as she faced the charge. Surely her heart would break. Surely she would die.

"O God, please forgive me and help me," Nan sobbed, as she surrendered all the pent-up feelings she had struggled with for three weeks. "My hope, my faith, have failed me!" Wave after wave of emotion threatened to engulf her as she reached out to God for help. At last she lay breathless and spent as a quiet resolve came into her heart.

Henry had said Cam was all right. She would cling to that hope, and when Pa went into town, she would go with him. She turned over on her back and stared at the ceiling in wonder.

Oh, dear Lord, I'm done for. I love him! Nan thought, wiping the tears from her eyes.

17

$\mathcal{A}$ DIM LIGHT GLOWED from the small window of the night watchman's shack. Inside a forlorn figure sat with his feet propped up on a chair, eating a sandwich. Furnishings were scarce, consisting of two chairs and a wobbly table. A lantern hung on a hook suspended from the ceiling. A dog padded in from the dark to sit by his side, tail wagging, hoping for a share.

"What is it you want, Brindle?" Cam asked, as the dog rested her head on his leg, looking with hungry eyes from the food in his hand to his face. "You want your share?"

Brindle gave an affirmative bark, sitting back to wait for one of the three sandwiches Cam always insisted Leola pack for him.

"Don' know where you put all this food!" she would grumble.

Unwrapping the bread and meat, he placed it on the floor for Brindle, watching as it disappeared in several gulps. Cam was grateful to have her for company through the long, dark nights.

Lately, Henry had been dropping by for a while, sometimes walking with Cam as he patrolled the lonely aisles between the large stacks of drying lumber. He wondered about this but didn't question Henry on it. He was glad to have his friend to talk to. It was with Henry's help that Cam had been able to sell his livestock, putting the money into a savings account at the bank. Each week he watched the amount grow as he put aside a portion of his salary.

Cam moved his feet to the floor, giving a glance up at the clock on the wall. He would have time to read for a while before his next walk-through. Cleaning up the crumbs Brindle had left, he took a book from his pocket and drew his chair closer to the light. He had been reading for only a few minutes when Brindle raised her head and gave a low woof. She got up and walked to the door to stand, sniffing the air.

"What is it, gal?" Cam asked, laying aside his book to take down the lantern.

Brindle gave off another low bark and took off down the wooden walkway leading into the docks of lumber stretched out into the water. Cam ran after her as she turned off into the center of the stacks. He could hear her excited yelps. When he reached her side he held his hand on her nose to quiet her. He could hear hurried footsteps retreating in the dark. Whoever had been there was gone. "Come on, gal, it was probably someone wanting to do a little night fishing."

Just to be sure, Cam decided to patrol every dock to be satisfied that all was secure. The first day he was on the job, Mr. Wilson had stressed the importance of keeping fishermen off the heavily loaded docks. It was dangerous enough for those who knew where to walk, Wilson had told Cam. Others could unknowingly step on a bad board and fall through to the snake-infested hyacinths below—something Cam did not particularly care to think about as he made his rounds.

When he got back to his shack, Henry was waiting there in the dark. Brindle ran to him, jumping up in greeting.

"What was that all about?" he asked Cam.

"Must have been somebody trying to sneak in for a little night fishing," Cam answered, going in to set the lantern on the table. Henry followed him into the little room. Taking a chair, he sat down, leaning it against the wall. His dark face glistened in the light. He had a worried look on his face.

"I don' know, Mista Cam, I don' like it. Somepin' ain't right!"

"What are you trying to say, Henry?" Cam asked, looking up from where he was petting Brindle.

"Well, I didn' want to say anythin' 'bout it 'cause I thought mebbe there wasn't nothin' to it, but when I was a leavin' the night fo' last, I saw somebody a sneakin' out from them piles of lumber. I tried to foller 'im but lost sight of 'im."

"Do you think there's trouble afoot?" Cam queried, watching his friend carefully.

"I'm not sho . . . yo' might want to keep yo' eyes open, mebbe make yo' rounds mo' often," Henry admonished.

The two talked on for more than an hour before Henry stood up and stretched.

"Reckon I'll mosey on. Jes' you be careful, friend," he said as he faded into the darkness outside, stopping to listen to the sounds of the night.

"Yo' make a pretty good target sittin' there in the light," he said in a low voice, and he was gone.

When Henry reached the street he stood for a moment thinking about the unknown visitor Brindle had chased from the docks. Could it be the same man he had seen? If so, what was he doing there? He decided it was time to do more watching out there at night. He would go fishing up that way tomorrow and see if he could get in by boat without Cam knowing.

Moving on out of the shadows, Henry carefully made his way up the back streets toward Dunn House. It wasn't safe for a black man to be found roaming around at that hour of the night.

After Henry was gone, Cam pondered over the casual admonition. Perhaps he should pay more attention to his actions. He made the decision to change his direction each time he made his rounds, going at a different hour.

Brindle nudged close, laying her head on his lap. The night was clear and cool, the stars gave off their dim light in the early, predawn sky. The sound of the night creatures beat off a rhythmic concert as if to herald the break of day. He heard the splash of a fish breaking the surface of the water after some morsel of food. A pinpoint of light appeared, moving slowly downriver. An early fisherman was setting out to check his traps.

As Cam kept his lonely vigil, the haunting specter of Nan's lovely face and dark, shining eyes floated before him. He had not seen nor heard from her since that day on the street. He knew Henry had been out to see them, because the bag containing their things was gone. Cam had not asked if he had seen Nan.

The memory of that moment in the woods, when his lips had first met hers, returned with all its poignant sweetness. Her face near his had been warm and inviting, her eyes full of wonder. A longing to see her swept over him so forcibly that he bowed, shaken before the onslaught. Miss Dunn had said that time would heal, but his love for Nan had grown deeper with each passing day. No longer was it the intense, passionate love of a youth for a mate, but a more self-sacrificing, compassionate caring. In this knowledge he would seek the strength to go on. He had been selfish to think his love for Nan was all that mattered. What right did he have to be jealous of someone else who could make her happy? Wasn't her happiness what he wanted too?

"O God, help me," Cam moaned, as he succumbed to the weakness he felt within his own flesh. "I cannot go on without Your presence in my life. Be my Father! Give me a faith that will hold me steady and give me peace."

When Cam lifted his head the first slanting rays of the sun were lighting the morning sky with a rosy hue. A quiet spirit of wholeness settled down over him as he sat watching the sunrise. Gone was the awkward, uncertain boy. Ahead lay a new direction and a new life! He was now a man and must bear the responsibilities of that manhood. He was at one with himself, the universe, and the Father!

A blue heron flew in to land on a post sticking up out of the water nearby, spreading its wings to catch the early warmth of the sun. Brindle got lazily to her feet to sniff at the big bird.

"Come on, Brindle, leave it alone. It's time to go," Cam said, and he walked back to the watchman's quarters. Blowing out the light, he hung the lantern on the hook over the table. The day watch would be coming soon.

* * *

A furtive figure made its way along the street in the dark, turning often to peer over his shoulder to see if anyone was following. Stopping at a small house uphill from the river, the figure paused once more to listen, fading into the shadows. Satisfied that no one had detected his movement, the man stepped up to tap on the door until he heard scuffling sounds in the room on the other side. A dim light glowed through the window.

"Who is it?" a hushed feminine voice called through the entrance.

"Digger. Let me in," he whispered hoarsely.

A key grated in the lock, and he slid noiselessly through the door. A buxom woman in her late 30s stood back to let him in. Red hair tumbled to her shoulders, dark eyes in a white face looked at the intruder with disgust.

"Digger, what are you doing here? You're supposed to be . . ."

"Don't say it!" Digger hissed, closing the door softly behind him, relaxing only when he heard the click of the latch.

"What went wrong?" she persisted.

"He didn't say nothin' 'bout there being a dog out there!" Digger growled, removing his hat to reveal a scowling dark visage. "It's gonna take more 'n one man to pull this job off. You tell him that! You hear? I'm not riskin' my skin for nobody! You tell him that!"

Digger jammed his hat angrily on his head. "You know where to find me. Now blow out that lamp!"

He waited for her to comply, then let himself out. He stood in the night, listening for a moment before moving off toward the river.

* * *

Clay Beardsley had just finished pulling on his shiny black boots when there was a tap on his door. He frowned with annoyance as he put on his coat to hide the revolver he wore in a shoulder holster. Answering the knock, he found a small boy in the hall with a message in his hand. Beardsley gave him a coin and turned back into the room, pushing the door shut with his foot.

As he read the note written in a woman's hand, a scowl appeared on his handsome face.

"The bungling idiot. Couldn't even set a simple fire," he muttered. "I'll have to take care of it myself."

He picked up his hat and left the room, turning the key in the lock. He would think about it over breakfast.

Beardsley descended the wide stairway, his eyes scanning the lobby below. Other than two men leisurely reading newspapers, it seemed deserted. The desk clerk was sorting the mail and putting the letters in the slots behind him.

He looked up with a nod of greeting as Beardsley stopped to pick up a paper.

"Good morning, Mr. Beardsley," he said pleasantly, pushing his spectacles back up on his nose. He glanced up at the clock. "You're right on time for breakfast, sir."

"I like to be punctual, Mr. Berry," Beardsley responded, satisfied with the clerk's observation.

He now recognized the importance of establishing routines and impressing them in the minds of other people since that close brush with the colonel's men. A man couldn't be too careful. He might need a good alibi.

Beardsley folded the paper without looking at it and sauntered into the hotel dining room. He was irritated when he saw someone else sitting at the table he always used—an issue he took up with the waiter in short order, passing him a sizable tip. For this morning, he would have to sit at a nearby table, but he was assured it would not happen again. The waiter served his coffee and he sat sipping it leisurely, his mind actively at work while waiting for his breakfast.

Things had been going well for him lately. He was beginning to gain some respect in the community by dressing well and living the lavish life-style of a successful businessman. It was easy to get people to forget when you started flashing money around.

Through his cleverness, he had outwitted George Fox up in Norwalk, passing himself off as a wealthy landowner from the South in town to visit a relative. When Mr. Fox had invited him home for dinner, he had carefully manipulated the conversation to talk about his fat holdings in Florida. Beardsley grinned with self-satisfaction at how well he had played his part. Faking dismay, he had declined to answer when they had asked if he knew anything about the property they held. But, at Mrs. Fox's insistence, he had finally admitted he had knowledge of the parcel. It was then he had painted a rather dismal picture of the land, describing it as mostly undrainable swamp with some high ground, full of snakes and mosquitoes.

"There's some young fella living out there, but they say he isn't worth much—too lazy to work," he had informed them, noting Mrs. Fox's triumphant look at her husband.

Beardsley had shown proper regret at learning that Cam was their nephew. And when he had left there that evening, they were practically begging him to take the land off their hands. He had waited a couple of days, however, to avoid suspicion, saying he wanted to think about it. It was a pretty good piece of work.

The waiter brought his breakfast and refilled his cup. Beardsley ate slowly and thoughtfully. He held deed to quite a lot of land now, with good stands of pine on it. If there was a good market for pine, he could start up a mill and produce lumber. Then when the land was cleared, he could turn some cattle in there. But, of course, the cypress mill would have to be reckoned with. Cypress was so hard to snake out of the swamps with mules, and if it was no longer plentiful, people would turn to the more available pine.

Pleased with his line of thought, Beardsley pushed back his plate and sat drumming his fingers on the table. Suddenly, an evil plan began to formulate in his mind. Since he had planned to start a small fire at the mill that would focus the blame on Cam, why not make it a bigger fire and burn the whole place down!

He would begin by laying the groundwork to discredit Cam, perhaps planting the suspicion that he had a drinking habit. Yes, that was it! They could plant a few empty whiskey bottles around out at the mill. Then the night of the fire, they could overpower Cam and douse him with liquor and who would know.

Satisfied with the plan, Beardsley picked up his paper and casually strolled out to the street. He would go see Belle tonight. She could get the boys together for a meeting. If Digger didn't want to be a part of it, he would simply have to take care of him. Stepping out into the bright sunlight, he headed for the mill.

* * *

That night Cam was returning from his second round through the maze of lumber when a familiar voice came from the darkness.

"Iffen I was yo' enemy, my frien', yo'd be a goner."

"Oh no, my friend, Brindle knew you were there," Cam replied, mimicking Henry. He set the lantern down on a post out on the dock and motioned for Henry to join him in the dark shack.

When Henry slipped in a moment later, Cam could see his dim outline as he seated himself on the floor.

"I've had some second thoughts about what happened last night, Henry," Cam said in a low voice. "After you left, I went back to look over the area where Brindle spotted that intruder. There was nothing there except a newspaper stuck on a board. I didn't think much about it at the time . . . figured the wind blew it there. But, this morning, I got to thinking it over and I realized that if the wind blew that paper there it would be yellowed or faded. It was neither. That newspaper had been carried there fresh from someone's house."

"Uh, huh," Henry grunted. "'Pears like somebody's wantin' to start hissef a fire, but Brindle is messin' up the act."

"Why would anyone want to do that?"

"Fo' one thing, Mista Cam, not ever'body in this here town likes yo'. Best yo' be careful and don' go rushin' out in them dark places so fast."

"I've thought of that, Henry," Cam said slowly, remaining quiet for a moment.

"Henry," he said finally, "I'd appreciate you not telling this to Harriet Dunn. No use worrying her. Don't even tell Leola."

"All right, Mista Cam, but yo' know how hard it is to keep anything from yo' woman."

"No, don't reckon I do, Henry," Cam chuckled.

Henry got to his feet. "Cain't stay long," he said in a matter-of-fact tone. "It ain't safe fo' me no mo' to be out on the streets of a night. A fella got caught out a coupla days ago. Some folks found him floating in the river, tarred and feathered. Iffen yo' will, take that lantern off someplace and I'll be a goin'."

As Cam obliged, Henry turned up his coat collar and pulled his hat low over his face before stepping out to move along the dock to where he had left his boat tied under one of the piers.

* * *

Hiram Wilson stared across the desk at his day watchman standing there before him, an empty whiskey bottle in his hand. In his judgment of men, he had never been overly impressed with this man. He was dependable enough on the job but had the habit of pointing out the weaknesses of the other workers in a childish, tattletale way. This time he was especially irritated at his accusation.

"Stevens, how do you know that Cam left that bottle there?" he said sharply, eyeing the man with an intense gaze.

"Well . . . uh . . . I don't know for sure. But who else could have put it in the shack! I came on duty and we talked for a minute, 'n he left," Stevens declared hotly, the blood rushing to his angular face, his narrowed glance darting around the room. This wasn't going as easy as he thought it would. He stood there uncertain of what to say next.

"Take that bottle and get out of here!" Wilson ordered in disgust, hitting his fist on the desk.

The startled Stevens beat a hasty retreat, leaving Mr. Wilson glaring after him. Leaning back in his chair, Hiram Wilson sat deep in thought. He couldn't have been wrong about Cam. That boy looked you right in the eye and had a direct, open honesty you could trust.

He got to his feet and walked to the window, thrusting his hands deep into his pockets. There was something going on here that made him uneasy. The report Cam had filled out told of an intruder. Now this . . . this allegation against Cam.

His thoughts went to Harriet Dunn. Cam had mentioned her in their talk that first day. Wilson had known her all of her life. Her father had been his close friend. Why not talk to Harriet about this matter? He turned back to his desk, glancing up at the clock. Perhaps he would eat there today if he could get away from the office in time.

Harriet Dunn was glad to see her old friend, who had been like a second father. She was delighted that he lingered after the other guests were gone, and she invited him into the kitchen for another cup of coffee, dismissing Leola so they could converse without interruption.

Hiram Wilson watched her face carefully as he finally brought up the subject of Cam. She seemed surprised when he asked her how long she had known him.

"You're here about the rumor going around town, aren't you?" Harriet Dunn asked intuitively, her eyes searching his face. "I overheard a comment by one of my guests today."

"It's more than that, Harriet. The day watchman brought an empty whiskey bottle into my office this morning. He said Cam left it in the shack."

"It's a lie!" she cried passionately. "That boy has never drunk since I've known him."

"Uh huh, I figured as much. Why don't you tell me about Cam," Mr. Wilson encouraged, watching the play of emotion on her face as she talked.

"I believe Clay Beardsley is behind this rumor, but once again, we have no proof," she concluded.

"Does Cam know about the rumor?"

"I don't think so. He sleeps during the day, and you know where he is at night. During his waking hours he does the chores and repairs for me here."

"Well, let's keep this between ourselves. I'll try to keep my eye on things at the mill," he said, getting to his feet. "It's been good to see you again, Harriet. You are as lovely as ever. I am surprised that some man hasn't captured your heart."

"Perhaps you would be more surprised to find that a wonderful man has won my heart," she responded demurely, the color mounting in her face.

"Oho! Who is the lucky fellow?" he asked, gray eyes beaming down at her and a broad smile creasing his face.

"Colonel Stothard of Savannah," she said softly, watching his reaction to the name.

"Good man! I met him up on the Oklawaha some time back. Invite me to the wedding, Harriet," he said genially, turning to go.

"Oh, you'll be there, I want you to take Papa's place. Will you give me away?" Harriet Dunn asked, following him to the door.

"I would be honored!" he answered, looking at her fondly. "Good-bye, Harriet."

As she watched his stalwart figure disappear through the front entrance, her thoughts turned back to Cam.

"I must talk to Henry," she murmured and went to look for Leola.

* * *

When Cam strolled out on the docks with Brindle at his heels, a cold wind was blowing in off the river. Stevens, the day watchman, already had his things together and was waiting to leave. Cam noticed that he kept pacing back and forth, nervously watching the clock. Brindle ambled over to sit at his feet.

"Call your dog, Fox!" Stevens said in a harsh voice, shoving Brindle aside with his feet.

"Come here, Brindle. Lie down!" Cam ordered, wondering at Stevens' sudden hostility.

"Stevens, why don't you go ahead and leave," Cam said. "Seems like you're anxious to go."

Stevens picked up his coat and walked off briskly without a backward glance. Cam watched him for a moment, then dismissed his strange behavior. He carried his lunch into the shack and took down the lantern to check the fuel. Finding it was scarcely half full, he reached for the can of kerosene that was always kept in the corner. It wasn't there. He looked all around the room, but it was nowhere to be found. Stevens may have set it down outside the door. Cam was puzzled when he could not find the can there either. He would have to make do with what he had by using the light only when he made his rounds. The reading he did each night to help pass the long hours would have to be postponed until after he made his last tour of inspection before daylight. He stuffed some matches in his pocket and picked up the lantern. Stepping outside, he called to Brindle, who was sniffing along the boards of the main dock leading out into a jungle of lumber.

"Come on, Brindle!"

The dog was trotting along the dock on an unseen trail, her nose close to the boards, tail wagging. She paused to look back at Cam, torn between the desire to obey or to follow her natural hunting instinct.

"Brindle! Come here!" Cam called again, giving a sharp whistle.

Brindle stopped, her head extended and nose high in the air, taking in a scent that beckoned her onward. Her body trembled with an innate hunger, but at Cam's sharp whistle she reluctantly turned to walk obediently back to her master.

"Come on, gal," Cam said gently, patting her on the head. "We'll sit out here for a while."

He sat down on the platform and leaned back against a stack of lumber. The wind he had felt earlier had died down, and the river was calm. Fishermen were rowing their boats in toward the public pier, their oars flashing in the failing light. One boat remained up the shoreline from the mill. Probably a night fisherman out for some channel cats, Cam decided.

It had grown quite dark before Cam lit the lantern in preparation for his first walk through the docks. Watching the feeble flame take hold, he wondered if Henry might come tonight. It had been two nights since his last visit. Cam let the shade down with a click and adjusted the wick. Calling to Brindle, he started out on the board walkway. The dog ran ahead, stopping to test the air then circling to pick up a trail.

"Brindle, it's probably only a bird's nest. Leave it alone!" Cam commanded.

18

$\mathcal{H}$ENRY FISHED FOR A WHILE, keeping enough distance that Cam could not recognize him. It was hard to be so near his friend these last few nights and not make his presence known. But this was the only way he knew to be there to help Cam. He was disturbed greatly by what Miss Harriet had told him after Mr. Wilson's visit. She had sent a message to Colonel Stothard, but he wasn't going to get here in time. The word was out along the river that something was coming off at the mill tonight. Those of the black race who had whispered a warning to him were frightened for their lives, scarcely pausing as they passed. "Stay away from the mill," they had said.

Henry frowned. There was no doubt in his mind that someone was about to attempt to discredit Cam. But who? Could it be that Beardsley? Moses, who worked at the mill part time, had told of seeing some fancy-dresser there talking to the day watchman, Stevens.

The darkness thickened and Henry pulled in his line. It was time to start rowing out to the mill docks. There was no light coming from the watchman's quarters. This worried Henry some. Cam usually had the lantern lit by this time and would have put it out on that post near the shack. He kept scanning the area for a light as he turned the boat and pulled hard on the oars. The blades cut quietly into the water with deep, powerful strokes. He had rowed within 100 feet of the piers before he caught the faint flicker of a light.

Henry let up on the oars, allowing the boat to drift, relieved as he saw the tiny gleam begin to move along the platform. Cam was making his first round. Knowing that Brindle would detect him, Henry waited patiently for them to pass before attempting to get the boat in near the docks. At last the way was clear, and he peered into the darkness to locate his point of entry. He was dismayed to find the tide had nearly closed up the path he had made through the tangled mass of river growth, slowing his progress. It was risky business moving a boat through these hyacinths at night without a light. He wasn't anxious to tangle with one of those big moccasins.

When he reached the edge of the first dock, Henry was satisfied he had gone as far as he dared. Securing the boat, he took up the pole and quietly poked the dense growth around him to move any snakes out of the vicinity. He might be in a hurry when he came back, and he sure didn't want any company!

Henry hesitated for a moment, listening to the sounds of the night around him. No one had to tell him the dangerous position he was putting himself into. If he was discovered and fell into the wrong hands, he would become the scapegoat for any devious plans carried out here tonight.

Leola's face came before him. She was sure some woman, and as soon as he could find steady work, they hoped to become man and wife. He felt as if a heavy weight was on his chest, squeezing the very breath from him, as he realized he was placing all that was dear to him on the line. A terrible premonition swept over him, leaving his brow and his palms wet with sweat. The temptation to leave was strong, yet he knew he could not desert his friend.

Henry took a deep breath and laid the pole across the seats of the boat. The dock with its heavy load of lumber loomed overhead. He reached for a firm grip on the edge, and finding a foothold on the lower structure, pushed himself up on top. He crouched there in the dark, straining to hear the least sound, hoping that the dog was with Cam in the shack. Assured that his presence had not been detected, he stood erect and moved swiftly across the platform, placing his feet near where the lumber rested on the boards, to keep from making a misstep.

Judging that he was pretty close to the center of the stacks, Henry climbed to the top of one. From there he could see the main walkway leading out into a maze of lumber. He sat down to catch his breath and pulled a piece of netting from his pocket. He took off his hat and draped the netting over his face, tucking it in around the collar to keep out the mosquitoes.

The time dragged by slowly as he sat waiting in the dark. What he would, or could, do remained a question. He had no weapon. It was not safe for a black man to be found carrying a gun. He would just have to wait and see what came off. If a fire was set, he would be there to help Cam fight the blaze.

Henry was unaware he had dozed off until he was awakened by a sound just below him. Chancing a look over the side, he could make out three dark figures.

"What about the dog?" he heard one whisper hoarsely.

"Don't worry about the dog. Stevens took care of that," came the reply.

They moved on to split up and position themselves behind the lumber where the main dock came out into the water. They were going to lay in wait for Cam! Henry wondered if he should risk trying to slip by them to warn him. There was no way he could make it without climbing through the understructure of the main platform, and that would take time. While he struggled with what course of action to take, he heard Cam calling to Brindle. When the dog did not respond, Cam shouted her name again and gave a loud whistle.

Henry could see him coming out the main walkway with the lantern in his hand. He watched transfixed as Cam came running toward where the men were hiding.

"Brindle!" Cam cried in a distressed voice, falling to his knees beside the prostrate dog, now visible in the light. "Oh,

Brindle," he moaned, setting the lantern aside to gather her up in his arms.

Henry momentarily forgot the three men lurking in the shadows as he felt his friend's anguish. He was about to cry out a warning when they jumped Cam, striking him on the head. Aware that he could not help him now, Henry watched in silent horror as they poured whiskey in Cam's mouth and on his clothing, then stuck the bottle in his inert hand.

In the dim light of the lantern, he recognized Digger, but the other two wore hats pulled down over their faces and he could not be sure. There was something familiar about the tall fellow with the broad shoulders. He seemed to be the one giving the orders.

"Now get the kerosene Stevens left for us and pour it around that stack of lumber over there! That's it! Hurry up!" he commanded as he pulled out a cigar and put it in his mouth. Striking a match, he cupped his hands to protect the flame and lit the cigar with great puffs of smoke.

Henry gasped with recognition as the light from the match revealed the man's features. It was Clay Beardsley!

Beardsley ordered the others to stand clear as he tossed the match into a puddle of oil, watching as it caught hold and spread.

"Better throw that dead dog to the alligators," Beardsley advised. "We don't want anybody asking questions about that."

"Yeah, that'll be a way to get rid of one of those ol' gators," Digger chortled, "that poison'll fix 'em."

"Stevens, grab that lantern and break it. We'll let the little rooster stew in his own juice!" Beardsley ordered harshly, exposing the identity of the third man.

"Ha! Ha!" Digger cackled. "He'll be a roast chicken yo' mean! Ha! Ha!"

"I didn't wanna be a party to no murder," Stevens complained as he complied. "You said you was just gonna set a little fire."

Henry ducked down as the three ran along the dock below him. The fire was already licking greedily at the base of the stack of lumber, giving off enough light that they would have seen him. Soon their footsteps faded into the night.

"Prob'ly got a boat out there," he muttered to himself. He hoped they would not find his.

The fire was getting brighter, and billows of smoke were beginning to rise. He had to get to Cam! Henry climbed down the dark side of the lumber he was on and ran to Cam's side.

"Mista Cam!" he called, trying to shake Cam into consciousness. "Yo' gotta wake up! We gotta get yo' outta here!"

Shouts were coming from the street. He could hear the sound of running feet as people began entering the dock area. Looking around, he could see that Cam was in no immediate danger. He would be found quickly.

"Best thing I kin do for yo', Mista Cam, is get outta here," Henry said, and with another glance at the fire he ran into the shadows to hide.

A crowd of men surged out into the main dock area. Peering out from his hiding place, Henry was shocked to see that the leader of the group was Digger! That would mean if they came in by boat, they did not go far when they left. They probably rowed to the other side of the mill. They would go back and move the boat later. No one would think anything of it.

"Come on, men, we gotta see what we can do!" he shouted importantly. "Anybody seen the night watchman?"

"Who's this?" cried another, catching sight of Cam's inert body in the firelight.

"That's him! Drunk as a skunk!" Digger cried. "He must'a fell down and broke that lantern and started the fire! Let's get him out of here and call the law!"

Henry watched until they had Cam safely away from the fire, then he faded into the night, running swiftly to where he had left his boat. He would have to hurry if he was going to get away before the fire lit up the whole sky. He dropped down into the boat, grabbed the pole, and pushed off, grateful that the hyacinths had opened up some. When he reached the open water, he rowed as fast as he could, his breath coming in short gasps like sobs, his arms aching from the exertion. By the time he had made it into the shadows of some trees along the shore, the fire had spread to other stacks of lumber, the flames shooting into the night air. Even the docks were ablaze.

"Well, that's the end of the mill," Henry exclaimed sorrowfully. "They's no way they's gonna put that fire out."

He rowed on, keeping to the dark areas as much as possible. He was glad when he reached a place he could tie up the boat without suspicion. Leaving everything as it was, he removed the netting from his face and discovered his hat was missing. It must have fallen off when he ran to help Cam!

Cam's first conscious thought was a terrible pain in his head. He tried to raise a hand to where it hurt, but something was binding it. There was a loud roar in his ears as if a freight train was bearing down on him. He struggled to free his hands.

"Hey! He's comin' around," a voice said. "Somebody run get Mr. Wilson!"

"Did somebody go for the sheriff?" another asked.

"Yeah. He should be here any time now," answered the first voice.

Cam opened his eyes to a circle of angry faces. He was lying on the ground with his hands tied behind him. Thick smoke hung in the air, and there was confusion everywhere.

"What'd ya' try to do, ya' crazy drunk, try to burn the whole town down?" cried a man Cam had never seen before.

"Here he is, Mr. Wilson. Here's the fella that started it!" bellowed a narrow-faced individual with a dark countenance.

"All right, Digger, step aside," Hiram Wilson said hoarsely, pushing his way through the crowd.

When he caught sight of Cam lying there bound with a rope, reeking of alcohol, he was stunned. A grim look of relief flitted across his haggard face. He had thought the young man was lost in the fire.

"Cam! What happened?" he cried.

"I'll tell you what happened!" Digger shouted for all to hear. "When we found him, he was drunk as a skunk and had fallen, breaking his lantern."

A cold shock came over Cam as he looked from one accusing face to another. They all thought he had done it! He looked back at Mr. Wilson.

"The mill . . . is it . . ."

"Gone, everything's gone!" Mr. Wilson responded to the unfinished question. A big man came elbowing his way through the crowd. Dressed in khaki, he wore a badge on his rumpled shirt. The stub of a cigar was in his mouth.

"Where is he?" he asked, anyone in general. "Oh, there you are, Hiram. Sorry to hear about all this."

"Right here, sheriff," Digger said with an air of importance. "We've got him all tied up for you."

"All right, I'll get him on down to the jail before this crowd gets ugly," the sheriff said, switching the cigar from one side of his mouth to the other.

"Can you walk, son?" he asked, bending his huge hulk to search Cam's face.

"Yes" was the low answer.

"Get him on his feet, somebody."

Two men jumped from the circle to lift Cam to his feet. As the sheriff led him away, Cam's eyes met briefly with those of Hiram Wilson who stood there, a ruined man, bewilderment on his ashen face.

"I . . . I'm sorry, Mr. Wilson, I let you down," Cam stammered as he was pushed on.

* * *

Harriet Dunn was awakened by the short blasts of the mill whistle. She threw back the covers and went to the window. A red glow filled the sky. The mill was on fire! All through Dunn House she could hear hurried footsteps as the men rushed from their rooms and down the stairs.

"Cam! Henry!" she exclaimed, fear gripping her heart. She reached for her robe, pulling it around her, and ran from her room. Sam McCullough was coming toward her in the hall, hurrying the best that he could on his crutches.

"Sam, you're going down there?" Miss Dunn asked, taking hold of his arm.

"Yes, ma'am," he replied, moving on down the hall.

"Sam, please, would you . . . would you send me word . . . about Cam?" she pleaded, her voice breaking off in a sob.

"I'll do my best, Miss Dunn."

She followed him to the porch, watching him as he carefully descended the steps and made his way out the walk.

"Please hurry!" she called after him.

The flames could be seen reaching into the air far above the buildings. Sparks and glowing embers were falling everywhere. To some, just waking up, dazed with sleep, it must have seemed the end of the world. Harriet could hear the roar of fire from where she stood. Leola came to stand beside her, mute with fear.

"Miss Harriet, th' Lawd is gonna have to be with us tonight, sho 'nough," she moaned, with trembling hands clenched under her chin. "My heart tells me sumpin' terrible's wrong!"

Harriet Dunn sank down into a rocking chair, a dark despair sweeping over her with a crushing blow. If Cam or Henry were caught in that fire, there was no way they could have survived. Oh, no! she thought. Surely God would not allow this to happen! A sob escaped her lips, causing Leola to look at her with concern. It had been a long time since Harriet had sought solace from the Lord. They had attended church before her mother died, but, gradually through the years, with the care of her father, and now Dunn House, she hadn't thought much about it. Her Bible was still on the table by her bed, but she hadn't opened it for several years. Neglect had robbed her of an experience she once found satisfying. Remorse flooded her soul as she searched for an inner peace that was not there.

"O God, please forgive me," she asked in an agonizing whisper. "Please, Father, let Cam and Henry be safe."

When she raised her head, the whole town was etched in stark outline against the orange glow of the burning wood. As she watched, an acrid layer of smoke, forced down by the heavy night air, began to settle down, blotting out the scene.

She got to her feet and walked to the railing Cam had built around the porch.

"Leola, why doesn't somebody come?" she burst out piteously.

"I don' know, Miss Harriet," Leola said, coming to comfort her. "But yo' hold on, somebody will. Now yo' jus' set yo'sef down here, and I'll go make yo' some coffee."

Leola had just picked up some wood to start the fire when she heard a familiar tap at the window. She dropped the kindling and ran to open the door. Henry stood there bare-headed and wild-eyed.

"What took yo' so long, man!" she exclaimed, pulling him into the kitchen.

"Woman, I've got a heap o' trouble! Yo' don' know what I been through! I had a hard time gittin' here! Ever'body is run-nin' roun' scared an' I didn' want them thinkin' I was a sneakin' roun' like I did sumpin'! I didn' know where yo' wuz an' I been sittin' out there in the dark a waitin'. Where's Miss Harriet?"

"She's out on the front porch. She's worried half sick 'bout Mista Cam!" Leola answered. "Yo' want I should go get her?"

"Hurry, woman, I gotta talk to her!" Henry urged. He sat down in a chair and held his head in his hands. He did not look up until Harriet Dunn came into the room followed by Leola, who closed the door after them.

"Henry!" Miss Dunn cried, a note of gladness in her voice. "Thank God you're safe! Where's Cam?"

"I don' know where he is right now, Miss Harriet, but I know they found him in time."

"I had to leave him there, Miss Harriet. If I was gonna hep him, I had to get away," Henry said woefully, shaking his head.

"Tell me, Henry . . . tell me what happened!" Harriet Dunn exclaimed, sitting down in the chair Leola brought her.

"Pull those shades, woman," Henry said, glancing over to-ward them, waiting until Leola complied before he spoke again.

"Well, Miss Harriet, I took my boat an' went out fishin' like I been a doin' and waited 'til aftuh dark . . ."

As Henry related to her the story of what had happened, Harriet Dunn's feelings ran the gamut of human emotion. When he had finished she sat in stunned silence.

"One mo' thing, Miss Harriet. When I hurried to hep Mista Cam, I musta los' my hat. Iffen they find that hat, they's gonna be a lookin' fo' somebody else. That Mista Beardsley's gonna find out somebody mighta seen him and he's gonna be a huntin' me," Henry whispered hoarsely, his voice failing him, hands gesturing helplessly.

"I'll take care of you, Henry," Miss Dunn said, rising to her feet. "You can stay in the storeroom. If worse comes to worst, we can hide you out at Zachariah Sparks' place."

"Leola, give Henry some food and take him out to the storeroom. Be careful that no one sees you. I'll see what I can find out about Cam."

Harriet Dunn left them there and went back to the porch for another look at the fire. The glow in the sky was beginning to dim. Dense smoke hung low to the ground. It burned her lungs and caused her eyes to smart. None of the men had returned to Dunn House, not even Sam McCullough. Dare she go to the mill? Would it be safe? If only she had a horse; she would not be afraid on a horse. Dandy! Why not ride Dandy? Cam wouldn't mind.

She went to her room and changed into riding clothes. Then taking a lantern from the back porch, she walked to the stall Cam had built for Dandy behind the storage room. It took only a few minutes for her experienced hands to saddle the horse and lead him out. The spirited Dandy pranced in anticipation of a run. She mounted him with an easy grace, and he moved out into the street.

"Run, Dandy, run!" she cried, thrilling to the moment.

The horse hardly needed urging, taking off with a clatter of hooves on the hard-packed clay of the road. When she reached the river, Harriet Dunn turned Dandy into the well-worn road that led south to the mill. The smoke grew thicker here, mixed with the fog from the river. Had she not been familiar with the landmarks, she would have had difficulty finding her way. Guiding Dandy with a firm hand, she reached the mill area where the air was more clear. People were standing around in groups talking. She saw Sam McCullough in one group with his back toward her.

She reined the horse in to a walk, working her way through the crowd. The bits of conversations she overheard brought fear to her heart. She rode on deeper into their midst and was appalled at what she saw. What was once the largest mill of its kind had been reduced to charred and twisted rubble, still smoldering. The devastation extended far out into the water where the docks were still ablaze, one stack of lumber igniting another in a chain reaction. The heat was intense. Men with smoke-blackened faces stood helpless, watching the end of an era, unable to do anything further to check the progress of the fire.

Harriet Dunn looked for Hiram Wilson and, spotting him surrounded by a group of men, she turned Dandy in that direction. He saw her coming and made his way toward her. She pulled the horse to a stop in a clearing and waited for him. She was unaware of the picture she made—her slender form sitting astride the handsome Dandy, dark hair cascading down her shoulders, blue eyes wide with anxiety. Many an admiring glance was sent her way.

"Harriet!" Wilson exclaimed when he reached her side. "You shouldn't have come here!"

"Cam," she asked through numbed lips, her face white. "Where is he?"

"Cam is in jail. The sheriff took him away quite a while ago. He wasn't hurt. Feelings are running pretty high against him, though. They think there was an accomplice," he explained, laying a hand on hers. "Harriet, I'm sorry. Right now, things look pretty bad for him. He's going to need counsel."

She nodded her head, understanding what he was telling her. Then, for the first time she noticed how he had aged overnight. Bloodshot eyes glared from an ashen face, his shoulders stooped. She placed her other hand over his.

"Hiram, I'm . . . I'm sorry," she stammered. "What will you do?"

"I don't know," he said wearily, brushing the gray hair from his eyes. "Everything I have is gone. I'm too old to start over again."

He pulled his hand away and dropped it to his side in a gesture of defeat. Tears flooded her eyes as she watched him walk away into the crowd. She turned Dandy to start back toward Dunn House.

"Good evening, Miss Dunn," said a familiar voice. Through her tears she saw a hand take hold of Dandy's bridle.

"Did you come to see the big fire?" Clay Beardsley asked in a mocking voice. "They caught the one who set it. I believe you know him?"

His black eyes glittered as they took in her white face, blue eyes glistening with tears. When she did not answer he went on talking. "If you were kinder to me, I could probably help him," he hinted, fire flashing in his eyes.

Harriet Dunn stared at him in horror at his suggestion. She could not believe her ears. Was this man so egotistical that he could not understand that a woman would detest him?

Encouraged at her silence, he let go of the bridle to lay his hand on hers. Coming out of her trance, she gave Dandy a hard kick with the stirrups. He responded with a great leap forward, knocking Beardsley to one side, and raced away in the smoke-filled night. She did not rein him in until she was almost to Dunn House, trotting him up to the barn. There was a light in the kitchen. Leola must be waiting up for her. She dismounted and led Dandy into his stall, removing the bridle and saddle with trembling hands. Her legs were so weak they could scarcely hold her up.

"I'll give you a rubdown in the morning, Dandy," she promised, giving him a pat on the neck.

After she had closed and locked the door, she hurried into the house. She was surprised to find it was only an hour before daylight. Leola was sitting at the kitchen table, head down, asleep. Rather than disturb her, Miss Dunn went on to her room to change her clothes and lie down for a while. Early in the morning, while the town was still in bed, she would seek out an attorney for Cam. She was awakened a short time later by a tap at her door. It was Leola.

"I saw yo' light on, Miss Harriet, an' wanted to know iffen yo' was all right."

"I'm fine, Leola. Cam is in jail; he is safe for the time being. I am going to get dressed now and go see an old friend of mine about representing him at the hearing."

"Do yo' want I should fix yo' something to eat befo' yo' go?"

"That would be good, Leola, thank you."

Harriet Dunn washed her face and combed her hair until it shone in the lamplight. She wrapped it in soft coils and pinned it high on her head. From her closet she took a brown skirt with a matching short jacket, choosing a peach-colored blouse to complete the outfit. It was a good choice, she decided as she looked in the mirror. The color added a blush to her cheeks and made the tired lines around her eyes less noticeable. Taking a handkerchief from the drawer, she put it in her pocket and went out, closing the door behind her.

19

$\mathcal{H}$ARRIET DUNN OPENED THE GATE and made her way up the broad walk. She had always loved coming to this big house with the wide verandas all around. Marcus Tyler Moore had given her father legal assistance on many occasions, and she had come here with him. After her father died, it was Marcus who helped Harriet save what she could from the creditors. She had not seen much of him in the last few years. Since Mrs. Moore's death, he had been gone a lot, getting more and more involved in the politics of the state.

She knocked on the door and stood waiting. Silas, Mr. Moore's faithful manservant, greeted her.

"Good mawnin', Miss Harriet, y'all are out early today! Come in, come in!" He stood back for her to enter, closing the door after her.

"Silas, is Mr. Moore in?"

"Yes he is, ma'am, but he's in bed asleep."

"Silas, please awaken him. I must see him now. It's . . . it's urgent!" Silas looked up the stairway and then back at her, hesitating for a moment. Mr. Moore had been out most of the night with the fire and all. He was not sure he should wake him up so early.

"Silas, please . . . I know it's early . . . but I must see him!" she pleaded as if reading his mind.

"In here, Miss Harriet," he said, opening the door to the drawing room. "I'll see what I kin do. Make yo'sef comfo'ble."

She sat down on the familiar settee to wait. The room brought back memories of her father. She had not been waiting long when she heard footsteps outside in the hall.

"Silas, bring some coffee to the drawing room," she heard Marcus Moore say in his quiet, mild-mannered way. Then the door swung open and a portly man in his 60s entered the room. He was dressed neatly in navy pin-striped trousers and a white shirt, opened at the neck. His broad face lit up at the sight of her, gladness shone in his eyes.

"Harriet! What brings you here this morning?" he said warmly, taking her small hand in his.

"I've got some trouble, Marcus, and I desperately need your help." Her voice broke and tears came to her eyes as all the pent-up emotion from the night before crowded to the surface.

"There, there," he said gently, concern showing in his face. "You just dry those tears and tell me about it. What's happened that's got you so upset?"

"I'm sorry Marcus," she sobbed, fighting for control, dabbing at her eyes with a handkerchief.

"Does this have anything to do with what happened last night?" he asked, watching her face carefully, taking note of the strain there.

He had known her a long time and had watched her grow into a handsome young woman. He had often wondered why she had not married.

She nodded her head with its shining crown of dark hair, then raised her tearful blue eyes to meet his.

"Cam . . . is . . . is like a son to me."

"I take it you're referring to the young man they have in jail for starting the fire?"

"Yes, were you there last night?"

"I was there at the beginning with Hiram, saw them take the accused away. There is a lot of circumstantial evidence against him. I was told he may have had an accomplice." Marcus paused, then asked with curiosity in his voice, "How did you come to know this boy?"

Harriet started at the point where Cam's mother died and the subsequent events leading up to the present, leaving out only her romance with Colonel Stothard and Henry's involvement in the fire. When she had finished her story, he sat in deep thought for a few minutes, his eyes on her face.

"Are you saying that you believe Cam is being blamed for something he didn't do?"

"Yes, Marcus, I am. There is nothing that Clay Beardsley would not do to destroy Cam. Whatever other ulterior motive he may have had in destroying the mill, his hatred for Cam played a big part in the outcome," she said with firm conviction.

"Of course, Harriet, as you know from past experience, you will have a hard time proving such an allegation under the circumstances," he said, getting up to stare out the window, his hands folded behind his back.

"Marcus, will you represent him, if I tell you I have such proof?"

Startled, he turned to look at her. How could she have proof? Of all the cases he had tried, this one was nailed shut. Besides, the whole town was convinced the boy was guilty. Sentiment was running strongly against him. He himself had heard the facts there at the mill. What could Harriet know? Should he lay his career on the line because of her love for the boy? There had been some talk of him playing a leading role in the state government, maybe the highest office.

He came back to where she sat and stood looking down at her. It made him realize how lonely he had been since Mrs. Moore had died. How could he turn away from those imploring eyes?

"Harriet, I . . . ," he said with a helpless gesture.

"Please, Marcus, you're the only one I can turn to," she entreated, leaning forward to gaze at him earnestly.

"All right, tell me your facts," he said, resigning himself to her importunity. He sat down opposite her to listen.

"What I did not tell you before," she began, "was that several days ago, Hiram came to Dunn House to see me. Accusations were being spread around town and at the mill that Cam had a drinking problem. He wanted to know how long I had known Cam. I told him the same story I have told you. He related to me that Stevens, the day watchman, had brought an empty whiskey bottle into his office that morning, claiming he had found it in their quarters where Cam had left it."

She paused as Silas came into the room with a tray containing a decanter of coffee and some warm muffins. She waited for him to pour, accepting the cup from him. When he had finished serving, Silas left the room and she continued.

"I was so disturbed by what he said that I hired a man to stay hidden on the docks to keep watch for Cam's safety. That man was there last night and saw it all. It was his hat they found. He lost it when he ran to check on Cam after the men had set the fire and gone."

Marcus Moore listened carefully to every detail, asking questions here and there to clarify points, as she told Henry's story.

"Where is this man now?" he asked as she concluded.

"I have him hidden. The town thinks there is an accomplice. But Beardsley knows that someone else was there to see his dastardly deed. He will be looking for that man!"

"I can see that you have a very low opinion of this man Beardsley."

"I detest him. He . . . he insulted me," she said, the blood rising in her face. "Last night I rode Cam's horse down to the mill to talk to Hiram. I wanted to find out if Cam was safe. As I was leaving, Beardsley grabbed Dandy's bridle, detaining me. He suggested that if I would be kinder to him, he would help Cam."

Marcus Moore got up to pour himself some more coffee. He had been hearing suspicious rumors about this Beardsley for some time, but there had been no substantiating facts. It was an old story in the years of reconstruction of the South after the Civil War. Hoodlums and murderers had donned an air of respectability to cover their crooked deals and crimes. It was one of the issues he felt strongly about as he watched honest homesteaders losing their land to scheming land-grabbers. Perhaps this was one he could put out of business once and for all. He finished his coffee and set his cup down.

"I'll go talk to the sheriff and look in on the boy today. There was some talk of a hearin' as early as tomorrow. I'll see if I can hold them to that. Your job is to keep that man safe until the day of the hearin'." He got to his feet.

"Do you have someone you can trust to bring him to the rear of the courthouse?"

"Yes, Zachariah Sparks, if I can get word to him in time," she answered.

"Good. We'll have to handle this in a very careful manner so as to not jeopardize that man's life."

He went to the door and called for Silas. When he had come, Mr. Moore instructed him to get the carriage and see Miss Dunn back to her home.

* * *

Leola was in the kitchen preparing the noon meal when Harriet arrived back at Dunn House. She went immediately to Leola to warn her that she should not go near the storage room except when it was absolutely necessary to get articles of food. She also told her not to speak with Henry when she was there, so that their voices would not be overheard.

"You understand that Henry is in great danger, Leola, and that you must help me protect him?" she said soberly. "He's our only hope."

"Yes'm, Miss Harriet, I'll be very careful. I think we have plenty of food in here to keep us, and I took plenty out to that man last night," Leola replied.

"Well, if you need anything, go to the store for it. Don't go near the storeroom. I'll go change and help you; I know you're tired." Miss Dunn started for the door then turned around, "Oh, yes, Leola, can you find me someone who will take a message out to Mr. Sparks . . . it's urgent."

"My sister's boy is comin' by here to chop some wood after while, Miss Harriet. He'll go."

"Good! Tell me when he comes."

* * *

Nan climbed to the wagon seat beside her father and they started out. She turned to wave at her mother who waited to close the gate behind them. She had been so afraid that they would not go when she saw the smoke this morning, and she had watched her father's face anxiously as he studied the dark cloud in the dawn sky. He had decided it was not a forest fire, the smoke would be billowing and moving. This smoke had just seemed to be hanging there in the east like a flat cloud, drifting off to the south. Feeling that it posed no threat to them, her father had hitched up the horse and made ready to go to town.

Nan had been looking forward to this day with mixed feelings of joy and apprehension at seeing Cam. What would she say? She had rehearsed the words in her head a thousand times, but nothing sounded right. Would he be glad to see her? She had to force these thoughts, which had plagued her for weeks, out of her mind, turning her attention instead to the forest around her.

They passed the turnoff leading to where Cam had built his cabin, and Nan felt a pang of regret for his sake. Yet, wasn't she glad that he was no longer in that lonely place?

Time stood still as Nan experienced great joy at the prospect of seeing Cam again. Her spirits soared, only to be crushed a moment later by the fear that he did not care for her anymore and she would lose him, then she would sink into a wretchedness that tore at her very spirit. The stress she was under was so wearing that she began to droop noticeably by the time they reached the end of the sandy trail.

Mr. Sparks called to the horse and flipped the reins, urging her to a fast trot. He had taken note of Nan's morose spirit and tried to point out things of interest to bring a smile to her face. But much of the time she seemed not to notice he had spoken.

"Nan," he said finally, "after we have eaten at Miss Harriet's, why don't you stay and visit with her until I get my runnin' around done."

She nodded her acceptance of the suggestion, grateful for the chance to talk to Miss Dunn. Maybe she would get to see Cam, if he was there. "O God, please let him be there," she prayed silently.

Leola was putting the food on the table when they walked into the dining room. To Nan it appeared she was more glad than usual to see them, rushing to return to the kitchen. When she returned, Harriet Dunn was right behind her. The grave expression on Miss Dunn's face let Nan know there was something terribly wrong. Her heart skipped a beat, and she felt slightly faint.

"Nan, Mr. Sparks, would you to come into the kitchen please. I must talk to you," she said, holding the door for them.

Mr. Sparks pushed back his chair and took Nan by the arm, leading her out. Once inside the kitchen, Miss Dunn led them to a room across the hall.

"This is Cam's room—we can talk here. Mr. Sparks, you can have that chair there . . . Nan, sit here beside me on the bed."

Nan glanced around the room, noticing the neat appearance, then sat down facing Miss Dunn. Her father pulled the chair toward them and sat down, his eyes on Nan's white face and dark, troubled stare.

"We have had a terrible night here in town," Harriet began, the strain showing in her voice. "Hiram Wilson's mill has been burned to the ground and Cam is in jail, accused of setting the fire. The whole town is in quite an uproar against him."

Nan broke down and started sobbing as Miss Dunn related the nightmare of events leading to Cam's arrest and Henry's escape. Harriet paused only to put her arms around the weeping girl, looking across at Zachariah Sparks, who sat with clenched fists resting on his knees. His face worked convulsively as he listened intently. "Henry came here, and I have him hidden in the storage room. He is our only hope of saving Cam. Beardsley will be looking for him and will suspect we are helping him. I need your help, Zachariah, to keep Henry safe until the hearing and to get him there without harm.

"Early this morning I went to see Marcus Moore. Thank goodness he was in town! He has agreed to represent Cam at the hearing tomorrow. He asked me to find someone I could trust to bring Henry to the rear of the courthouse. He will tell us the time." Harriet Dunn sat waiting for him to speak. Up to this point he had said nothing.

"I was just thinking of the Missus out there alone with the little ones. She won't know and she'll be worried," Mr. Sparks said, finally.

"Leola has a nephew coming by soon. I was going to send him out with a message to you. If you like, we can send him out with a message to Mrs. Sparks. He is a very trustworthy young man and could even stay the night there," Miss Dunn offered hopefully.

"That'll do," he responded brusquely, his eyes on Nan's tear-stained face. "Where will we stay?"

"You can have this room, and Nan can stay with me."

"All right," he said, rising to his feet. "Let's get something to eat and then I need to figure out a plan."

"Go into the kitchen, Mr. Sparks. Leola will have your plate ready there. Nan and I will be there in a minute."

When he had gone out and closed the door, Harriet took Nan by the shoulders and looked her in the eyes.

"Nan, Cam will be all right. He will come through this, you'll see. We'll trust God, you and I together, for his deliverance."

"It's not that, Miss Dunn, it's . . . it's just that I talked awful to Cam . . . I . . . I hurt him so . . . and now this! How can he ever want to see me again!"

"I know all that is true, Nan, but Cam still loves you deeply. I'm sure of that," Harriet responded, hugging the girl close. "We must be strong for his sake. He needs us. Tell me, do you love Cam?"

Nan pushed herself back and sat looking at her hands. When she raised her eyes, they were shining with a soft light. "I love him so much . . . it's . . . it's killing me," she said. "I tried not to because I didn't want to be doomed to life on a homestead like Ma."

"Cam didn't want that for you either, that's why he planned to leave the homestead and get a job in town. Beardsley didn't know that when he bought out that land forcing Cam to move. Cam's love for you went far above his loyalty to his uncle. He planned to work and save his money so he would have something to offer you. He wanted so much to tell you all this the day you had your quarrel."

"And I spoiled it all," Nan said quietly. "Miss Dunn, do you think he will forgive me?"

"I'm sure he will, Nan," Miss Dunn responded, taking her hand. "After all this is over, go to him. Come, let's go see if your father found something to eat. You must be hungry too."

Mr. Sparks had finished his meal and was lingering over a cup of coffee. Miss Dunn sat down with Nan across the table from him. Leola promptly brought them a plate of hot food.

"I think I'll take a walk over town and stop by the jail. Maybe they'll let me see the boy. You got anything you want to send down there?" he said.

"Cam will need some clean clothes. You could take him some. Leola could fix him some food too. We'll have them ready," Miss Dunn replied, turning to Leola.

* * *

Harriet Dunn sat in her office trying to concentrate on the bookwork before her. It was getting late in the afternoon and Marcus Moore had not stopped by, nor had Mr. Sparks returned. Nan was out on the back porch. Harriet could hear the swing moving. She closed her ledger and got up to walk to the front door. Relieved to see Mr. Sparks coming down the street toward her, Miss Dunn went to the back and called softly to Nan.

They were both waiting when he walked through the door. He motioned them into the kitchen before he spoke.

"I wasn't able to see Cam. No one has been allowed in except Marcus Moore. Sheriff Neubeck took the clothes and lunch. Said he'd see that Cam got them. I asked how Cam was doin'. He said he was doin' pretty well—been readin' most of the time. When I asked him what he was a readin', he said it looked like a Bible!"

"Cam has read his Bible every day since I have known him," Harriet Dunn said in answer to the unspoken question she saw in Nan's eyes. "It was his mother's, and he seems to find comfort in reading it."

Leola appeared in the door. "Miss Harriet, Mista Mo' is heah to see yo'."

"Bring him on back, Leola, and close the door, please."

"I'm sorry it took so long to get back to you, Harriet, I . . ." Marcus Moore began, breaking off his speech when he noticed she was not alone.

"It's all right, Marcus," Miss Dunn assured him, "this is Zachariah Sparks and his daughter, Nan. They are friends of mine, also Cam's. Mr. Sparks will see that Henry gets to the courthouse safely tomorrow."

"Well, that'll be just fine! It's good to meet you, Mr. Sparks. You too, Miss Nan. Now, here is the way it'll go. The hearing is set for ten o'clock in the morning. The judge will read a statement of charges and will take a sworn witness from those who were there. Then he'll ask the accused how he will plead. Of course, Cam will say he's not guilty. Then the judge will ask if there is any proof of innocence. That's where you come in, Mr.

Sparks," he said, turning to Zachariah. "Bring Henry to that back door leadin' into the judge's chambers and we'll keep him there until I call for him. Mind you, lock that door once you get him inside."

"Do you have a plan to get him down there?" Mr. Moore asked.

"I been thinkin' on it. Miss Harriet can use some wood, so I thought I would haul her in some and unload it in the back near the storage room. While I'm unloadin' the wood, I'll be loadin' Henry. I'm pickin' up a load of feed this time in and have a lot of sacks in the wagon. I'll hide him under those."

"Sounds like it ought to work, Mr. Sparks. I guess I won't need to tell you to be extremely careful. We have a lot ridin' on Henry's safety," Marcus Moore warned.

"I've got a powerful shotgun under the wagon seat. I'll use it if I have to!" Mr. Sparks replied with passion.

"I guess that's about all, then . . . Let's see . . . ," Marcus Moore said, thoughtfully stroking his chin. "Oh yes, I'll have them save a seat for you and the young lady, Miss Harriet. That way you'll not have to come so early. Just tell the man at the door who you are. I'll be goin' now . . . keep that witness safe! See y'all tomorrow."

"Thank you, Marcus," Harriet Dunn said, walking with him to the door. "I will always be indebted to you for helping Cam."

"He's a fine young man, Harriet. I will do my best. Goodbye."

She stood at the door until he had boarded his carriage, waving as he pulled away from the gate. As she walked slowly back to where the others waited, a nagging thought kept forcing its way into her mind. Leola must not leave the house either. For if Beardsley got hold of Leola, he would soon find out where Henry was. She hurried out to the kitchen.

"Where's Leola?" she asked.

"She took up a basket and said she had to go to the store," Nan answered.

"How long ago?" Miss Dunn asked sharply.

"Just after you walked out with Marcus Moore. Why?" queried Mr. Sparks.

"Beardsley will know that if he can get Leola, he will find Henry! Go after her, Zachariah, hurry!" Harriet Dunn cried.

Almost an hour went by before Mr. Sparks returned. His face was grave as he faced her. "There was no trace of her. No one at the store had seen her."

"Zachariah, we are going to have to move Henry into the house somewhere, and soon! We will not be able to wait until dark. We must think of something!"

"Do you have a wheelbarrow?" he asked.

"Yes, it's under the house. The lattice is hinged in the corner near Cam's room. You'll find it there."

"I'll go bring in a sack of those potatoes out there. Nan, you come along and keep a sharp eye out. If you see anything, give that funny little bird call."

"Miss Harriet," Zachariah said from the doorway, "you just stand here and open this door when I get close. If I can't lift him, I'll have to dump him in."

"You'll need the key, Zachariah. Leola keeps it there on a nail by the door. Yes, that's it."

Harriet Dunn waited by the door for Mr. Sparks' return. Henry had been locked in the dark storage room, alone and in fear of his life, for nearly a whole day, held captive for what he knew. She wondered how she could tell him about Leola. What would he do?

"O dear God, if only the colonel would come in time!" she murmured prayerfully, leaning her head against the wall. It had been almost a week since she had sent the telegraph. There was no one else left to turn to.

Her strength nearly failed her as she thought of her faithful cook in the hands of some ruffians, being beaten, perhaps worse. A silent sob tore at her breast as she listened for Zachariah's step.

* * *

Colonel Stothard had pushed his men hard once they had unloaded their horses from the train at Jacksonville. Riding hard, stopping only to rest their mounts, they had rushed on toward their destination. By midafternoon they had reached the forks in the road just outside of town and had made camp in a thick stand of pines just off the road. The men had wearily unsaddled their spent animals and now sat in a circle around the fire sharing a hurriedly prepared meal, their first of the day.

The colonel sat with his back against a stump, watching these loyal men who had been in his employ for some time. They ate quietly, too tired for the usual lighthearted banter that went on in the camp. Like himself, they were a breed of men dedicated to making the new South a safe and decent place for their families and for the generations to come.

He felt a sense of guilt at asking any of them to ride further, but he must know if Harriet was safe from harm. He pulled the telegraph from his pocket and read it again, as he had done many times on the way down. It was sent in the code they had agreed on. "The bees are in town, someone is being stung." Fear for her safety struck him again. Why hadn't he insisted that she return to Georgia with him the last time he was down to Dunn House. She had promised to set the date for their wedding soon, and he had not pressed her on the subject again.

Captain Brevard laid his plate aside. He had noticed the colonel had scarcely touched his food. His heart went out to this man he had known and served under so long. Harriet Dunn was a woman to capture any man's heart. He, too, had battled with the desire to have her as his own, but loyalty to Colonel Stothard had held him steady. She was the colonel's lady.

He got up, stiff and sore from long hours in the saddle, and went over to Colonel Stothard.

"Colonel," he said, trying to keep his tone light, "what do you think about me taking one of the boys and riding into town to nose around? We can see what is going on and then, when it gets dark, you can ride in to Dunn House."

"Good idea, Captain!" Colonel Stothard exclaimed with apparent relief. "Please hurry back and let me know if . . . what's going on."

"And, Captain," he went on, his voice thick with emotion, "thank you!"

Captain Brevard walked toward his horse. He was bone tired, but his concern for the colonel and his lady spurred him on. He knew Colonel Stothard hated to ask any of them to ride further.

As he threw the saddle on his mount, he looked at the weary faces of his men. He would need a fresh face, one who would not stand out in the crowd as a stranger or be recognized, to mingle on the street and listen. That would leave him free to go to Dunn House to check on Miss Dunn.

"Saddle up, Wes, let's ride," he ordered, noting the relief on the rest of the men's countenances.

Wes got to his feet and saddled his tired horse. Soon the sound of their movement from camp had died away, leaving those left behind to stare mutely at the fire.

The two men split up shortly and Wes rode on ahead. They were to meet back at camp as soon as possible. While he waited for Wes Scott to get a substantial lead, Captain Brevard dismounted and checked the cinches and put on his riding gloves. Climbing back on his horse, he pulled his hat low over his face and started out, holding his mount to a leisurely gait. His eyes took in every movement around him as he approached town. There seemed to be an unusual amount of activity. Several buggies passed him going into town. There was a smell of burnt wood in the air.

He rode on down the wide clay street and turned off toward Dunn House. The town was full of people, carriages, and wagons. He kept his head low and casually stepped down from the saddle to tie his horse to the railing in front of the boardinghouse.

Inside, Harriet Dunn was so engrossed in helping Mr. Sparks get Henry into the house that she did not hear the quiet step behind her. When she became aware of the tall figure looming over her, she nearly fainted, grabbing the door for support. A familiar voice broke into her consciousness as an arm shot out to steady her.

"Miss Dunn, don't be frightened, I've come to see what kind of trouble you are in," Captain Brevard said quietly, leading her trembling body to a chair.

Hurriedly, she told him of Henry's plight and that she was there at the door to help Mr. Sparks bring him into the house.

He left her there to check on Sparks. Soon Henry was carried into the safety of the kitchen. Nan fixed a pot of coffee while Harriet Dunn told Captain Brevard all that had happened.

He listened intently, asking questions when necessary, watching the play of emotions on her face. When she came to Leola's disappearance, she paused to give a troubled look at Henry. As she went on, Henry gave a cry and dropped his head in his hands, moaning in grief. When she stopped speaking, the captain got to his feet.

"You will be safe here in the house for the present. Stay inside and keep Henry away from the windows. I'll ride out to report to Colonel Stothard. He and the men are camped just outside of town. To keep from being recognized, he plans to ride in as soon as it is dark enough. We don't want to tip Beardsley off that we are in town. I'll send some of the boys on in earlier to keep watch. Meanwhile, we'll start a thorough search for your cook. Go on with your usual activities, feed your guests and try to act natural." He bowed slightly, touching the brim of his hat and with a light step, he was gone.

Harriet Dunn breathed a great sigh of relief. It was comforting to know that Colonel Stothard and his men had arrived and would soon be here. Her pulse quickened at the thought of seeing him again. She glanced at the clock. It would soon be time to serve the guests. Putting her feelings aside, she turned to the business at hand.

"Zachariah, take Henry into the linen room. It's there at the end of the hall next to Cam's room, where you will stay. Lock the door, the key is in the lock," she said, indicating the passage to the hall.

"Henry, try not to worry. Captain Brevard and his men will find Leola. I'll send you some hot food as soon as Nan and I get it ready."

"I sho hope so, Miss Harriet, iffen they don' find my woman, it's all over with me," he said dejectedly.

Captain Brevard found it difficult to hold his horse in check until he reached the edge of town. Every minute counted, but he couldn't afford to attract attention to his coming and going. Once on the open road, he spurred his horse into a fast gallop.

Colonel Stothard was pacing the ground when he arrived at the camp. Wes Scott had ridden in shortly before and was telling the colonel what he had found out. The other men had gathered in a tight bunch to listen.

Bringing his mount to a sudden stop with a spray of sand, the captain dismounted in a singular motion, handing the reins to a comrade.

"Colonel, things are pretty bad. Miss Dunn is safe so far. Mr. Sparks is with her," he reported, trying to reassure him. "But, here's what we have to contend with," he continued, as he told them the whole story.

"I let Miss Dunn know you would be coming in as soon as it was dark, but with all the people in town, I'm not sure you would be noticed much. What do you think, Wes?"

"I agree," Wes answered.

"The way I see it, we might be better off to get you in there now. If Beardsley and his men find out Henry's whereabouts, they will be watching the place come dark," Captain Brevard declared.

Colonel Stothard nodded his approval and turned away to stalk toward King, who was hobbled close by.

"Douse that fire, somebody, and saddle up," Captain Brevard ordered tersely, taking his reins back. "Bonham, you ride in with the colonel! Wes, you take Joe and ride to Dunn House and stay out of sight. Beardsley will probably make a move on that storage room out back if he finds out from the cook they were hiding Henry there. He won't know he's been moved. Keep your eyes and ears open and if you pick up on anything, pass the word." He climbed into the saddle.

"Good hunting, boys! Keep your hats low and spread yourselves out. Wes, you and Joe ride on ahead and get in place. Make sure it's safe for Colonel Stothard."

Wes and Joe rode out of camp and disappeared through the trees. The waiting was hard. Colonel Stothard stood with his hand on King's bridle, staring at the spot where Wes and Joe had ridden out of sight. King reared his golden head and pawed the ground in anticipation of moving on.

"All right, Bonham, you and the colonel can ride out. Take those side streets and come around the other way. I'll be right behind you a short distance away. The rest of you choose your routes and come on in."

20

LEOLA WAS LYING FACEDOWN where she had fallen when she lost consciousness. The stinging, bleeding welts on her face, arms, and legs brought her to the realization of what had happened to her. Her captors had whipped her until she had fainted, trying to make her tell where Henry was. One eye was swollen shut, throbbing with each heartbeat. The pain was so intense, it was all she could do to keep from crying out.

Knowing she would not survive another merciless beating with the whip, she forced herself to remain still, even though her muscles were twitching with pain.

There was the sound of movement in the room as the door opened, casting a dismal ray of light across the floor near her face. She opened her good eye and saw an ant crawling along the dirt floor. A boat whistle could be heard in the distance, letting her know she was somewhere near the river.

"She talk yet?" said a voice she recognized as Beardsley's.

"Naw! She passed out on me," answered her assailant.

"Throw some water on her and bring her to! We don't have time to waste!"

Footsteps approached her and a foot shoved her over on her back. She gasped and sputtered as a torrent of water hit her in the face. "Now, are you gonna talk or do you want some more of the whip?" the man snarled.

199

Leola cringed with fear as he raised the whip to bring it down across her mouth, bringing blood from where it cut into her lip.

"No!" she moaned in agony. "The storage room."

"Let's go," Beardsley said curtly.

"What about her?" asked the man with the whip in his hand.

"Leave her. She's not going anywhere. We'll take care of her later," Beardsley snapped.

They went out, closing the door. Fighting to keep from losing consciousness, Leola pulled her bruised and bleeding body slowly toward the door. I's gotta get outta here befo' they come back, was her only thought. After what seemed an eternity, she was able to raise up enough to unlatch and push open the door. As she struggled out she fell down the high steps, hitting her head. How long she had been lying there, she didn't know. It was getting dark and she knew they would come for her soon.

"Gotta move," she muttered through the blood-caked lips, trying to raise herself up. A rustling sound nearby struck fear to her heart. A dark form came stalking around the corner of the shack. Leola whimpered, trying to move away. There was a gasp and she heard quickened footsteps.

"Captain, over here," she heard a low voice say.

"Aw, she's been beaten pretty bad. Easy now, let's get her out of here quick!" the captain exclaimed.

Leola felt hands lift her and carry her to where a horse was waiting. As gently as they could they placed her facedown over the saddle and that was the last she knew.

Somehow, Harriet Dunn, with Nan's help, managed to get enough of a meal put together to satisfy the hungry people who showed up at Dunn House for the evening meal. Thank goodness Leola had baked plenty of pie and cake ahead to add to the fare.

While Nan poured another cup of coffee for lingering guests, Miss Dunn cleared away the plates, taking them to the kitchen. Someone was coming through the hall. Oh no, she thought, I don't have enough food left to feed more guests. Wearily brushing the hair back from her face, she started for the door. She would just have to turn them away. She paused, taken aback that the steps were coming on to the kitchen. The door swung open and the colonel strode through.

"Harriet!" he cried huskily, taking her in his arms to hold her close. "I got here as soon as I could! You're going to be all right. Captain Brevard and his men are looking for Leola."

He held her back at arm's length to look in her eyes, which were filled with tears of relief. He could see in her face evidence of the strain she had been under.

"Harriet, dear, I want you to come back with me. I cannot go on this way. There are too many miles between us. Please tell me you will come!"

"Yes, Alexander, I'll go with you this time," she responded, her tired eyes shining with a soft light. "Just give me a few days after all this is over to get things in order."

He crushed her close again. His lips kissed her forehead. "Harriet dear, I don't want to be apart from you again," he said passionately.

"Nor I, Alexander. I love you."

Robert Bonham had stayed behind as Colonel Stothard walked toward the kitchen. He seated himself in the empty sitting room where he could see the doorway leading into the cooking area and anyone entering from the outside. He picked up a newspaper, going through the pretense of reading it. Several guests were leisurely enjoying their last cup of coffee. The big redheaded man with the beard was Mr. Sparks, he remembered. The girl serving the coffee was his daughter. He had seen them when he was here before. He settled down patiently for a long wait. The soft chair felt good after a long day in the saddle.

* * *

Wes Scott crouched lower in the shadows as he detected a slight sound. He wondered if Joe had heard it from where he was positioned. He strained his eyes through the murky darkness but could see nothing to cause alarm. He had just about decided it was made by someone on the porch when he heard the swoosh of the fire. The noise he had heard was the striking of a match! Whoever had set it had come up from their blind side and made off.

"Joe!" he yelled, running toward the burning building, which was going up like a tinder box. "Grab something, fast!"

Harriet Dunn saw the flames through the kitchen window. "Dandy!" she gasped. "He's in the stall back of the storage room!" She ran to unlock the back door. Strong hands pulled her to one side as the colonel rushed out with a roar.

"Wes! Get that horse out of there!" he shouted, running to help. Wes broke the lock on the stall and grabbed the excited Dandy by the mane, leading him out. The stall was already filling with smoke. He left the trembling horse in the care of the colonel and ran back to get the bridle and saddle.

Upon hearing the shouts, Bonham laid the paper down and quickly stepped into the hall to guard the front entrance. He observed Mr. Sparks and Nan going out to stay with Miss Dunn. The other guests were gazing out the windows of the dining room. His place was here. He was confident Wes and Joe could handle things outside.

The storage room was a total loss. As she stood there surveying the ruins, Harriet Dunn shuddered at the thought of what would have happened to Henry.

"Come, Harriet, you need to be back in the house," Colonel Stothard urged gently, guiding her away from the crowd.

Nan held the door open for them, her black eyes filled with sympathy.

"Take care of her, Nan," the colonel said. "I need to talk to Wes and Joe a moment." He went out, closing the door behind him.

"Pass the word that a black man died in this fire," he instructed his men. "And let's hope it reaches Beardsley's ears. I trust we will hear from the rest of the men soon."

They were all gathered around the dining room table when Wes walked in. The supper guests were all gone and the crowd outside had dispersed. The excitement of a second fire in two days was over.

Wes was glad to report that he had heard several onlookers relaying the message that Henry had died in the fire.

"That ought to be satisfying to those who wanted him dead," he added.

Harriet Dunn gave a worried glance at the clock. The hour was getting late and still no word from Captain Brevard. Her heart was heavy as she despaired of ever seeing Leola again. Beardsley would have disposed of her once he had gotten the information he wanted. She would have to tell Henry something soon. The price of his loyal friendship to Cam had been very high. Tears of gratitude for these faithful friends filled her eyes.

Bonham came to the door and beckoned for the colonel to come with him. Harriet could hear their voices as they talked in the hall. When the colonel returned to where she was, he knelt before her, taking her trembling hand in his.

"Harriet, they have found Leola. Captain Brevard and his men are bringing her in. She's alive, dear, but in bad shape. She will need some care," he explained in a calm voice.

"Oh, thank God!" she cried. "When—how soon?"

"I don't know. Their progress has been slow. They have had to stop a lot."

"I'll get some bandages and salve together. Nan can put on some water to heat. I'll go tell Henry and make a pallet in the linen room with him. He can watch over her."

* * *

Cam swung himself to a sitting position on the hard bunk. Today was the hearing. He had slept little during the night. The lonely hours of isolation were beginning to wear on him. They had not allowed him to see anyone except Marcus T. Moore, the attorney Miss Dunn had sent. Mr. Moore was a kind man, saying only that Cam should not give up hope. The jailer who brought his meals each time would place them on the shelf and leave without saying anything.

When Sheriff Neubeck had questioned him, no one believed his story. They had found no sign of Brindle. The night of the fire, he had overheard someone say there was enough evidence against him to put him in prison and throw away the key. Everything in him wanted to scream his innocence as he sat there gripping the edge of the crude bed. It was all so wrong!

He dropped his head in his hands as despair began its brutal attack. This time Beardsley had won. While he continued his evil gains, Cam would be tucked away in prison for a crime he did not commit, the victim of an unscrupulous man with a consuming hatred for him.

His mind went to Nan. Would Beardsley get her too? What must she think of him now? He was no longer a homesteader. He had been branded a criminal!

Locked in a desperate struggle between instinctive survival and futility, Cam remembered what his mother had once said to him. "Cam, truth crushed in earth shall rise again. What people say cannot hurt you, if you are innocent, but the way you react to what they say can. Hold your head up, Cam! Be true to yourself! Trust the Father!"

What was it he had read in her Bible last night? "The Lord is the strength of my life; of whom shall I be afraid"?

"Help me, Lord. Give me the strength I need," he murmured prayerfully, surrendering it all to the Father. A sense of peace swept away the dark despair, replacing it with assurance. The Lord of the universe was on his side! He had a Father who cared for him!

"Here's your breakfast, son," Sheriff Neubeck said, breaking into his thoughts. He unlocked the cell door and set down the plate and cup on a shelf.

"You'll need to get ready to go over to the courthouse for your hearing. I'll come for you in a little while."

Cam lifted his head to look at the sheriff with a steady gaze. "Yes sir, I'll be ready," he replied respectfully, running his hand over his tousled head.

Sheriff Neubeck went out and locked the cell. He paused for a moment, looking at Cam. Of all the prisoners he had locked up, this boy did not belong there. Something was different about this young man. Maybe it was the way he looked you in the eye with that direct manner he had. The respect and manners he displayed showed he had come from a good family. Unlike most prisoners he had brought in, he had not heard one word of complaint from him.

"I'll be back," he said finally, noting that Cam had made no move to get his food.

Cam got up and picked up the clean clothes Miss Dunn had thoughtfully sent to him and began to dress.

* * *

It was not yet daylight when Miss Dunn got up to check on Leola and found her much improved. Henry had been overjoyed when they had brought her in, calling to her to hold on as Harriet Dunn had washed and dressed her lacerated skin. He had watched over her carefully during the night, dozing off and on as she rested, holding her in his arms when she whimpered in fear.

"You are doing much better this morning, Leola," Miss Dunn encouraged, smiling down at her as she dressed her wounds. "The swelling has gone down some in your eye."

Leola tried to respond with a smile, but her lips were too swollen and sore. Giving her cook a pat on the shoulder, Harriet Dunn got to her feet and walked to the door.

"Henry, I'll get you something to eat and send some broth for Leola. It would help if you would feed her for me." She went out, closing the door behind her.

When she entered the kitchen, Nan was putting long pans of biscuits in the oven. A pot of grits was bubbling on the stove, and the smell of coffee was in the air. The girl had been a tremendous help and seemed to know what to do without much instruction. Expertly she was slicing ham and putting it in a skillet to fry. Harriet Dunn smiled to herself. Little did Nan know she was preparing to become the overseer of Dunn House. What a moment that would be when she could tell Cam and Nan.

Colonel Stothard came in shortly, looking very handsome in his khaki riding habit.

"Good morning, ladies," he hailed, sniffing the air. "If I wasn't spoken for, Nan, I'd follow you around the world for a cup of that coffee!" He was delighted to see the color come into Harriet Dunn's cheeks.

"You'll not have to do that, Colonel," Nan retorted light-heartedly, "you just sit at that table there and I'll pour you a cup!"

It was nine o'clock when they fed the last of the guests and cleared away the dishes from the table. Leaving a large pot of stew simmering on the back of the stove for the noon meal, Nan and Miss Dunn hurried to get ready to go to the courthouse.

With a promise to send a carriage for them, Colonel Stothard had left earlier to join his men. Mr. Sparks had gone to hitch up his wagon and prepare to take Henry to the back of the courthouse as instructed. Only Robert Bonham remained behind, keeping his vigil over Dunn House.

Wes Scott brought the carriage to a halt and helped Miss Dunn and Nan down to the ground. Pushing the crowd aside, he saw them safely into the courtroom.

A hush fell over the roomful of people as Miss Dunn and Nan took their seats down front. Harriet Dunn presented a lovely picture in her light blue dress and matching hat. Nan looked all around the room, but Cam was nowhere to be seen. She saw Clay Beardsley standing in the back and turned her eyes away from his bold gaze. The bailiff came in and laid some papers on the judge's desk. An expectant hush fell over the crowd. A door opened to the left and the sheriff entered with Cam, who was dressed neatly in the clean clothes Miss Dunn had sent him. He held his head high and walked to the chair indicated by the sheriff, keeping his clear blue eyes straight ahead. As he sat down, he glanced up and met Nan's eyes. Cam gave a perceptible start and turned away before seeing her smile of encouragement.

Marcus Moore walked in to casually take a seat. No one seemed to think much of his presence there. It had been a habit of his to drop in on the local scene occasionally. It was good politics.

The judge entered and rapped his gavel to quiet the people. Picking up the papers on his desk, he looked them over briefly, laying them before him.

"This hearing is now in session. Would the accused please stand," he said in a sonorous tone, looking over his glasses at Cam.

When Cam had complied, standing tall before his bench, the judge began to read the list of charges against him.

In the back of the courtroom, Clay Beardsley grinned with satisfaction. Everything had gone as he had planned. The little rooster would be gone once and for all! There were no witnesses left. The next step would be to start up his mill. His dark glance went to Harriet Dunn. What a woman! She had strength and fire. He liked that in a woman. When he was successful she would find him attractive. All women had their price. She would come around. He was so engrossed he did not see the several men who were edging in around him.

The judge was about done; it would soon be over. Digger was off to the left of him. He turned a dark, bearded visage to give Beardsley a triumphant glance. Little did he know that he would soon be behind bars and that the man beside him was one of the colonel's men. Stevens, who had no stomach for such things, was not present; he had chosen to stay outside and was now in the custody of Captain Brevard and the colonel, who had taken him into the same door through which Cam had entered.

"How does the accused plead?" the judge was saying.

"Not guilty!" Cam said with a ring in his voice.

"Do you have proof of innocence?"

Marcus Moore sprung to his feet. "Yes, your honor, we do. We have a witness who was there the night of the fire."

A bit surprised, the judge hesitated and then said, "Call the witness in, Mr. Moore."

Clay Beardsley's hand went toward the gun he had under his coat. He felt a hard prod in his back as a voice spoke in his ear. "I wouldn't do that, Mr. Beardsley. Let's be nice and still and see the show."

Marcus Moore strode to the door through which the judge had come. Opening it he called, "Bring him in!"

Henry came into the courtroom with Mr. Sparks right behind him. Henry's eyes widened as he saw the large number of people. Marcus Moore led him to stand before the judge.

"Don't be afraid, Henry. Just tell the judge what you saw the night of the fire."

Beginning feebly, Henry seemed to gain confidence as he spoke. "Well, Miss Harriet was consid'rable worried 'bout Mista Cam, and she hired me to go down to the mill every night and watch out fo' 'im." The crowded courtroom grew totally still. The judge listened carefully as the story unfolded, perceptively visualizing the well-laid plot. When Henry finished, Marcus Moore turned him around to face the crowd.

"Do you see these men in the courtroom, Henry?"

"Yes, suh."

"Would you point them out, Henry?"

"Yes, suh, there's Mista Beardsley," he said, pointing at Beardsley, "and there's Digger. I don't see that Mista Stevens."

"He's right here, Mr. Moore," Colonel Stothard said in a loud voice for all to hear, pushing Stevens in the room ahead of him.

Marcus Moore placed his hand on Cam's shoulder and turned to face the judge. "Sir, I think you have no other alternative than to find this young man innocent of the charges brought against him."

Contemplating the entire incident for a moment, the judge stood to announce, "Not guilty! All charges are dismissed. Sheriff, take the guilty parties into custody," and he dismissed the court with a rap of his gavel.

Nan tried to get to Cam, but the crowd pressed in around him. Colonel Stothard came to usher them out a side door to the waiting carriage. She would have to wait until later. Surely Cam would be back to Dunn House before she had to leave for home.

Nan was busy helping Miss Dunn serve the noon meal when Cam returned to Dunn House. He came in the back entrance and went directly to his room, closing the door. He did not come in to eat. Harriet caught Nan's questioning glance and shook her head. Nan set the platter of biscuits down and turned away as tears of disappointment flooded her eyes. A great sob welled up within her, and she hurried from the room. What could she do? Pa was planning to start for home as soon as he had eaten, and she would not have a chance to talk with Cam!

Harriet Dunn hurriedly poured the coffee in the remaining empty cups and followed Nan into the kitchen.

"Nan, dear, I know what you are going through. It's going to be all right, you'll see. Cam is probably exhausted from his ordeal and needs time to himself." She put her arms around the distraught girl to comfort her.

"It's not that," Nan sobbed. "Pa's wanting to go home right after dinner, and I won't be able to see Cam for a long time!"

"Look, Nan, I'm going to need someone to help me until Leola gets well. Why don't I ask your father to let you stay here to work for me. Would you like that?"

"Oh, yes. Yes! Would you?" Nan responded quickly, her face lighting up at the prospect.

"Good! Now dry your tears. I'll talk to him. You can bring the dessert in soon. The guests are probably about ready for it."

* * *

Nan was glad that Miss Dunn had persuaded her father to allow her to remain in town and work at Dunn House. All afternoon, while she was baking pies, Nan found it difficult to keep her eyes from wandering to Cam's closed door. In the passing busy hours she vacillated between the overwhelming desire to see him and the frustration of not knowing what to say or do when she did.

The supper hour came and still Cam did not appear. Nan was thankful that other than the regular boarders, there were fewer people to serve, since most had left town after the hearing. Those who did come to eat did not linger for very long.

Harriet and Nan wearily cleared the table and carried the dishes to the kitchen. Miss Dunn put the food away while Nan scraped the plates and stacked them for washing.

Colonel Stothard came in to suggest that Miss Dunn take a relaxing carriage ride with him. Nan urged Miss Dunn to go on, leaving the cleanup to her, assuring her that she did not mind. In fact she welcomed the task to keep her mind busy.

It was getting late when she finally dried the last plate and put it away. The kitchen was warm from the long hours of cooking. She brushed the damp hair back from her face. Picking up the wet towels, she went out to the back porch to hang them on the line to dry. The evening air was refreshing, and she sat down in the swing to cool off. The blackened scar of the burned storage shed was a repulsive sight. It recalled unpleasant memories she wanted to push from her mind. Long shadows reminded her it would soon be time to light the lamps.

With a heavy sigh, Nan got up and slipped quietly back into the house. Cam was sitting in the kitchen with his back to her, his head in his hands, a forlorn, lonely figure. He gave no indication he had heard her step.

Nan felt as if her heart would burst as all the pent-up longing to be with him, to talk to him, to . . . oh, what was she thinking! The blood rushed to her face and pounded in her temples, yet, she knew what she must do. Walking silently up behind him, she placed her arms around his shoulders, resting her chin on his head. She felt him stiffen as she spoke.

"Cam, please hear me out. I have liked you since you first came home with Pa. And . . . and when you kissed me that day in the woods . . . well . . . I have fought loving you. Please don't think badly of me, Cam, I just didn't want to be the wife of a homesteader. I've seen what it did to Ma, and I didn't want that. But it's different now, Cam . . . I . . . I love you. Please forgive me . . . and if your proposal of marriage is still on . . . I . . . I accept," she finished almost inaudibly.

He sat so still, she thought he had not heard her. Then he jumped to his feet, breaking her hold on him. He walked to the other side of the room.

"Nan," he cried in a strangled voice, "I can't ask you to marry me! I have nothing to offer you, no job, no home, nothing! I don't even have a homestead!"

"Cam, I'm saying I love you!" she gasped, leaning on the chair for support. Tears sprung into her eyes and she dropped her head. "I felt . . . I thought you loved me," she faltered.

"Nan, I care too much for you to drag you into a life of drudgery," he said more calmly, coming back to take her by the shoulders. "Please understand. I prayed for the strength to love you as I should . . . to want the very best for you . . . to want you to be happy."

"Cam, I love you. If you want me to be happy, ask me to be your wife," Nan implored, fighting with all the feminine instinct she possessed. She reached her arms to wind them around his neck and leaned against his chest. She could hear the rapid beating of his heart.

He gave a shuddering groan and gathered her in his arms. He was like a drowning man. He could no longer resist his love for her.

"Nan," he said thickly, burying his face in the fragrance of her hair, "will you marry me?"

"Yes . . . oh, yes, Cam!" she said softly, raising her radiant face to his.

Cam was sitting at the table eating the supper Nan had warmed up for him when Miss Dunn and the colonel returned. He looked up at them with a happy grin.

"I think Nan has something she's dying to tell you."

A red tide flooded Nan's face as she turned to face them. "Cam has asked me to marry him and I have accepted," she said shyly, her dark eyes shining with a soft light.

Miss Dunn gave a glad cry and hugged Nan to her. "How wonderful! Has a date been set?"

"We are going to send word to Preacher Underwood tomorrow and let Nan's folks know. Nan would like to be married here in town. If all goes well, we are planning for a week from Saturday evening."

"You can be married here at Dunn House if you like," Harriet offered.

"Nan?"

"Oh yes, Cam, that would be perfect!"

"Fine! It's settled then," Miss Dunn said happily.

* * *

Saturday dawned clear and bright. Cam had gotten up before daylight and made a pot of coffee. With Henry's help he had worked tirelessly to clear away the unsightly charred remains of the burned storage building. Today, they should complete the new one.

Cam poured himself another cup of coffee and went out to the porch to sit on the step. Henry was just reining in his mule at the back gate.

"Morning, Henry, there's coffee!"

"Mawnin', Mista Cam! I done had coffee with Leola."

"How's she doin?"

"Oh, she's doin' fine! She's a gettin' sassy agin. That's a good sign. She's plannin' big t' be here t' hep Miss Nan 'n Miss Harriet with the weddin'."

"I'm sure they will be glad to hear that!" Cam laughed. He drank the rest of his coffee and set the cup down. "Well, I guess we had better get started on finishing up that roof."

It was nearly noon when they stood back to survey their handiwork.

"There she is, Mista Cam, good as new."

"Henry," Cam said, turning to face him, "I've not said this in words before, but you have been a true friend. We have been through a lot together . . . and I'll not forget the risks you took to stick by me. I'm getting married today and I will be taking on a different set of responsibilities, but, I want you to know I will always have time for you."

"I know, Mista Cam, I know," Henry acknowledged, shaking his head.

Nan came to the porch to call to them. "Are you two hardworking fellows wantin' anything to eat?"

"Hey there, Miss Nan!" Henry called to her. "You sho do look pretty today!"

"Hey, yourself, Henry!" she answered with a happy note in her voice. "When is Leola coming?"

"I'm a fixin' t' go get her now, Miss Nan. I'll be eatin' over there."

* * *

The wedding ceremony was over so soon that, to Cam, it seemed like a dream. The guests who had lingered long enough for some of Leola's cake and lemonade were leaving, anxious to get home.

Cam and Nan waved good-bye to the last of them and walked arm in arm back to the kitchen. Miss Dunn and Nan's mother were busy making sandwiches and coffee. Colonel Stothard and her father were sitting at the table talking.

"Where are the children?" Nan asked her mother.

"I've already tucked them in bed. They were worn out."

At Harriet Dunn's insistence, Zachariah Sparks had decided to stay over until morning. Nan was delighted. It was good for her mother to get away from the loneliness of the homestead for a while.

Miss Dunn set a plate of sandwiches on the table and turned to Colonel Stothard. "Shall we tell them now, Colonel—uh—Alexander?"

The colonel stood to his feet and came to stand by her side. Her face was flushed with happiness.

"Alexander has asked me to marry him and I have accepted. As soon as I can wrap up my affairs here and pack, I will return to Savannah with him. We will be married there. I have been concerned about what to do with Dunn House. Henry and Leola want to marry, and they would be dependent upon Leola's wages here and what Henry makes at odd jobs. Cam, you and Nan need a place of your own to live in. We have talked it over and have come up with a solution to all of our problems. We have decided to give Dunn House to you as a wedding present. You can live here and run the boardinghouse with Henry and Leola's help."

Cam stood transfixed, trying to grasp the full impact of her words, looking from one to the other.

"Cam, Dunn House will be your home." Her voice broke. "Alexander and I want you and Nan to have it."

He looked down at Nan, who had grabbed his arm tightly. Her eyes were filled with tears of happiness.

"How can I . . . how can we ever thank you . . . ," he stammered, trying to overcome the emotion he felt for these kind and wonderful friends.

The coffeepot boiled over on the stove, coming to his rescue, as the women turned to see about it. While Nan assisted with the cleanup, Cam slipped out into the darkness. He sat down on the step to listen to the sounds of the night as he had done many times with his mother. As he thought about her, he wondered if she would know that everything was all right with him.

He looked up to see the North Star shining through the branches of a great oak tree. Just as that beacon of light had guided many a lost soul to safety, his mother's Bible and prayers had sustained him and led him to the Father.

Cam heard a quiet step behind him. Nan sat down beside him and slipped her hand into his, laying her head against his shoulder.